THE SILENT POOL

Titles by Patricia Wentworth

THE SILENT POOL

PATRICIA WENTWORTH

HarperPerennial

A Division of HarperCollins*Publishers*

HarperCollins books may be purchased for educational,
business, or sales promotional use. For information
please write: Special Markets Department, Harper-
Collins Publishers, Inc., 10 East 53rd Street, New York,
NY 10022.

First HarperPerennial edition published 1990. Reissued
1992.

LIBRARY OF CONGRESS CATALOG CARD NUMBER 92-52672

ISBN 0-06-092333-4

92 93 94 95 96 WB/MB 10 9 8 7 6 5 4 3 2 1

THE SILENT POOL

CHAPTER 1

It was Miss Silver's practice to open her letters at the breakfast table. True to the maxims instilled into her when still extremely young, she was in the habit of giving duty the first place in her life. A call for her personal or professional assistance, whether by post or telephone, would therefore naturally precede any dalliance with the morning papers, of which she took two—one of that aloof and lofty character which made even the most world-shaking events seem to be taking place at an immense distance and to have very little bearing upon daily life; the other frankly given over to headlines, a lively presentment of politics, and such immediate and pressing matters as who had been married, murdered, or divorced.

She picked up the letters and sorted them out. There was one from her niece Ethel Burkett, who was the wife of a bank manager in the Midlands. She opened it at once. Roger, the youngest of the three boys, had not been very well when Ethel wrote last, and it was a relief to read in reassuring phrases that he was now quite himself again and had returned to school. A piece of family news followed. Mrs. Burkett wrote:

"You will, I know, be delighted to hear of the safe arrival of Dorothy's twins, a boy and a girl. They are fine babies, and she and Jim are perfectly delighted. Really, after ten years of having no children and being dreadfully unhappy about it, they haven't done so badly, have they—first a boy and then a girl, and now both together. Personally I feel that they should stop there!"

Jim being Ethel Burkett's brother and Miss Silver's nephew, this was intelligence of a most gratifying nature. Two coatees and three pairs of infant socks had already been despatched to Dorothy Silver, but it now became imperative that the gift should be doubled. She remembered with pleasure that she had plenty of the sock wool, and that only yesterday she had noticed some very attractive pale blue balls in Messiter's wool department which would be just the thing for the little coatees.

Leaving the rest of Ethel's letter to be read at her leisure, she turned to one from her other niece, Gladys. It contained, as she had expected, a number of complaints and more than one hint that an invitation to stay with "dear Auntie" would be some slight mitigation of her lot. Miss Silver had a kind heart, but it did not dispose her to pity Gladys. She had married of her own free will. Her husband was a most worthy man if rather dull. He had been no less so when she chose to marry him. He was now not quite so well off—very few people were. But Gladys, having married to escape the necessity of working for her living, considered it a grievance that she was now obliged to sweep, and dust, and cook. She did all three very badly, and Miss Silver felt a good deal of sympathy for Andrew Robinson.

A glance at the untidy scribbled page having assured her that the letter was just what she expected, she laid it aside and took up a letter with the Ledbury postmark. She knew Ledshire well and had many friends there, but this large, distinctive handwriting was strange to her, the paper thicker

2

and more expensive than most people could now afford. She straightened out a double sheet and read:

"Mrs. Smith presents her compliments to Miss Maud Silver and would be glad if she could make an appointment for some time between 10 a.m. and noon tomorrow, Thursday. She expects to be in London, and will ring up from her hotel to confirm the appointment and decide upon the hour."

Miss Silver observed the sheet with interest. It had been cut down by a couple of inches, obviously in order to remove an address. The writing showed signs of hurry, and there were two blots. She decided that it might be interesting to see this Mrs. Smith and to find out what she wanted.

But she had time not only to finish her breakfast but to read, first dear Ethel's letter, so warm, so full of the details of a happy family life, and afterwards with frowning distaste that from Gladys Robinson, which differed only from many of her previous efforts in that it went so far as actually to ask for money—"Andrew keeps me so short, and if I take it out of the housekeeping he goes on dreadfully. He doesn't seem to think that I must have clothes! And he is quite disagreeable if I so much as speak to anyone else! So if you possibly could, dear Auntie—"

Miss Silver gathered up her letters and the newspapers and went through to the sitting-room of her flat. She hardly ever came into it after the briefest absence without feeling a gush of gratitude to what she called Providence for having enabled her to achieve this modest comfort. During twenty years of her life she had expected nothing more than to be a governess in other people's houses, and to retire eventually upon some very small pittance. Then suddenly there had opened before her a completely new way of life. Equipped with strong moral principles, a passion for justice, and a gift for reading the human heart, she had entered upon a career as a private detective. She was not unknown to Scotland Yard. Chief Detective Inspector Lamb had a high esteem for her. If it was sometimes tinged with exasperation, this did not interfere with an old and sincere friendship. Inspector Frank Abbott in moments of irreverence declared that his esteemed Chief suspected "Maudie" of powers alarmingly akin to witchcraft—but then it is notorious that this brilliant officer sometimes allows himself to talk in a very extravagant manner.

Miss Silver having laid the newspapers upon the top of a small revolving book-case, put her nieces' letters into a drawer of the writing-table and deposited Mrs. Smith's communication upon the blotter.

The room was a pleasant one. To the modern eye it contained too many pictures, too much furniture, and much too many photographs. The pictures, in frames of yellow maple, were reproductions of Victorian masterpieces—Sir John Millais' *Bubbles* and the *Soul's Awakening*, Mr. G. F. Watts' *Hope*, and a melancholy Landseer *Stag*; the chairs in walnut profusely carved but surprisingly comfortable with their curved arms and capacious laps; the photographs almost a guide to the fashions of the past twenty years in much older frames, relics from an age devoted to silver filigree and plush. These photographs were, in fact, a record of Miss Silver's cases. In serving the ends of justice she had saved the good name, the happiness, sometimes even the life of these people who smiled at her from the top of the book-case, and from any other place where it had been possible to find room for them. There were a great many pictures of the babies for whom she had knitted shawls and socks and little woolly coatees. As she stood by the writing-table she looked about her with pleasure. The sun slanted in between her peacock-blue curtains and just touching the edge of the carpet, showed how well the colours matched.

As she pulled out the writing-chair and sat down, the telephone bell rang. Lifting the receiver, she heard a deep voice say, "Is that 15 Montague Mansions?"

She said, "Yes."

It was a woman's voice, though almost deep enough to have been a man's. It spoke again.

"Is that Miss Maud Silver?"

Miss Silver said, "Speaking."

The voice went on.

"You will have had my letter by now—asking for an appointment—Mrs. Smith."

"Yes, I have had it."

"When can I see you?"

"I am free now."

"Then I will come at once. I suppose it will take me about twenty minutes. Good-bye." The receiver was hung up. Miss Silver replaced her own. Then she took up her pen and began to write a short but severe letter to her niece Gladys.

She had made some progress with the much more agreeable task of answering dear Ethel's letter point by point, when the front door bell rang and she was obliged to put it away. A moment later her devoted Emma Meadows was opening the door and announcing,

"Mrs. Smith."

CHAPTER 2

A stooping elderly woman came into the room. She had a fuzz of grey hair under a shabby felt hat with some incongruous and rather dusty veiling in a straggle about the brim. In spite of what was almost summer weather she wore one of those fur coats which disguise the original rabbit under the name of seal-coney. It was old-fashioned in cut and evidently long in wear. Beneath it there was some black woollen garment with an uneven hem. Black shoes, solid and low in the heel, and rubbed black gloves completed the picture.

Miss Silver shook hands and invited her visitor to be seated. She appeared to be somewhat out of breath, and as she crossed the floor a limp became noticeable.

Miss Silver gave her time. She took the chair on the other side of the hearth, reached for the knitting-bag which lay on the small table at her elbow, and taking out a ball of fine white wool, began to cast on the number of stitches required for an infant's vest. Such a good thing that she had plenty of this exceptionally soft wool, since Dorothy's unexpected twin would require a complete outfit.

In the opposite chair, Mrs. Smith had produced a large white handkerchief and was fanning herself. She had been breathing rather quickly, but she now laid down the handkerchief and said,

"You must excuse me. I'm not much in the way of climbing

stairs." Her voice was gruff and her way of speaking abrupt. There was just the least suspicion of a London accent.

Miss Silver had finished casting on and was knitting rapidly after the continental fashion. She said in her pleasant voice,

"Pray, what can I do for you?"

Mrs. Smith said, "Well, I don't know." She was pleating the edge of the linen handkerchief. "I've come to see you professionally."

"Yes?"

"I heard about you from a friend—no need to say who it was. In fact from first to last of my business it's a case of least said soonest mended."

Knitting was so much second nature to Miss Silver that she was able to give full attention to her client. She said,

"It does not matter at all who recommended you to consult me, but I must warn you that my ability to help you will depend a good deal on whether you can make up your mind to be frank."

Mrs. Smith's head came up in the manner which used to be called bridling. She said,

"Oh, well, that would depend—"

Miss Silver smiled.

"Upon whether you felt that you could trust me? I cannot help you at all unless you do so. Half measures are quite useless. As Lord Tennyson so beautifully puts it, 'And trust me not at all or all in all.' "

"That," said Mrs. Smith, "is a bit of a tall order."

"Perhaps. But you will have to make up your mind. You did not really come here to consult me, did you? You came because you had been told about me, and because you

7

wished to make up your mind as to whether you could trust me or not."

"What makes you think of that?"

"It is the case with so many of my clients. It is not easy to speak to a stranger of one's private affairs."

Mrs. Smith said with energy,

"That's just it—they are private. I wouldn't want it to get about that I'd been seeing a detective."

There seemed suddenly to be a considerable distance between herself and Miss Silver. Without word or movement, this small governessy-looking person appeared to have receded. With her neat curled fringe, her dated dress—olive-green cashmere—the bog-oak brooch in the shape of a rose with a pearl at its heart, the black thread stockings, and the glacé shoes, too small for the modern foot, she might have stepped out of any old-fashioned photograph-album. And with that effect of withdrawal, she might have been just about to step back again. The astonishing thing was that Mrs. Smith discovered that she didn't want her to go. Suddenly and quite passionately she didn't want her to go. Before she knew what she was going to do she found that she was saying,

"Oh well, of course I know that anything I tell you would be all in confidence and perfectly safe."

"Yes, it would be perfectly safe."

Mrs. Smith's manner had changed imperceptibly, and her voice too. It had a naturally deep tone, but some of the gruffness went out of it. She said,

"Well, you're right, you know—I did just come to have a look at you. When I tell you why, I daresay you will see for yourself that it was quite a sensible thing to do."

"And now that you have seen me?"

Mrs. Smith made a quite involuntary gesture. Her hand

8

lifted and fell. It was a small thing, but it did not go very well with the rabbit coat and the rest of her appearance. She would have done better to go on pleating the linen handkerchief. That slight graceful gesture was out of key. She realized it a moment too late, and said with a little more accent than before,

"Oh, I'm going to consult you. Only of course it's a bit difficult to begin."

Miss Silver said nothing. She continued to knit. She had seen so many clients in this room—some of them badly frightened, some of them dazed with grief, some in great need of kindness and reassurance. Mrs. Smith did not appear to come into any of these categories. She had her own plan and her own way of carrying it out. If she had made up her mind to speak she would speak, and if she had not made it up she would remain silent. Suddenly and abruptly it appeared that she had made up her mind to speak.

"Look here," she said, "it's this way. I've got an idea that someone is trying to kill me."

This was not the first time that Miss Silver had listened to these or similar words. She sustained no shock of disbelief, but said calmly and firmly,

"What grounds have you for thinking so, Mrs. Smith?"

The black gloved hands were plucking at the handkerchief.

"There was some soup—it tasted—odd. I didn't take it. There was a fly on a drop that was spilled. Afterwards it was lying there dead."

"What happened to the remainder of the soup?"

"It had been thrown away."

"By whom?"

"By the person who brought it to me. I told her there was

9

something wrong with it, and she flushed it down the sink in the bathroom."

"There is a sink in the bathroom?"

"Yes. I don't go downstairs so much since I have been lame. It is convenient to be able to do the washing-up on the spot."

"And it is done by someone who brought you the soup. Who is this person?"

"I suppose you might call her a—help. I have been a bit of an invalid—she looks after me. And you needn't start suspecting her, because she would a good deal rather poison herself than me."

Miss Silver said briskly,

"You should have kept the soup and had it analysed."

"I didn't think of it like that. You see, it was mushroom soup—I just thought a wrong one had got in. Not that Mrs.—" She pulled herself up with a jerk. "I mean, anyone who was a good cook would know a toadstool from a mushroom, wouldn't they?"

Miss Silver ignored this.

"You imply that you did not think much of the incident at the time. Will you tell me what has made you think more seriously of it now?"

Dark eyes looked from behind the dusty veiling. There was a little pause before Mrs. Smith said,

"It was because of the other things that happened. One thing—well, it mightn't mean much, but when there are a lot of things happening one after another it makes you think, doesn't it?"

Miss Silver's needles clicked. She said gravely,

"If there were several incidents, I should like you to begin with the first one and then tell me about the others in the order in which they occurred. It was some time after the episode of the mushroom soup that you first began to suspect that there was anything wrong?"

"Well, it was, and it wasn't. It wasn't the first thing that happened, if that is what you mean."

"Then will you please begin at the beginning and take things in their right order."

Mrs. Smith said, "Oh, the first thing was my accident—five—no, six months ago."

"What happened?"

"It was one of those dark afternoons just before you put the lights on, and I was going down the stairs. And the bother is I can't swear to anything, because you know how it is when you have a fall, you don't really remember a lot about it. The first thing I knew I was down in the hall with a broken leg—and I can't swear I was pushed, but I've got my own ideas about it."

"You think that someone pushed you?"

"Pushed me or tripped me—it doesn't much matter which. And it's no use you asking me who could have done it, because it might have been anyone in the house, or it mightn't have been anyone at all. Only no one is going to get me to believe that I just went crashing down those stairs on my own."

Miss Silver said, "I see—" And then, "And the next thing?"

"The soup, like I told you."

"And after that?"

Mrs. Smith frowned.

"There were the sleeping-tablets. That was what made me feel I had better come and see you. The doctor gave me some when I broke my leg, but I don't like those sort of things. They've got a way of getting hold of you, and I've seen too much of that. So I've never taken one except when the pain was pretty bad. There was about a half bottle of them, and I suppose I might have had six or seven in the six months. And then just the other day I thought I'd take one. Well, you know how one does, I tipped the bottle up on to my palm and quite a lot of tablets came out. I was just looking at them and not thinking anything, when all at once it seemed to me there was one that was different from the others. If it had come out by itself, I don't know that I should have taken any notice—sometimes I wake up in the night and think about that—but seeing it there among the others, it seemed to me it was bigger than it ought to be, and that someone had been messing it up. I took a magnifying-glass and I looked at it, and you could see where it had been cut open and stuck together again. It gave me the cold shivers and I couldn't throw it out of the window quick enough."

Miss Silver gave a short hortatory cough.

"If you will allow me to say so, that was extremely foolish."

Mrs. Smith said heartily,

"Of course it was, but I didn't stop to think, any more than if I'd got a wasp on my hand and was shaking it off."

"This happened recently?"

"Monday night."

Miss Silver put down her knitting, went over to the writing-table, and came back with an exercise-book in a shiny blue cover. Propping it on her knee, she wrote in it in pencil, heading the page with the name of Smith followed by a query. This done, she looked up with the bright expectancy of a bird on the alert for a suitable worm.

"Before we go any farther I should like to have the names and some description of the other members of your household. Their real names, if you please."

Mrs. Smith was observed to hesitate. Then she said with a shade of defiance in her voice,

"And what makes you say that?"

Miss Silver gave her the smile which had won the confidence of so many clients and said,

"I find some difficulty in believing that your own name is really Smith."

"And why?"

Miss Silver's pencil remained poised.

"Because ever since you came into this room you have been acting a part. You did not wish to be recognized, and you presented an extremely convincing portrait of someone very different from yourself."

There was a faint mocking inflection in Mrs. Smith's voice as she said,

"If it was convincing, in what way did it fail to convince you?"

Miss Silver looked at her gravely.

"Handwriting," she observed, "is often quite a reliable guide to character. Yours, if I may say so, did not lead me to expect a Mrs. Smith. Also the paper on which your letter was written was not what she would have employed."

"That was stupid of me." The deep voice now had no trace of a London accent. "Anything else?"

"Oh, yes, Mrs. Smith would not, I think, have troubled to put an eye-veil on to so old a hat. She would not have worn an eye-veil at all. It occurred to me at once that you did not wish me to have too good a view of your eyes. You were, in fact, afraid that you might be recognized."

"And did you recognize me?"

Miss Silver smiled.

"Your eyes are not easily forgotten. You kept them down

as much as possible, but you needed to look at me, because that was why you had come here—to look at me and to make up your mind about consulting me. You disguised your voice very well—the slight accent and the jerky way of speaking. But it was by one slight, almost involuntary movement that you really gave yourself away. It is, I imagine, one which is habitual to you, but I had seen you employ it in the character of Mrs. Alving in *Ghosts*. Your left hand just rose and fell again. It was the simplest thing, but there was something about it which was very effective, very moving. It has remained in my memory as part of a very notable performance. When you made that same movement just now I felt quite sure that you were Adriana Ford."

Adriana broke into deep melodious laughter.

"I knew as soon as I had done it that I had slipped up over that hand business. It was out of character. But I thought the rest of it was pretty good. The coat is a treasured relic of Meeson's—she's my maid—used to be my dresser. And the hat is one she was going to throw away. Frankly, I thought it was a masterpiece, veiling and all. Anyhow it was my eyes I was afraid about. My photographs have always rather featured them." She pulled off the hat as she spoke. The fuzzy grey wig came too. Her own hair appeared, short, thick, and beautifully tinted to a deep Titian red. She said in a laughing voice, "Well, that's better isn't it? Of course the hair is all wrong with these clothes and no proper make-up, but we can at least see each other now. I hated having to peer at you through that damned veil."

She tossed hat and wig on to the nearest chair and straightened herself. The stoop was no more hers than the rabbit coat. Adriana Ford's back was straight enough.

This was no longer Mrs. Smith, neither was it the tragic

14

Mrs. Alving, the terrifying and heart-shaking Lady Macbeth of a decade ago, or the warm and exquisite Juliet of thirty years back. Stripped of her disguise, here was a woman who had lived for a long time and crowded that time with triumphs. There was an air of vigour, there was an air of authority. There was humour, there was a capacity for emotion. The dark eyes were still beautiful and the brows above them finely arched.

Miss Silver saw these things and the something else for which she looked. It was there in the eyes and in the set of the mouth. There had been wakeful nights and days of indecision and strain before Adriana Ford had brought herself to play the part of Mrs. Smith and bring her troubles to a stranger. She said,

"Perhaps you will now give me the particulars for which I asked you."

CHAPTER 3

Adriana Ford laughed.

"Persistent—aren't you?" she said. The laughter passed. She went on in her deep voice, "You want to know who was in the house, and what they were doing, and whether I think any one of them has been trying to kill me—don't you? Well, I can give you a list of names, but it isn't going to help you any more than it has helped me. Sometimes I think I'm imagining the whole thing. I came to see you because quite suddenly I felt I couldn't just sit and wait for the next thing to happen. Quite a lot of people come and go at Ford House. I'll give you their names and tell you who they are, but I want it to be clearly understood that I'm not suspecting anyone or accusing anyone, and that if I say the word, you will tear up any notes you may have taken and forget everything I've told you."

Miss Silver said,

"I have already assured you that whatever you say will be in confidence. Always provided that no tragic event should necessitate the intervention of the law."

Adriana's hand rose and fell. It was the gesture Miss Silver had remembered—slight, graceful, and expressive.

"Oh, after me the deluge! If I'm murdered, you can do what you like!" The words were spoken on an impulse which spent itself and died. A frown followed, and quick words. "Now why did I say that? I didn't mean to. We had better get on with those names." She tapped with her fingers upon the arm of her chair. "I don't know how much you know about me, but everyone knows that I've retired from the stage. I live three miles from Ledbury in an old house down by the river. It is called Ford House. I bought it twenty years ago. I fancied it because of the name. I was born Rutherford, but I went on the stage as Adriana Ford. Some of my relations have stuck to the Scotch Rutherford, but some of them call themselves Ford—after me. I'm the last of my own generation. Now, I'll begin with the staff at Ford House. Alfred Simmons and his wife, butler and cook. They've been with me for twenty years. They live in, and so does Meeson, whom I suppose you can call my maid. She used to be my dresser, and she is devoted to me. She came to me when she was only a girl, and she's about sixty now. Then there are two women who come in daily—a girl called Joan Cuttle, a silly

16

irritating creature, but you can't imagine her wanting to poison anyone, and a middle-aged widow whose husband used to be an under gardener. Her name, if you want it, is Bell. Outside, there's a gardener called Robertson, and a young man under him, Sam Bolton. He looks after the car and does odd jobs."

Miss Silver wrote down the names in the blue exercise-book whilst Adriana fell into a frowning silence. In the end she said,

"Well, that's all the staff, and I can't think of a single reason why any of them should want me out of the way."

Miss Silver coughed.

"No legacies?"

"Well, of course! What do you take me for? Meeson's been with me for forty years, and the Simmons for twenty."

"Are they aware that you have provided for them?"

"They would think very badly of me if I didn't."

"Miss Ford, I must ask you to be exact. Do they actually know that you have provided for them?"

"Of course they do!"

"And to a considerable extent?"

"I don't do things by halves!"

"Any other legacies to the staff?"

"Oh, no. At least—that is—five pounds for every year of service. A hundred would cover the lot."

Miss Silver drew a line across the page.

"We have now disposed of the staff. May I ask who else resides at Ford House?"

Adriana's fingers traced the outline of a carved acanthus leaf.

"My cousin Geoffrey Ford and his wife Edna. He is in his late forties. His means are not what he would like them to

17

be, and the life of a country gentleman suits him. He began by coming for visits, which have prolonged themselves into a more or less permanent stay. He is agreeable company, and I like to have a man about the house. His wife is one of those tiresome well-meaning women. She interferes with the servants and calls it doing the housekeeping. She would like to keep everything locked up and dole it out in daily doses. And she is ridiculously jealous of Geoffrey."

Miss Silver held her pencil poised.

"When you say ridiculously, do you mean that she has no reason to be jealous?"

Adriana laughed a little harshly.

"Far from it! I should say she had every reason! But what does she expect? She is older than Geoffrey, and she could never have been attractive. No one has ever been able to make out why he married her. As far as I know, she has no money. Well, so much for Geoffrey and Edna. Then there's Meriel."

Miss Silver wrote down the name and repeated it on a note of enquiry.

"Meriel?"

"Oh, Ford—Ford. At any rate that's what she's been called for the last twenty-three years or so. And it's no use your asking where she comes in, because she doesn't. You may say that she was thrown on my hands, and there she's likely to remain. She frightens the men away. An intense creature— probably a misfit anywhere."

"What does she do?"

"The flowers." Adriana's mouth twisted.

"You have never thought of giving her a profession?"

"Oh, I've thought of it, but all she has ever wanted to do was to go on the stage or to dance—starting at the top. She

18

has no idea of working, and she has no real talent. In fact the whole thing is a grievance."

Miss Silver wrote against the name of Meriel Ford—Emotional, disappointed, discontented.

She looked up, to find Adriana's eyes fixed on her with a doubtful expression.

"Those are all the regular people, but of course there were visitors. I suppose you don't want to know about them."

"Do you mean that there were visitors staying in the house at the time of the incidents which have alarmed you?"

"Oh, yes."

"Then I think you had better give me the names."

Adriana leaned back.

"Well, there was Mabel Preston for one. She was there for the day when I broke my leg, but of course she couldn't have had anything to do with it."

"And who is Mabel Preston?"

Adriana made a face.

"Oh, an old friend, and an unlucky one. She used to be quite well known as Mabel Prestayne, but she married a wrong un and went downhill. He spent everything she earned, and when she couldn't earn any more he went off and left her, poor thing. I have her down once in a way, but I must say I didn't want her just then."

Pencil poised, Miss Silver enquired,

"Has she any interest in your will?"

Adriana looked rueful.

"Well, she has. I help her a bit, and she is down for an annuity. But it wouldn't be of any advantage to her really. In fact I should think she would lose by my death, because I give her things from time to time—clothes, you know—that sort of thing. You can put Mabel out of your head. It's

19

really not worth your while to write her down. I've known her for forty years, and she wouldn't hurt a fly."

"Have you any other names to give me?"

"There is my young cousin, Star Somers—you will know about her. She is very pretty and attractive, and she has had quite a success in comedy. She doesn't live at Ford House, but she runs up and down because her little girl is there with a nanny. Star divorced her husband about a year ago. He comes down sometimes to see the child, but he doesn't stay in the house. Another occasional visitor is Star's cousin, Ninian Rutherford. They're like brother and sister and very fond of each other—their fathers were twins. He comes to stay when she is there."

Miss Silver wrote down the name. Then she said,

"And which of these people was staying in the house when you fell on the stairs?"

Adriana's eyes looked back at her with a mocking expression.

"Oh, all of them, except Robin Somers. No, let me see—I believe he was there too. He doesn't come down as a rule when Star is at Ford, but it was Stella's birthday—the little girl, you know—and he actually remembered it. Star wouldn't see him—she was furious. There was a party—just a few children from round about—and I had been in the thick of it, but I went upstairs to try and get Star to come down, and she wouldn't, because of Robin. So he must have been in the house when I fell. . . . The date? Oh, March the fifteenth."

Miss Silver wrote that down too.

"And the incident of the mushroom soup?"

"Oh, that was in August. And I can't give you the exact date, so it's no use your asking me. I only remember about my fall because it was Stella's birthday. But it would have been a week-end, if that is any use, because Star was there, and Mabel—and, yes, I suppose most of the others too, but not Robin. At least not that any of us knew. But as to the tablet, you can see for yourself it might have been put into the bottle by anyone and at any time. In fact," said Adriana with a radiant smile, "anyone might have done any of the things, or they may all have been just nothing at all." She opened the old fur coat and threw it back with a buoyant gesture. "Now that I've told you all about it, you can't think how much better I feel. You know how it is, you think of things in the night and they get hold of you. I expect the whole thing is just imagination from start to finish. I slipped and fell. The fly on the drop of soup just happened to die—flies do. And as to the tablet, I suppose it might have been a different sort that got in by mistake, or one that hadn't turned out quite right—something like that. I had better just put the whole thing right out of my mind."

Miss Silver was silent. Her face was grave and composed. She thought Adriana Ford was talking to convince herself, and she wondered whether the effect would be more than a transitory one. It was a little while before she spoke again.

"As you have said yourself, you have very little to go upon. The fall might have been quite accidental, and the evidence as to the soup is far from conclusive. The tablet does give grounds for thought. It is a great pity that you threw it away. Since you have come to consult me, I will give you the best advice I can. Short of changing your household and your whole mode of life, there are certain things which you could do."

Adriana's fine brows lifted.

"As what?"

"You could make a point of having your meals with the

rest of the family. Separate meals make it a great deal easier to tamper with food. That is the first point.''

''And the next?''

''Allow your household to suppose that you have been making alterations in your will. If there is anyone who believes that your death will profit him or her, such an announcement would cast doubt upon the matter and thus remove a possible temptation.''

Adriana threw out her hands in a sweeping gesture.

''Oh, my dear Miss Silver!''

Miss Silver said sedately,

''That is my advice.''

Adriana flung back her head and laughed. It was a deep and musical sound.

''Do you know what I am going to do?''

''I think I can guess.''

''Then you are even cleverer than you think. I'm going to take out a new lease of life, and I'm going to live it my own way. Things happened when I was sitting here telling you I thought there was someone who wanted me dead—I didn't believe it any more, or if I believed it I didn't care. I'm going to live. And I don't mean just to drag on, an invalid on a couch—I mean really live. I've got a car hired for the day and Meeson waiting in it, and when I go out of here I'm going shopping, and I'm going to get a lot of new clothes, and I'll have my hair touched up—it wants it. And I'll go back to Ford and I'll make a big splash there. My parties used to be famous. I don't know why I stopped giving them—the war, and then I couldn't be bothered—but I'm going to start all over again. And I'll keep a good look out, I can promise you that. If there is anyone who wants me out of the way, they are not going to find it so easy!''

CHAPTER 4

The drawing-room at Ford House was a great deal too full of furniture. It was a large room with three long windows looking to the terrace, but it was not as light as it ought to have been because the old painted panelling had deepened to what was practically sage green, and the heavy grey velvet curtains obscured a good deal of the glass. In the days when Adriana Ford had entertained there these moss and lichen shades had made a wonderful background for her flaming hair and her whole magnificent exuberance. In her absence it was the furniture which dominated the scene—towering Chippendale cabinets crammed with china; a grand piano in ebony and mother-of-pearl; tables in ormolu, in marqueterie, in walnut inlaid with satinwood; monumental sofas; enormous chairs; a marble mantelpiece like the entrance to a tomb; a clutter of ornaments. Adriana had lighted it all like a torch. Without her it was a gloomy has-been.

Star Somers sat lightly on the arm of one of the chairs. She did not seem to belong to the room at all. She was in grey, but not the storm-grey of the velvet curtains. Her beautifully cut suit had the light silvery shade which went well with her name. A diamond brooch flashed from the lapel. A row of pearls crossed the neckline of a delicate white shirt. She was as exquisite off the stage as upon it. If the light had been twice as bright as it was, it would have disclosed no fault in the perfect skin, the lovely eyes, the pale gold hair. And the perfection owed practically nothing to art. Nature had given her eyelashes just that deeper tinge which flattered the grey eyes, and she wore no rouge and needed none. When she was pleased her colour rose, when she was sad it ebbed. Her charming mouth was emphasised by a most attractive shade of lipstick. At the moment her eyes were wide, her lips parted, and her colour high.

"You weren't going to tell me!" she said. "You've actually let Nanny go off without telling me!"

Edna Ford, who was her cousin Geoffrey's wife, looked down a long pale nose. Everything about her was pale—the hair which always reminded Star of sun-dried grass, the light blue eyes with their sandy lashes, the thin colourless lips set in a disapproving line. Even the embroidery upon which she was engaged had a pale and faded look, the background dull, the colours indeterminate, the pattern formal. Every time she put the needle in and drew it out again she managed to convey the fact that Star was making a fuss about nothing. There was going to be a scene. These theatrical people were all so emotional. And why couldn't Star sit down in a chair like anybody else instead of perching herself up on the arm like that? The covers were showing signs of wear anyhow, and it was going to cost the earth to replace them. Since it was Adriana who would have to foot the bill, there was really no need for her to worry about it, but she kept her voice even with an effort and said,

"But you knew she hadn't had her holiday."

Star looked at her reproachfully.

"But I never can remember about dates—you know I can't. And you didn't tell me—you didn't tell me a thing. You know perfectly well that I would never, never go all the way to America unless I was quite, quite sure about Stella."

24

Edna prayed for patience.

"My dear Star, I don't know what you mean. You seem to forget that Stella is not a baby any longer. She is six years old. I shall be here, and Meeson, and Mrs. Simmons, and that nice girl Joan Cuttle who comes up from the village. Surely between us we can look after one little girl—and really Nanny will only be away for a fortnight."

The grey eyes brightened, the soft voice shook.

"When six people are looking after a child everybody thinks someone else is doing it, which simply means that no one does it at all! And you know perfectly well that Meeson has her hands full with Adriana! Mrs. Simmons is a cook, not a nurse! She's always complaining she's got too much to do anyhow! And as for this Joan Cuttle, I don't know a thing about her, and I'm not leaving Stella with someone I don't know through and through! This is the most wonderful chance for me, but I'd rather throw it up than not be sure about Stella! Nanny must come back!"

Edna allowed herself a faint smile.

"She has gone on one of these motor-coach trips—France—Italy—Austria—"

"Edna—how frightful!"

"I have no idea where she is. She can't possibly come back."

Star's eyes brimmed with tears.

"Even if we did know, she's as obstinate as the devil—she probably wouldn't come." A bright tear splashed down upon the diamond brooch. "I shall just have to cable out to Jimmy and say he must let someone else have the part. It was absolutely written for me, and he'll give it to that frightful Jean Pomeroy. She'll ruin it of course, but it can't be helped. Stella must come first!"

"My dear, you are just being theatrical."

Star gazed at her, more in sorrow than in anger. Her colour had faded. She produced a small handkerchief and brushed it across her eyes.

"Of course you wouldn't understand. I can't expect you to—you've never had a child."

An unbecoming flush showed that the thrust had told. The little mournful voice went on.

"No—that is what it will have to be. Jimmy will be furious. He has said all along that there wasn't anyone else who would be *right*. It's just me! But I always have put Stella first, and I always will. I can't and I won't leave her unless—unless—" The handkerchief dropped. Her colour flowed back. She clasped her hands and said with leaping enthusiasm, "I've got an idea!"

Edna was prepared for anything.

"You can't take her with you—"

"I shouldn't dream of it! Of course it would be fun—oh, wouldn't it! But I shouldn't think of it for a moment! No, what I have just thought about is Janet!"

"Janet?"

Really Star was too difficult to follow. She jumped from one thing to another and expected you to know what it was all about.

"Janet Johnstone," said Star. "She was the minister's daughter at Darnach—that place where I used to go and stay with the Rutherford relations. Ninian and I used to see a lot of her. Stella would love her. And I shouldn't have a single moment's worry—you couldn't with Janet. Dependable, you know, without being stuffy. You hardly ever get it, do you? But Janet isn't—not the very least bit. She would be perfect."

Edna stared.

26

"Is she a children's nurse?"

"No, of course she isn't! She's Hugo Mortimer's secretary. You know—the man who wrote *Ecstasy* and *White Hell*. And he's gone off on a three months' holiday, shooting, or fishing, or something, so she'll be on her own, and she could quite easily come down here for Nanny's fortnight, and I could go off without a care in the world."

"But, Star—"

Star jumped down from the arm of the big chair. She was as light and graceful as a kitten.

"There aren't any buts! I'll go and ring her up at once!"

CHAPTER 5

Janet lifted the receiver. Star Somers' charming voice came to her.

"Darling, is that you?"

"It used to be."

"How do you mean, it used to be?"

"Everything has been rather intensive. We worked up to the last minute—I've been a machine. But it's over. He went off on Tuesday."

"How grim! You want a holiday."

"I do."

Inwardly Janet reflected that since Hugo had rushed off at the last moment without signing the cheque for her salary, a holiday was not going to be so easy to achieve. She had laid it out before him, she had handed him his fountain pen,

27

and the telephone-bell had rung. It was while she was answering it that Hugo had blown her a kiss and rushed for
his train, leaving the cheque right in the middle of his writing-
pad without a signature. She had written to him of course,
but whether he would ever get the letter was quite another
thing. If he made a plan, it would not be with any set intention
of carrying it out, but merely to have something from which
he could break away. The stimulus of the unexpected! It
wasn't always very convenient for other people. It wasn't
being at all convenient for Janet Johnstone. She heard Star
say,

"Darling, you can have a marvellous holiday this minute!
You haven't fixed anything up, have you? You told me you
hadn't just before Hugo went."

"No, I haven't had time."

"Then that's perfect! You can come down here tomorrow!
It's a lovely place, and no one will bother you!"

When you have played together as children and shared
most things in your teens, there is not much you do not know
about each other. What Star knew would send her off to take
up her part in Jimmy Du Parc's new musical show with a
mind completely at rest. What Janet knew made it perfectly
clear to her that Star had a game of her own. She said in the
voice which had just the least touch of a Scottish lilt,

"You had much better tell me straight out what you want."

"Angel, I knew you would come to my rescue—you always
do! You see, it's Stella. That fool Edna has let Nanny go away
on some ridiculous holiday trip, and I'm due to start for New
York tomorrow—no, it's the day after! But there's no time—
you do see that, don't you? And I can't go unless I can feel
quite sure about Stella. And I would with you. Edna isn't any

28

good with children. She hasn't ever had any. I've just been telling her so, and I don't think she liked it!"

"And how many children am I supposed to have had?"

"Darling, you're an angel with them—you always were! It's a gift! You will do it, won't you? You'll adore it really! It's a wonderful old house, and the gardens are a dream. A bit gone off now, of course, from what they used to be, because there are only two gardeners now instead of four, and I don't suppose there ought to be as many as that. It would be a take-in for everyone if it turned out that Adriana had run through all her capital, and I don't really see how she can be doing everything out of income—not nowadays. Surtax, you know, darling—it's frightening! You can't save a penny! Fortunately for us, Adriana could, and did. At least that's what we hope! Only we don't know who she will leave it to—and *honestly*, what's the good of splitting it? A little here and a little there, it would just be frittering! You do see that, don't you?"

The silvery voice ceasing for a moment, Janet was able to say,

"I don't see anything at all. Nobody could. And I haven't said I'll do it yet."

"Darling, you did! And you simply must, or I'm sunk! Suppose I don't go, and that frightful girl Jean Pomeroy gets the part! Jimmy will give it to her—I know he will! And suppose she makes some ghastly kind of hit in it! She *might*— just to spite me!"

Janet said,

"Star, stop talking! You're making my head go round. And you haven't told me a single thing. Where are you speaking from?"

"Darling, Ford House of course! I came down to say good-

29

bye to Stella and make sure everything was all right, and what do I find? Edna has let Nanny go prancing off to the continent on a motor tour!"

"Yes, you told me that. Ford House—that's where Adriana Ford lives, isn't it?"

"Darling, you know it is! Everyone does! You're just being difficult! And she had an accident six months ago, so Edna runs the house more or less!"

"Who is Edna?"

"She's my cousin Geoffrey's wife. Rather distant—the sort where you have the same great-grandfather. No one has been able to make out why he married her. She hasn't even got money! And they've no children. People do do the oddest things, don't they?"

Janet let that go.

"Is he there too?"

Star's voice ran up to new heights.

"But of course! I told you they hadn't got a bean. They live here. You'll probably think him charming—he can be if he likes."

"Does he do anything?"

"He goes out with a gun. But Mrs. Simmons has got to the point when she won't cook any more rabbits—anyway the staff won't eat them!"

"I was coming to the staff. Who is there?"

"Oh, plenty really. You won't have to do a thing. The Simmons are butler and cook, and there's Meeson who looks after Adriana—she used to be her dresser. Devoted, but she won't lift a finger for anyone else. And a woman from the village, and a girl called Joan Cuttle—what a name! And of course Meriel does the flowers."

"And who is Meriel?"

30

"Well, darling, there you have me! Nobody quite knows. One of those intense creatures with a lot of hair. And no one knows whether Adriana had her surreptitiously, or whether she just picked her up somewhere and adopted her, which is exactly the sort of thing she might have done. When I really want to annoy Geoffrey I tell him I'm quite sure she is a daughter, and that Adriana will leave her everything!"

"How old is she?"

"Oh, I don't know—twenty-three—twenty-four—so I don't suppose she could be really, because Adriana must be eighty, though no one knows about that either. She has always been a clam about her age. But she's my grandfather's sister, and I've got a sort of idea she was older than he was, only it's all rather hush-hush—because of the Scandals, you know, before she blossomed out into being world-famous. I mean, once the public takes you seriously as Ophelia, and Desdemona, and Juliet, they stop thinking about your private life. I believe she was too heart-wringing as Desdemona. And then, of course, later on there were things like Mrs. Alving and the other Ibsen females—and Lady Macbeth—quite overpowering! So no one bothered any more about whether she had lived with an archduke or had an affair with a bullfighter. She was just Adriana Ford, with her name in letters about three feet high and people tearing the box-office down to get seats."

It sounded a bit overpowering. Janet said so.

A new flow began.

"Darling, you practically won't see her. She broke her leg six or seven months ago, and it left her with a limp, so she wouldn't let anyone see her walk. It was one of her special things, you know, the way she moved and walked, so she's been saying she couldn't. Of course the doctors have always

31

said she could if she wanted to, and the other day she went up to town and saw a specialist, and he said she had simply got to lead a normal life and get about as much as she could. Edna was telling me about it before she came out with this horrid thing about Nanny. She said Adriana was going to start coming down to meals and everything, so you'll be seeing her a little more than I said. But honestly, that will be all to the good, because Edna is the world's worst bore. As a matter of fact, Adriana always has spent most of her time in her own set of rooms, with Meeson to wait on her and everything just as she likes it. If she takes a fancy to you she'll send for you, and you must be sure to go. It's a sort of royal command and frightfully impressive. Darling, I must fly! Come round to the flat at nine o'clock, and we'll fix everything up!"

CHAPTER 6

"That is the very last one of Stella." Star held out a large photograph in a folding leather case. "You haven't seen her for simply years, and of course she's changed."

The picture showed a thin, leggy child with straight dark hair cut in a fringe and a face which had lost its baby roundness and was developing features not yet adjusted to each other. The nose had more of a bridge than is usual at six years old. The brows were straight and dark above deep-set eyes. The mouth was wide and rather shapeless.

"She isn't a bit like me," said Star regretfully.

"No."

"Or Robin. He was terribly goodlooking, wasn't he? And of course Stella may be—you never can tell, can you? But it will be in her own sort of way, not ours. She has got wonderful eyes—a sort of mixture of brown and grey, much darker than mine. Janet, you will write me every single thing she says and does, won't you? I'm a fool about her—everyone tells me I am—but that's the way it is. Someone said to me the other day, why didn't I have her with me instead of leaving her down at Ford House? I nearly scratched her eyes out, and I said, 'Oh, it would be a bit of a tie, you know'." Tears rushed into her eyes. "It isn't that—I don't care about anyone else, but I want you to know how it is. I never stop missing her—I don't honestly. But it's better for her to be down there in the country. She's got rabbits, and a kitten, and children do get something out of being in the country that you can't give them in town. Do you remember us at Darnach? It was heaven, wasn't it!"

Janet laid the photograph down upon the bed. There was an open suit-case before her, and she was packing it with Star's filmy underclothes. She had known perfectly well that Star would have been relying on her to do the packing. The mention of Darnach might have been without any special intent, or it might not. She was to know in a moment, because Star said,

"You don't ever see Ninian now, do you?"

Janet was folding a pale blue negligée. She laid it in the suit-case and said,

"No."

Star brought her over an armful of stockings.

"Well, I can't see why not. I ran into Robin the other day, and we had lunch. I really didn't mind—much. And Robin and I were married, whereas you weren't even properly engaged to Ninian. Or were you?"

Janet distributed the stockings.

"It depends on what you call properly."

"Well—you didn't have a ring."

"No, I didn't have a ring."

There was a little pause before Star said,

"Did you break it off, or did he? I asked him, and he wouldn't tell me—just cocked up one eyebrow and said it wasn't my business."

Janet said, "No."

"Because if it was on account of Anne Forester—Was it?"

"She was what you might call a contributory cause."

"Darling, how *stupid!* He didn't care for her—not the least bit in the world! It was just a flare-up! Don't you ever have a pash yourself and get over it? I have dozens! I see a too utterly expensive hat and feel as if I should die if I didn't have it, or a mink I can't possibly afford, or anything like that, and after a little it wears off and I don't give a damn! Anne Forester was like that. He couldn't possibly have afforded her, and she would have bored him stiff in a week. You see, I do know Ninian. We may be only first cousins, but in a way we're much more like twins, as our fathers were. It's something quite special. So I know what it was about Anne. And there's another reason why I know—because of what happened with Robin and me. We just had a pash for each other, and we got married on it and crashed. There wasn't anything there really—not for either of us. Only I can't be sorry about it, because I've got Stella, and she is real—I've got Stella. Now, with you and Ninian there is something real. He matters to you, and you matter to him—you always did, and you always will."

34

Janet had been bending forward over the suit-case. Her hands went on putting things into it, folding them carefully, laying them straight. She was a little taller than Star, but not much. And she was penny-plain to Star's twopence coloured—an agreeable shade of brown hair and eyes that matched it, eyebrows and lashes a little darker—a face with nothing striking about it except that the chin gave the impression that she would be able to make up her mind and stick to it, and the eyes had a straight and friendly look. Star had once said, "You know, darling, you'll go on getting more attractive all the time, because the niceness will go on coming through." She watched her now and wished that Janet would speak. She never would about Ninian, and it was stupid. Things you don't talk about lie in the dark and fester. You want to get them out into the light, even if you have to drag them. But when Janet straightened up and turned round, all she said was,

"There—that's done. And you'd better not touch it, except to put one or two last things in on the top. Now, what else is there to do?"

"Well, we haven't settled anything about the business side yet."

Janet frowned.

"There wouldn't be any business side, only Hugo forgot to sign my cheque, and as he is probably well off the map by now, there is no saying when I can get hold of him. You can lend me ten pounds."

"Darling, you can't live on ten pounds!"

Janet laughed.

"You don't know what you can do till you try. Only this time I'm not trying. I shall have a fortnight nice and free in Ford House, and I've got something in the savings bank.

With your ten pounds, I shall get through, even if Hugo doesn't communicate—and he probably will, because he'll want to know if there's anything about his play. I ought to be going."

Star put out a hand and caught at her.

"Not yet. I always feel safe when you are somewhere about. I don't mean with me, but when I know I can just ring you up and say come along and you'll come, like I did tonight. And when I think of being right over on the other side of the Atlantic I get a horrid kind of shivery feeling, as if there was a lump of ice right down inside me and it wouldn't melt. You don't think it could be a presentiment, do you?"

"How could it?"

Star said weakly,

"I don't know—nobody does. But people have them. One of my Rutherford great-aunts had one. She was going on a pleasure trip, I don't remember where, and just as she was going to step on board she had a most dreadful cold feeling and she couldn't do it. So she didn't. And everyone else was drowned. That was her portrait in Uncle Archie's study. In a little lace cap and one of those Victorian shawls. She married an astronomer, and they went to live in the south of England. So it just goes to show, doesn't it?"

Janet let this go by. She had known Star for so many years that she did not expect her to be logical. She said cheerfully,

"Well, you needn't go if you don't want to—need you? You can always send Jimmy Du Parc a cable to tell him you've got cold feet and he can give Jean Pomeroy your part. It's perfectly simple."

Star pinched hard.

"I'd rather die!" she said. "And you don't believe in pre-sentiments, do you?"

"I don't know. What I do know is that you can't have it both ways. If you want this part you'll have to go to New York for it. It isn't going to come to you."

"It's a *marvellous* part! I should be right on the top of my own particular wave! Janet, I've got to do it! And as long as you are with Stella I shall know that it'll be perfectly all right. You do think it will be all right, don't you?"

"I can't see why not."

"No—I'm just being silly. I do hate going on journeys. Not when I'm actually doing them—that's rather fun—but the night before. It's like looking from a nice bright lighted room and not wanting to go out into the dark."

Janet laughed.

"You are not very likely to find it dark in New York!" she said.

When she had gone, Star picked up the telephone receiver and dialled quickly. The voice that answered was as familiar to her as her own.

"Ninian—it's Star."

"It would be!"

"I've rung you up three times, and you've always been out!"

"I do go out!"

"Ninian, I've just had Janet here—"

"Epoch-making intelligence!"

"That idiot Edna has let Nanny go off on holiday some-where on the continent."

"That bourne from which no traveller returns!"

"Oh, she'll return all right, but not for a fortnight—and I'm off to New York."

"I know you are. I'm coming to see you off."

"Well, you wouldn't be if it wasn't for Janet. I couldn't go away and leave Stella without somebody."

"Well, I should have said Ford House was rather over-stocked with women."

"I wouldn't leave Stella with one of them! What I rang up to say was that Janet is going down to look after her."

There was something of a pause. Then Ninian Rutherford said,

"Why?"

"Why what?"

"Why ring me up?"

"I thought you might like to know."

He said in his most charming voice,

"Darling, I don't give a damn, and you can put that in your pipe and smoke it!"

Star gave an exasperated sigh and hung up.

CHAPTER 7

Janet went down to Ford House next day. She sat in the train to Ledbury, and something kept telling her that she was running into trouble, and that she was a fool to be doing it. Staying in town would have meant bread and margarine with a sprinkling of cheese and an occasional herring washed down with cups of weak tea but it might have been preferable to a fortnight with Star's relations. She didn't know them, and they didn't know her. When she thought about them

38

she got the sort of feeling you have when you open the door at the top of steps going down into a cellar. There was a place like that in the Rutherfords' house at Darnach. The door was in the passage outside the kitchen. When you opened it there were steps that disappeared into the darkness, and a cold air came up that was tinged with mould. Going down to Ford House felt like that.

Janet took herself quite severely to task about the feeling. She did have that sort of feeling sometimes, and when she had it she blamed a Highland grandmother. Three-quarters of her derived from Lowland Scots who made common sense and a firm adherence to principle their rule of life, but the Highland grandmother was not always to be silenced. Ninian had once declared that she would be unbearable without her—"Too 'dull' and good, for human nature's daily food."

She pushed Ninian out of her mind and shut the door on him. Since she had been doing this for nearly two years, it ought by now to have been easy, but push and shut as she would, there was always something that got left behind or that came seeping back—the way he looked when his eyes laughed at her, the black look of his anger, his quick jerking frown. She supposed they would stop hurting in the end, but at the moment the end was quite a long way off.

At Ledbury she took a taxi, and was driven three miles along country lanes to Ford village. There was a green, a general shop, a church, a garage with a petrol pump, and the entrance to Ford House—tall stone pillars with no gates between them, a squat-looking lodge to one side, and a long unweeded drive stretching away between trees and over-grown bushes.

They emerged upon a gravel sweep. Janet got out, and the driver rang the bell. Nobody came for quite a long time. The

39

bell was an electric one. Janet had begun to think it must be out of order, when the door was opened by a girl in a washed-out cotton dress. She had pale, prominent eyes and she poked with her head, but her voice sounded amiable as she said,

"Oh, are you Miss Johnstone? I didn't hear the bell with all the noise that's going on. That Stella—I never heard a child scream like it in my life! She's been something dreadful ever since Nanny went. I only hope you'll be able to do something with her. Slapping's no good, for I've tried. Nothing to hurt her of course, but sometimes it stops them—only not her. All she does is carry right on till you don't know whether you're on your head or your feet."

While she spoke the driver dropped Janet's suit-case on the step, pocketed his fare, and drove away.

Janet walked into the hall. Someone was certainly screaming, but just where the sound came from, she could not be sure.

"There!" said the girl. "Did you ever hear anything like it?"

"Where is she?" said Janet quickly.

But the words were hardly spoken before they were answered by Stella herself. A door at the back of the hall was pushed open and a screaming child ran out. And then in an instant half way across the floor she stopped dead, stared at Janet's suit-case, at Janet herself, and said,

"Who are you?"

Janet went to meet her.

"I'm Janet Johnstone."

The child was the child of the photograph. She showed no sign of having just emerged from a screaming fit. The dark straight fringe was neat, the fine pale skin unmarked by tears. The beautiful deep-set eyes were fixed in an appraising stare.

40

"Are you Star's Janet?"

"I am."

"That played with her and Ninian at Darnach?"

"Of course."

"You mightn't have been. I know three other people called Janet. Ninian plays lovely games—doesn't he?"

Janet said "Yes" again.

The eyes looked through and through her. They were of so dark a grey that they might almost have been black. Janet wondered what they saw. The thought went through her mind, and as it passed, Stella put out a hand and said,

"Come along and see my room. Yours is next door. It's Nanny's really, but she's gone away on a holiday. I screamed for two hours."

The little hand was cold in hers. Janet said,

"Why?"

"I didn't want her to go."

"Do you always scream when you don't want things and they happen?"

With simple determination Stella said, "Yes."

"It sounds very unpleasant."

The dark head was vigorously shaken.

"No, I like it. Everyone else puts their hands to their ears. Aunt Edna says it goes through and through her. But I don't mind how much noise I make. I was screaming when you came."

Janet said, "I heard you. Why? Why did you scream?"

They had reached the top of the stairs. Passages ran away to the right and to the left. Stella tugged at her hand.

"We go this way." They took the right-hand passage. "I didn't want you to come."

"Why?"

41

The child caught her breath.

"I wanted to go with Star in an aeroplane. It would be fun. So I screamed. Sometimes if I scream long enough I get what I want—" Her voice trailed away, the clasp on Janet's hand tightened, the dark brows drew together. "I don't always, but sometimes I do. And it's no good trying to stop me. Joan slapped me just before you came, but it only made me worse."

"Was that Joan who let me in?"

Stella nodded vigorously.

"Joan Cuttle. Aunt Edna says she's such a nice girl, but I think she's a sissy. She can't even slap properly. She just flaps with her hand—it doesn't hurt a bit. Anyhow I oughtn't to be slapped—it's bad for me. Star would be very angry if she knew. Do you think I am a problem child? Uncle Geoffrey says I am."

Janet said, "I'm sure I hope not."

They had arrived at what was evidently the nursery. It had a lovely view over green lawns that went down to a stream, but after the merest glance her hand was tugged again.

"Why did you say you hoped not? I think it's in*tres*ting."

Janet shook her head.

"It sounds very uncomfortable, and you wouldn't be happy."

The dark eyes were lifted to hers in an odd deep stare. Stella said mournfully,

"But I don't scream when I'm happy." Then she jerked her hand away. "Come and see my room! Star had it done for me. It's got flowers on the curtains and blue birds flying, and there's a blue carpet and a blue eiderdown, and a picture with a hill."

It was a pretty child's room. The hill in the picture was the

42

hill that stood over Darnach with the Rutherfords' house at the foot. The name of the hill was Darnach Law, and she and Star and Ninian had climbed over every foot of it.

Nanny's room, which was to be hers, opened out of Stella's. It had the same outlook, but a good deal of heavy mahogany furniture made it dark. There were pictures of Nanny's relations on the mantelpiece, and a many times enlarged photograph above it. Stella could tell her who everyone was. The young man in uniform was Nanny's brother Bert, and the girl next to him was his wife Daisy. The picture over the mantelpiece was done from quite a little one of Nanny's father and mother on their wedding day.

Stella knew everything about the people in the photographs. She was in the middle of a most exciting story of how Bert's youngest was in a ship that was blown up in the war—"and he swam for miles and miles and miles, and it got dark and he thought he was going to be drowned—" when the door opened and Edna Ford came in. Stella finished the story in a gabbling hurry—"and an aeroplane came and he wasn't, and Bert and Daisy were ever so glad."

Edna Ford shook hands in the rather limp manner in which she did most things. She had a washed-out, faded look, and she wore the least flattering of clothes. Her tweed skirt hesitated between brown and grey and dipped at the back. The jumper, of an indeterminate mauve, clung closely about stooping shoulders and a singularly flat chest. Nothing more trying to face and figure could have been devised. The sallow skin, the light dry hair, were cruelly emphasised. She said in a complaining tone,

"Really, Miss Johnstone, I don't know what you must think. Stella had no business to bring you up like this. But of course with no proper staff this is the sort of thing that happens. A small convenient house would be so much better, but it is out of the question. Someone has to look after my aunt. Simmons does what he can, but he is not strong, and we spare him as much as possible. I don't know what we should do without Joan Cuttle. I believe she let you in. So helpful and good-natured, but of course not really trained. Such a nice girl though. The Simmons are old servants of my aunt's, and Mrs. Simmons is a very good cook. And then, of course, there is a woman from the village, so I suppose it might be worse. I am really not strong enough to do a great deal myself. Now let me see, Joan will bring up your case— she said you only have the one. And then perhaps Stella ought to go to bed. Star said she would ring up at seven— there's an extension in your room. And I only hope she will be punctual, because we dine at half past, and it does put Mrs. Simmons out if anyone is late."

CHAPTER 8

Star rang up at half past six, which was better than being late. The call must have cost her pounds, because she went on talking in a perfectly care-free manner while the pips kept mounting up. Janet and Stella made a game of it. They sat side by side on the bed and played snatch-the-microphone, so that at one moment Star found herself impressing upon Stella that she was an exceptionally sensitive child and mustn't be crossed, and in the next blowing kisses along the wire to Janet. As this had the fortunate result of making Stella

44

laugh, nothing could have been more reassuring for Star. The good-byes were said in a much happier atmosphere than anyone would have thought possible, and it was only at the last that there was a sob in the high, pretty voice.

"Janet—are you there?"

Janet said, "Yes."

"You will keep her safe, won't you? I've got the most dreadful cold feet."

"Star, you're just being silly!"

Stella bounced on the bed beside her.

"Me—me—it's my turn!" She butted Janet out of the way. "Star, it's me! You are being silly! Janet says so, and so do I."

"Darling, are you all right—are you happy?"

"Of course! Janet is going to tell me about going up Darnach Law and getting lost in the mist. You didn't tell me about that—"

"Janet will," said Star.

"And when I'm quite grown up I shall go there, and I shall climb all over the hill! And I shall come with you in an aeroplane when you go to New York, and I shall sit up all night and see you act!"

They were still talking ten minutes later when Janet took the receiver.

"Better ring off now, Star. Have a good time, and send us all your notices."

Stella bounced and echoed her.

"Send me every single picture—promise!"

In her packed-up flat Star felt cold and cut off. They were going to do very well without her. Not that she wanted Stella to miss her—she didn't, she really didn't. But that cold feeling persisted, and the Atlantic was dreadfully wide.

Down at Ford House Stella went happily to bed. There were going to be so many things to do tomorrow that she was in a hurry to get there and begin doing them.

Janet put on a brown taffeta dress with a little turnover collar and fastened it with a deep-coloured cairngorm brooch which had belonged to the Highland grandmother. As she went down the wide staircase, there were hurrying steps behind her. A dark girl passed her in a rush, and then, as if the impulse which had taken her there had petered out, turned no more than a dozen feet away from the foot of the stairs and stood waiting, her hands clasped at her breast, her foot tapping the floor.

Janet did not hurry herself. She continued her staid descent. This, she supposed, was Meriel, and all that she or anyone else knew about Meriel was that Adriana Ford had picked her up somewhere. She looked at her and saw a creature slight to the point of attenuation, with masses of hair tossed together above an artificially whitened face, eyes dark behind darker lashes, and thin lips painted scarlet. She wore a black dress with a spreading skirt and very long sleeves coming down over long white hands. A string of pearls fell to her waist. Janet thought they were real. Very difficult to tell, of course, but she thought so all the same. As she reached the bottom step, the scarlet lips opened to say,

"I suppose you are Janet Johnstone." The voice was husky, the tone aggressive.

Janet smiled briefly and replied,

"I suppose you are Meriel Ford."

The black eyes flashed.

"Oh, we're all Fords here, and none of us have the slightest right to the name. It should be Rutherford really. Adriana just thought Ford sounded better for the stage. Adriana

Ford—that's pretty good, isn't it? Rutherford would have been too long. And then, of course, when she bought this place it all fitted in too marvellously. Ford of Ford House!" She gave a low laugh. "And Geoffrey and Edna followed suit, so we're all Fords together! Have you seen Adriana yet?"

"Not yet."

Meriel laughed again.

"Oh, well, if you had come down a month ago you might have stayed your fortnight and never set eyes on her. She has been like that ever since her accident in the spring—up in her own room and only seeing the people she fancies. But she has taken a turn just the last few days—went up to town to see a doctor and came back with a lot of new clothes and all set to start entertaining in a big way. She has been coming down to meals and generally sitting up and taking notice. But I believe she is staying in her room tonight—probably because you are here. She doesn't always fancy strangers. Are you a nervous person?"

"I don't think so."

Meriel surveyed her.

"No—you haven't enough temperament. Adriana won't care about you one way or the other. Between people who have temperament it's love or hate, you know." The thin shoulders were shrugged. "It doesn't really matter which. It is the emotion that counts. One might just as well be dead as have no emotions. But I daresay that seems like nonsense to you."

"It does rather," said Janet equably. She moved on across the hall.

The meal was well cooked and well served. Simmons had been a good butler. He knew his job, and within the limits of his strength he could still put up a good performance with Joan Cuttle helping in the background.

Geoffrey Ford came in when the soup was already on the table—a goodlooking fair-haired man a little run to seed. His eye travelled over Janet in the manner of an expert. There was a gleam of interest, almost immediately quenched by a definite lack of response. He liked a woman who could give him glance for glance, but here there was no answering spark, beckoning only to withdraw behind dropped lashes. He got a steady look and a pleasant answer when he spoke to her, but he thought not even Edna's jealousy would be able to find anything to feed on in Miss Janet Johnstone. He had a mental shrug for the conclusion.

When dinner was over he vanished into the smoking-room. Janet endured two hours of Edna's conversation against a background of jazz music evoked by Meriel. As fast as one programme ended she started fiddling with the knobs and roamed Europe in search of another. Sometimes the throbbing rhythms were just a whisper behind a barrage of intruding stations, sometimes they blared at roaring strength, sometimes a heterodyne tore shrieking across the beat. But loud or soft, clear or jarring, Edna plied her embroidery-needle and went on talking about the dullness of life in the country, the difficulty of getting household help and keeping it when you had got it, and other kindred subjects. She had a good deal to say on the question of Stella's upbringing.

"She is really getting too old for a nurse, and Nanny doesn't fit in—nurses practically never do. She doesn't like the Simmonses, and they don't like her. I'm always afraid of there being a flare-up, and I really don't know what I should do if they gave notice. And then there is Joan. Such a nice girl, but Nanny is always picking on her. I am sometimes quite sorry there is this class at the Vicarage. For Stella, you know. I suppose Star told you. The Lentons have two little girls, and Jackie Trent comes in. His mother neglects him dreadfully. She is a widow, and a very flighty person. She lives in the cottage opposite the church, and he makes the class up to four. And a cousin of Mrs. Lenton's helps in the house and teaches them. She isn't really strong enough to take a regular job, so it's all very convenient. Only sometimes I think it would be better if it wasn't, because then Star would be obliged to do something about Stella. She would really be a great deal better at school."

Janet was very glad indeed when ten o'clock struck and Edna, folding up her work, remarked that they kept early hours. She took a book to bed with her, read for an hour, and slept until seven in the morning.

The first thing she saw when she opened her eyes was Stella sitting cross-legged on the end of the bed. She wore a blue dressing-gown embroidered with daisies. Her eyes were fixed on Janet in an unwinking stare.

"I thought you'd wake up. People do if you go on looking at them. Nanny won't let me wake her—she's most strict about it. She looked after a boy called Peter once, and he used to come rampaging into her bed as soon as it was light. She told him and she told him, but he *would* do it. So she went away and looked after someone else."

They were just going down to breakfast, when there was a knock on the nursery door. At Janet's "Come in!" there entered a little roundabout woman with a thick mop of grey hair and a bustling way with her.

"Good-morning, Miss Johnstone. Meeson's the name, and Mrs. for choice. Not that I ever fancied a man enough to marry one, but it sounds better, if you know what I mean.

49

When you're getting on in years, as you might say—more to it than just plain Miss. And Miss Ford, she sends her compliments and will be glad if you will visit her whenever you get back from taking Stella to the Vicarage."

Stella frowned.

"I don't want to go to the Vicarage. I want to stay here and see Adriana, and have Janet tell me about Darnach."

Meeson put out a plump hand and patted her shoulder.

"Well then, ducks, you can't. And none of those screaming games, *if* you please."

Stella stamped her foot.

"I wasn't going to scream! But I shall if I want to!"

Meeson said easily, "Well, I shouldn't if I were you." She turned back to Janet. "Shall I tell Miss Ford you'll come, then?"

"Oh, yes, of course."

The Vicarage was no more than the length of the drive and about another hundred yards away. It sat comfortably next to the church with a riot of climbing roses almost hiding the walls. Two little fair-haired girls watched at the gate for Stella, and just as Janet turned to come away, a small white-faced boy ran up to join them. She thought he had an uncared-for look. There were stains on the grey pullover, and a hole where a stitch in time would have saved a good many more than nine.

CHAPTER 9

Back at Ford House, Janet took her way along the left-hand corridor at the stair head. Knocking on the end door, she was bidden to enter by a voice which didn't sound as if it belonged to Meeson. She came into a large L-shaped room with the sun pouring in through two of the four big windows.

Adriana Ford lay on a couch on the shady side. Cream brocade cushions propped her. She wore a loose wrap of the same material trimmed with dark fur. A green velvet spread covered her to the waist. Janet must have seen these things as she came in, because she remembered them afterwards, but at the time she was only aware of Adriana herself—the fine skin, very carefully made up, the great eyes, the astonishing dark red hair, cut short and square. There was no effect of age, there was no effect of youth. There was just Adriana Ford, and she dominated the room.

Janet came up to the couch. A long, pale hand touched hers and pointed to a chair. She sat, and Adriana looked at her. It could have been unnerving, but as far as Janet was concerned, if Adriana wanted to look at her she was welcome. She certainly hadn't anything to hide. Or had she? Ninian walked in among her thoughts and angered them. Her colour rose.

Adriana laughed.

"So you are something more than a brown Scotch mouse!"

Janet said, "I hope so."

51

"So do I!" said Adriana Ford. "We're a terrible household of women. That is what one comes to—we start with women, and we go back to them. And I'm lucky with Meeson—she was my dresser you know, so we can enjoy ourselves talking about old times. And I didn't think then I'd be cast for a part like this—the Interminable Invalid! Well, this doesn't amuse you. Star sent you down here to look after her brat. Has it treated you to one of its screaming fits yet?"

Janet showed a dimple.

"She only screams when she can't have something she wants."

"It's a simple code! I've told Star a dozen times the creature ought to go to school. She's quite intelligent, and she's too old for Nanny. Well, I suppose you've met everyone. Edna is the world's worst bore and Geoffrey thinks so. Meriel wants the moon and she isn't likely to get it. We're an odd lot, and you'll be glad when you can leave us. I'd be glad enough to get away myself, but I'm here for keeps. Do you see much of Star?"

"Off and on," said Janet.

"And Ninian?"

"No."

"Too busy for his old friends? Or just the changeable kind? I hear he made a hit with that queer book he wrote. What was it called—'Never to Meet.' No money in it of course, and no sense, but just a flash of genius. All the clever boys who were at college with him patted him on the back and wrote him up, and the Third Programme did a dramatized version which I don't suppose I should have listened to if it had been by anyone else. His second book has got more stuff in it. Have you read it?"

Janet said, "No." She had made herself a promise about

52

that, and found it hard to keep. Not to read his book was the sign and symbol that she had turned Ninian from her door. Out of a corner of her mind there came the whispered echo from Pierrot's song:

> *"Ouvre moi ta porte*
> *Pour l'amour de Dieu!"*

Janet fetched Stella at half past twelve, and was presented with a programme for the rest of the day.

"Now we go home, and you brush my hair, and look at my hands and say you can't think how I get them so dirty, and I wash them, and you look at them again, and then we go down and have lunch. And after lunch I have my rest— only if it's fine I have it in the garden on a li-lo with a rug. You can have one too if you like. Aunt Edna does, but Nanny says it's a lazy habit. The rugs are in the nursery cupboard, and we must always remember to bring them in."

They went out after lunch, across the green lawn and through a gate into a garden with a pool in the middle of it. There was a stone seat, and a summerhouse, and a yew hedge which kept the wind away. Beyond the hedge there were tall hollyhocks that topped it, and borders bright with phlox and marigold, snapdragon, gladiolus, a late tangle of love-in-the-mist, and the high plumes of golden rod. In the summerhouse there were garden chairs, and a locker full of cushions and li-los.

Stella directed the proceedings with zest.

"We'll have lots of cushions. You can sit on the seat, and I'll have my li-lo by the pool. It's my very favourite place. Sometimes there are dragonflies, and nearly always there are frogs, but Nanny doesn't care about them. And when we are

53

quite comfortable you can tell me about getting lost in the mist."

The sun was warm, the sky was blue. A green dragonfly hovered above the pool like a quivering flame. Janet saw these things with the eyes of her body, but with the eyes of her mind she climbed and stumbled in a mist on the slopes of Darnach Law with Ninian's hand on her shoulder steadying her.

Stella's high voice chimed in.

"Wasn't Star there?"

"No. She had a cold. Mrs. Rutherford wouldn't let her go out."

"What a pity."

"She didn't think so. We were wet through. There is nothing that soaks through everything like a mist."

Stella said in a sleepy voice,

"Star doesn't like to get wet." She yawned and snuggled down among her cushions. "I do. I like to get all soaked—and come in—and have a lovely fire—and hot—buns—for—tea—" Her voice trailed away.

Janet watched her, and saw the sleeping face relax, the cheeks softly rounded, lips parted, and eyelids not quite shut. With all that restless energy gone, there was a defenceless look. She wondered whether Stella was climbing Darnach Law in a dream.

She began to wish that she had brought a book. She had not expected to have time for reading, and she did not care to go and fetch one now, in case Stella should wake and find herself alone. She fell to watching the dragonfly. It had settled now, and clung motionless to a sun-warmed stone. She had never seen one so near before—the brilliant eyes, the gauzy wings, the long apple-green body, and all that shimmering motion stilled.

There was a step on the paved path. Ninian Rutherford came through an arched gap in the hedge and said with a question in his voice,

"Nature study?"

It was an extremely charming voice—fit, as his old Scotch nurse used to say, to wile a bird from her nest. It had wiled Janet once, but she was armed against it now. Or was she? She looked up and met his laughing eyes. If there was something behind the laughter, it was gone before she could be sure of it. They might have met yesterday and parted the best of friends. The two-year gap was to be ignored.

He came round the pool and sat down beside her.

"Well, how are you getting on, my jo Janet?" It was the old jesting name, the old jesting tone.

"And what were you looking at?" He sang under his breath:

> "Keek into the draw well,
> Janet, Janet.
> There ye'll see yer bonnie sel',
> My jo Janet!"

She said in her most matter-of-fact tone,

"I was watching a dragonfly. I had never seen a green one before. Look!"

But he was looking at her.

"Have you been slimming? You're a bit on the thin side."

"If I'm here for a fortnight I shall probably have to slim. The milk is practically cream, and Mrs. Simmons is a wonderful cook!"

55

He laughed.

"It's the one bright spot. Honestly, darling, you'll be bored stiff. It was like Star's nerve to push you into looking after her brat! But whatever possessed you to let her do it? I'd have seen her at Jericho! But you never did have any sense."

The colour rushed into her cheeks.

"If there's one thing I've got, it's just that!"

"Sense?" His eyes teased her. "You haven't got as much as would lie on the edge of a sixpence—not if it means looking after yourself and seeing people don't exploit you, and not working your fingers to the bone for them!"

She lifted a pair of small brown hands and let them fall in her lap again.

"I wouldn't just call them worked to the bone myself."

"Metaphorically speaking, they are. It's just what I said— you've no sense. You let Star foist this job on you, and you let that fellow Hugo work all the flesh off your bones, the damned ass!"

"He is not a damned ass!"

"He is—and a poseur into the bargain!"

He was as dark as Star was fair. Janet suddenly realized that Stella was like him. There was the same nervous energy, the same black frown, and the dark spark of anger in the eyes. It danced there now as he leaned towards her and said,

"You don't know how to fight for yourself—that's the trouble with you! You would be a bonnie fighter if you'd give your mind to it—I give you that! But you don't! You're thinking about the other person all the time, or you're being too proud to bother!"

Just where were they going? They both knew well enough what he meant when he said she was too proud to fight. She had been too proud to fight for him. If he wanted Anne

Forester, it wasn't Janet Johnstone who would crook a finger to beckon him back.

"Ninian, you're talking nonsense."

"And why not? I can talk better nonsense than that if I've a mind to!"

He had leaned near enough to give her the feeling that she was hemmed in, his arm along the back of the seat, his slim length easy. She put out a hand to hold him off, and he laughed.

"Ninian, you'll wake Stella."

He said in a laughing voice,

"Well, I don't want to do that! Let sleeping tigers lie! How do you get on with her?"

"Very well."

"Had one of the famous screaming fits yet?"

"She only has them when she's bored."

"So she won't have one with you—is that it?"

"Of course."

"Our sainted Edna is enough to bore anyone. No wonder Geoffrey strays. And her face was her fortune, you know. At any rate it was all the fortune she had. So why on earth Geoffrey married her just has to take its place as one of those insoluble mysteries along with the Man in the Iron Mask and Who Killed the Princes in the Tower. It's pretty certain Richard didn't, because if he had, Henry VII would have tumbled over himself to accuse him after the battle of Bosworth. I hope you admire the versatility of my conversation. Or perhaps Hugo is so brilliant that no one else can compete!"

Janet allowed the dimple to come out. It was an attractive dimple.

"You don't get much brilliant conversation when you are taking things down in shorthand."

"You don't mean to say you take down all that tripe in squiggles and dashes!"

"Dashes are Morse, not shorthand."

"Darling, I can't believe it. Shorthand! The only thing I can think of that would be worse would be a clattering typewriter, or Bernard Shaw's reformed spelling! It would dry me right up!"

The dimple remained. Janet said nothing.

He struck the back of the seat with his hand.

"This is where you ask me how I do my stuff!"

"But I know—on odd bits of paper, all up and down and across, and someone has to sort it all out for you."

"I have to do it myself, darling. Janet, it serves you right!"

"How does it serve me right?"

"You might have had the job for keeps, but no, you went into a huff and walked out. I'm not angry, you know—I'm just sorry for you having to take down that stuff of Hugo's."

"It's very good stuff." She spoke soberly. The dimple had disappeared.

Ninian ran an enraged hand through his hair and said,

"All right, it is, then! And so what? You work for him, and you don't have to bother with my wretched bits and pieces! He's a best-seller, and I'm not and probably never will be, so it's all for the best! And you wouldn't change your job for the world!"

Janet looked at him calmly. There was something gratifying about being able to put Ninian in a rage. She said,

"It's a good job."

"Oh, quite a labour of love!" The hand that had been laid along the back of the seat shot out and took her by the wrist. "Is it?"

"Is it what? Ninian you're hurting!"

"Is it a labour of love? I don't mind in the least whether I'm hurting you or not! Does he make love to you—does he kiss you?"

She looked down at the brown hand, which felt more like a handcuff than reasonable flesh and blood. But then, when was Ninian reasonable? Her lips trembled, but she would not let them break into a smile. There was a decided increase in her Scottish lilt as she said,

"It wouldn't be your business if he did."

The grip on her wrist tightened. She wouldn't have thought it possible, but it happened—quite painfully.

"Does he?"

"You're breaking my wrist!"

He laughed.

"That would put a stop to the shorthand!" He let her go as suddenly as he had snatched at her. "You shouldn't make me angry! You've got the trick of it, and I suppose you like playing cat-and-mouse with me!"

"I do not."

"Well, you'd better be careful, or one day you'll go too far."

He looked past her and saw Stella's eyes fixed on him. That she had only just opened them was apparent. They were still dark with sleep, the pupils contracting visibly as the light reached them. She said, "Ninian—" in a wavering voice. She had come out of a dream, and he was there. She stared, scrambled up, and flung herself upon him.

CHAPTER 10

Meeson came knocking on the nursery door just as Stella was ready for bed.

"Please, Miss Johnstone, Miss Ford would like you to come up and have coffee with her after dinner. She is not coming down tonight."

It was a royal summons and admitted of no refusal.

As she went downstairs half an hour later she found Ninian at her elbow.

"So we are bidden to the presence. You seem to have made a hit with Adriana."

Janet frowned.

"Have you seen her?"

"Oh, yes—I have the entrée. The polite guest loses no time in paying his respects to his hostess."

"You're not staying here!"

"Darling, where else? I do, you know, from time to time. Adriana and I are buddies, and after all she is 'my aunt', as our dear Edna says. A horrid title—even Stella won't use it!"

The meal was certainly enlivened by Ninian's presence. He placed himself between Edna and Janet and kept a stream of conversation flowing. Geoffrey responded, Edna thawed, and really things might have been very pleasant if it had not been for Meriel, who sat wrapt in silence, her gaze set darkly upon Ninian's face. It was plain that she resented his choice of a seat and the fact that she had not been quick enough to reach the place next to him in time to take it from Janet, who had been sitting on that side of the table at previous meals. Meriel had been last into the room, and she just hadn't had a chance. By the time she was in a position to see what was happening, Ninian was pulling out Janet's chair and fairly putting her into it. There was nothing left for Meriel to do but fall into a gloom.

It was half way through dinner before she suddenly found her voice and, leaning half across the table, began to remind Ninian of this, that, and the other.

"That dance at Ledbury—wonderful, wasn't it? Do you remember, you said I was the best dancer in the room?" She gave a low reminiscent laugh. "Not that it was such a very great compliment, because of course most English women can't dance at all—no fluidity, no grace, no temperament. You know, I always feel I might have done something with my dancing if Adriana had recognized my possibilities and had me trained—one must begin young. But of course she was entirely taken up with her own affairs—she always is. And now it is too late." Her eyes dwelt soulfully upon Ninian, her voice went down into tragic depths.

He extricated himself deftly.

"Oh, well, you would soon have got bored with having to practise seven or eight hours a day. A great deal too much like hard work, I should say." He turned to Geoffrey. "Did you see that Russian girl when she was over? I thought she was pretty good myself."

As they came out of the dining-room, Ninian announced to all and sundry,

"Janet and I have got to tear ourselves away. Coffee with Adriana."

61

"Do you mean she asked you—both of you?" Meriel's voice was angry.

"She did."

"I shouldn't have thought she would go out of her way to ask a stranger."

"Wouldn't you? But then you don't think very much, do you?"

She said,

"What's the use? It doesn't get you anywhere." Her eyes were suddenly imploring.

Janet looked away. She murmured an excuse to Edna and turned towards the stairs. After no more than half a dozen steps Ninian came up with her. She waited until the hall below was empty before she said,

"All she wants is to have a scene. You shouldn't bait her."

"There is nothing for her to have a scene about."

He glanced sideways at her. Her head was high. She looked, not at him, but straight ahead. She said,

"Do you expect me to believe that you haven't been flirting with her?"

He gave a rueful laugh.

"I don't know about expecting you to believe it, but it happens to be the truth. As you say, all she wants is to have a scene, and it doesn't very much matter what it's about. She's bored stiff, and she wants a spot of limelight and a nice juicy emotional part. Honestly, she scares me! I'd as soon flirt with an atom bomb!"

Janet said severely, "Why doesn't she get herself a job? I'm not surprised she's bored down here with nothing to do."

He laughed.

"Better keep off telling her that if you really don't want a scene!"

"Why?"

"You're being stupid. A job would mean work, and our darling Meriel has no urge to work. Money to spend and nothing to do, with rows of admirers helping her to do it—that, quite frankly, is her ambition. And she'll never leave Adriana, because out of sight could be out of mind, and she might get left out of The Will. That is all we think about in this house, darling. No one knows how much Adriana has got, and nobody has any idea who is going to get it when she is gone, so naturally no one thinks about anything else. Geoffrey would like a flat in town and his freedom. Edna dwells fondly on the thought of a nice little all-electric house full of the gadgets from exhibitions like Beautiful Homes For The Million. Meriel wants a film world in which she glides about in marble halls and sleeps on a tiger skin."

"And you?" said Janet. "What do you want?"

"What I can't get."

They had reached the top of the stairs and were standing there. His voice had a very undermining sound in it. She said,

"It used not to be money."

He laughed.

"We've changed all that. Every sensible person wants money."

"A sensible person knows that you have to earn it."

"Janet, you're a prig!"

"I daresay."

"It's a revolting thing to be."

She made a small pushing movement with her hands.

"Very well then, away with you!"

He burst out laughing.

"Come along! We're keeping Adriana waiting."

They found her on her couch, the velvet spread drawn up to her waist, rings on the long pale fingers, no other jewelry except the double row of pearls. The coffee had not yet arrived. She wanted to talk to them first. She would ring for it when she was ready.

"And I'll see you one at a time to start with." She spoke to Ninian. "You can go into my dressing-room and wait. There's a comfortable chair, and a book of my press notices."

He laughed.

"Do you think I need press notices to tell me how wonderful you are?"

The door shut. Janet was waved to a chair. She thought, "It's like being in some kind of a queer dream." And then Adriana was saying,

"I am going to ask you a question. I want an honest answer to it. Is that agreed?"

There was no change in Janet's face, or in her voice as she said,

"It would depend on what you asked me."

"Meaning you wouldn't undertake to be honest?"

"I mightn't know the answer."

"Oh, I think you would, or I shouldn't be asking. Well, here it is. You and Ninian and Star grew up together. There isn't much that children don't know about each other, and I want to know just how far you think Ninian is to be trusted."

Janet sat there silently. Adriana's eyes searched her. The question echoed in her mind. In the end she said,

"There are different kinds of trust."

"That is true. Did he fail you?"

Janet did not speak. After what seemed like a long time Adriana said,

64

"That is not my affair? I suppose not. But this is—would he fail me?"

"I don't think so." The words sprang to her mind, to her lips. She gave them no conscious thought. They were there. Adriana said,

"You didn't take long over that. In other words, he would play fast and loose with a girl, but he wouldn't pick a pocket."

Janet said, "No, he wouldn't pick a pocket."

Adriana's voice went deep.

"Sure about that? He wouldn't play a lying part for money? He wouldn't try and scheme, and pull strings for his own advantage?"

Janet heard her own voice very clear and steady,

"Oh, no, he wouldn't do that."

"Why?"

"It isn't in him."

"As sure about it as that?"

"Oh, yes."

"That is how you thought of him when you were children. How do you know he hasn't changed?"

"I should know it if he had."

Adriana laughed.

"Well, you don't beat about the bush, anyhow! How well do you know Robin Somers?"

If Janet was startled, she did not show it. If the change of subject was a relief, she did not show that either. She said,

"It's two years since I've seen him."

One of Adriana's pale hands rose and fell.

"That is no answer at all. It's two years since Star divorced him. How well did you know him before that?"

Janet considered.

"I used to see him—not very often. He could be charming."

"Did he charm you?"

"Not very much."

"What did you think of him?"

"I don't see that matters, Miss Ford."

"I don't care about being Miss Ford. Call me Adriana. And if it didn't matter, I shouldn't be asking you."

Janet said, "I didn't like him very much. I thought he was selfish."

Adriana laughed.

"Men are—and so are women."

"He was making Star unhappy."

"Was he fond of her?"

"In his own way."

"And of Stella?"

"I suppose so."

"And what do you mean by that?"

"Well, he didn't bother about her, did he? She was down here, and he was up in town—how often did he come and see her?"

"Not very often."

Janet said with finality,

"She talks about Ninian, but she doesn't talk about her father."

Adriana smiled.

"That might mean that she cares too little—or too much. She is an odd child—it might be quite difficult to tell. Well, you don't like him, and he made Star unhappy, and of course that damns him!" The smile mocked her. "Would you take his word about anything?"

There was no hesitation at all about Janet's "Oh, no."

Adriana laughed.

"So now we know! Well, that's all for the moment, and

66

it's your turn for the dressing-room. Send Ninian in. You needn't read the press notices if you don't want to."

She found Ninian absorbed in them and reluctant to put them down. He went through to the sitting-room with a laughing "I'm like all her other adorers, I can't be torn away!" As he shut the door between the two rooms, Adriana said sharply,

"Don't stand there muttering behind my back! What did you say?"

"Oh, just that I couldn't put your notices down. The critics certainly did you proud."

"Well, I was good—I was damned good. And the gallery could hear my lowest whisper, which is more than you can say about practically anyone on the stage today. Oh, yes, I was good all right. And now I'm a has-been, and no one cares how good I was."

He came and sat down beside her.

"Darling, don't wallow! I know you get a kick out of it, but I don't. You enriched your generation, and what anyone can do more than that, I don't know. It's an achievement— and how many people achieve anything at all?"

She put out a hand, and he lifted it to his lips and kissed it lightly.

"Well, what do you want with me?"

"Oh, just to ask you a question or two."

His dark eyebrows rose.

"About?"

"About that girl Janet."

"What about her?" His eyes still smiled, but she thought they had a wary look. He said, "Darling, her life is an open book—there is simply nothing to tell. She is one of those

67

incredible creatures who just go on doing things for other people and not bothering about themselves."

"It sounds dull."

"She is a great deal too intelligent to be dull."

"Well, you have made her sound as if she had all the dull virtues."

"I know. But she isn't. You didn't really think so yourself."

"You would say, then, that she was reliable?"

"Do you see Star having her down here to look after Stella if she wasn't?"

"Star isn't exactly a model of common sense."

"No, but she knows Janet. When you've grown up with people there isn't much you don't know about them."

"Would you say she was a good judge of character—Janet, I mean, not Star."

"Oh, yes, she looks right through you and out at the other side. At least that is what she has always done with me."

Adriana's large dark eyes were fixed upon him. She said with devastating frankness,

"Why didn't you marry her?"

"You had better ask her."

"No use—she wouldn't tell me."

"And what makes you think that I will?"

"Are you going to?"

"Oh, no, darling."

She said,

"You might do worse. All right, go and fetch her in. And tell Meeson we are ready for our coffee."

When Meeson came in with the tray she had a beaming smile. It was plain that she thought the world of Ninian. He jumped up, put an arm round her, and told her she got better

looking every year, to which she replied that so did he—
"And get along with you, ducks! No good telling the tale to
the old uns. They've heard it all before, and if they don't
know what it's worth by now they never will. All the same,
I always did say if there's a dangerous time in a woman's
life, it's when she's just about made up her mind she's been
through the wood once too often and come out with the
crooked stick."

"Gertie, you talk too much," said Adriana.

"When I get a chance I do—stands to reason! Nobody
wants just to stand and look on, now do they—not if they
can help it! All right, all right, I'm going!"

"No, wait! You made the coffee up here?"

"On me own gas ring."

"And where did you get the milk?"

"Out of the big jug in the fridge. And the sugar is what I
got in Ledbury last time I went shopping there for Mrs. Simmons. So what?"

Adriana waved her away, and she went out, shutting the
door with some unnecessary force.

Ninian raised his eyebrows.

"And what is all that about?"

"Oh, nothing at all."

"Meaning if I don't ask questions I won't be told any lies?"

"If you like to put it that way. Do you still take all the sugar
you can get?"

"I do. Especially when it's the fancy barleysugar kind. I'll
even go so far as to have Janet's share when she's given up
taking it."

Janet said, "I haven't."

"But a really unselfish woman would let me have it all the
same."

"Then I'm not really unselfish."

Adriana watched them. She was weighing what each had said about the other, and weighing just how far it would bear the very considerable strain that might be placed upon it. They were young, they had everything before them—trouble and heart-ache, and the moments which make up for it all. She had had her share of them. She had walked among the stars. If she was offered her life over again, she wondered if she would take it. She supposed she would, so long as she didn't know what was coming. That was what sapped the strength and slowed the heart—to watch the inevitable approach of something which casts its threatening shadow across your path, stealing up behind you, reaching forward to darken the coming day. Stupid to think of that when she had made up her mind that the shadow was only a shadow and held no threat. Stupid to have these moments when nothing seemed to be quite worth while. Oh, well, when you were up you were up, and when you were down you were down. That had always been her way, but nobody had ever got her down for long. And she had had a good run, a long run. A long run had its drawbacks—you got stale. And yet you were sorry when it came to an end. But it wasn't the end yet, and what was the use of thinking about it? She pulled herself up against the cream brocade cushions and said,

"I'm going to throw a party. Gertie and I have been making out lists."

CHAPTER 11

Janet came out of Adriana Ford's room and went along to the nursery. She was thinking what an extraordinary person Adriana was, and that she couldn't possibly be as old as Star had said. There was something alive about her, something that would always take the middle of the stage, whether she held it with that tragic look, with gay talk about her new clothes and the parties she meant to give, or with the searching questions which came crashing in among your own most private affairs. What did she mean, asking those questions about Ninian, and why did she need to ask them of a stranger? He was her own relation, and she had known him all his life. What could Janet tell her that she did not know already? Janet was wondering why she had answered her at all. And then the door opened behind her and Ninian was following her into the room. He said, "Well?" with a question in his voice, and she said, "Good-night."

He laughed.

"Oh, I'm not going away—far from it! We are going to have a nursery crack."

"We are not!"

"Darling, we are. I wouldn't dream of locking the door and taking away the key. I shall use only moral suasion."

"Ringan, go to bed!"

The old Border form of his name came without her meaning to use it. It had been common coin when they were children, but even then the elders had frowned upon it as smacking too much of the vulgar. It was an odd variant for Ninian, and she had always wondered about it, but it came easily to her tongue.

His look softened.

"It's a long time since you called me that, my jo Janet."

"I didn't mean to. I don't know why I did."

"You're a cold, hard lass, but you slip into being human just once in a way. And now stop talking about yourself and tell me what you think of Adriana."

Janet's colour rose.

"I was not talking about myself!"

"All right, darling, have it your own way. But I want to talk about Adriana. What did you think of her?"

Janet frowned.

"She is not like anyone else."

"Fortunately! Imagine a houseful of Adrianas! Spontaneous combustion wouldn't be in it! You know, that is the trouble with Meriel—she is the imitation, the bad copy, the local dressmaker's version of a Paris model. She gets the mannerisms here and there, but she doesn't begin to have Adriana's courage and drive, to say nothing of her talent. Amazing person! What did she say to you when she sent me out of the room?"

"That's asking."

"Don't I get an answer?"

She shook her head. He said,

"Did *she*?"

She shook her head again.

"Does that mean she didn't, or that you won't tell?"

"You can please yourself."

He laughed.

72

"You are a very aggravating woman. What would you do if I was to shake you—call for help?"

"I might."

"Then I can tell you who would come—Meriel. She is the only one near enough. And what fun that would be—for her! A part to play after her own heart! Brutal seducer checked! An angel to the rescue! Foolish inexperienced damsel rebuked and warned!"

"Ringan, go to bed!"

She had meant her voice to be, not angry, but quietly firm. She could not help being aware that it held a trace of indulgence.

He leaned against the mantelpiece and looked at her with smiling eyes.

"How are you going to get me to go? Do you think you could push me?"

"I shouldn't dream of trying."

He nodded.

"Just as well. It's the world to a winkle that I'd kiss you. So what? If you're thinking of an appeal to my better feelings, you've known for a long time that I haven't got any."

She made no answer. He was trying to play on her, and she wouldn't have it.

He stretched out a hand and just touched her on the wrist.

"I haven't, have I? *Have I?*"

"I suppose you have your share."

"But such a small one? It wants a lot of encouragement. You might be quite surprised if you would take it on."

Janet's colour burned.

"You might try Anne Forester."

He shook his head.

"She wouldn't be any good at it." Then suddenly, and in a different voice, "Janet, you know she wasn't anything!"

"I know nothing of the kind."

"Then working for Hugo has had a most disintegrating effect upon your brain. You used to be quite intelligent, and if you had used one grain of common sense you would have known that Anne was only a play."

Janet was standing up very straight. If she could have added three inches to her height it would have been a great support. She did her best as she said,

"That would be so nice for Anne!"

"Oh, she was playing too. There wasn't anything serious in it at all, on either side. It was just one of those here-today-and-gone-tomorrow kind of things."

"Like the affair you had with Anne Newton—and Anne Harding?"

He burst out laughing.

"Of course! And anyhow they were all Annes. There's never been another Janet! You know, darling, what is wrong with you is that serious disposition—too many forebears living in manses and preaching long Scottish sermons. A man can kiss a girl without wanting to spend the rest of his life with her. I tell you, none of the Annes meant a thing, and they were not a bit more in earnest than I was—I swear they weren't. That sort of thing just doesn't mean anything at all."

Janet's smile flashed out, the dimple appeared.

"That is what Hugo said."

"He did, did he?"

"Oh, yes."

"And suited the action to the word no doubt. And I suppose you let him kiss you!"

"Why not?"

74

He took her by the shoulders.

"You know very well why not. Janet—did he? Did you let him?"

She stepped back, but not in time. Meriel stood in the doorway with the air of a tragedy queen. She had on the dress she had worn at dinner, and a shawl of crimson silk with a fringe that dripped to the floor. It was falling off one shoulder. She caught at it and said in a dramatic voice,

"I am interrupting you! I suppose you expect me to apologise?"

Ninian turned round in a leisurely manner and said, "Why?" The question was accompanied by rather a bleak stare.

"I was afraid I had startled you."

"But how could it have been anything but a pleasant surprise? Won't you come in and make yourself at home? I am sure Nanny always has a welcome for you. Janet wouldn't wish to lag behind—would you, darling?"

Janet had been standing just where she was, the colour still in her cheeks but her whole look grave and composed. Appealed to directly, she said,

"Yes, do come in. I was telling Ninian that it's time for bed. But it isn't really so late. Adriana was getting tired, so we came away."

Meriel came into the room holding the red shawl about her.

"I suppose she asked you to call her Adriana?"

"Oh, yes."

Ninian said abruptly, "Well, I'm off. Don't run through all the confidences tonight, or you will have none left for tomorrow." He paused on the threshold, and from behind Meriel's back he made a schoolboy grimace and blew a kiss.

Janet saw the door close behind him with some relief. Meriel alone she could cope with, but Ninian goaded by Meriel was capable of practically anything, and there had been the light of battle in his eye. She turned to the unwelcome guest.

"I'm afraid it's rather cold in here."

Meriel said deeply, "It doesn't matter." She laid her arm along the mantelpiece and assumed a graceful droop. "He can't bear to be in the room with me—you must have noticed it."

"It is a pity to fancy things."

"Oh, but it's not fancy. It is only too painfully evident. You *can't* have helped noticing it. So I felt—I had better explain."

"There isn't any need."

Meriel drew a long sighing breath.

"Oh, no, it is obvious, as I said. And I would rather you knew. It is so difficult with a stranger to pick one's way among other people's affairs without either hurting or being hurt. It will be easier for us all if you know just how we stand. Ninian has been here a good deal, you know, and—well, I expect you can guess what happened. He began to care for me more than I wanted him to." She fixed dark soulful eyes on Janet's face. "I tried to stop him—I did indeed. You mustn't blame me—at least not more than you can help. I had my own troubles. Geoffrey and I—no, I won't say any more about that. Edna doesn't understand him, doesn't make him happy, but we would never do anything to hurt her. I do want you to know that."

Janet had very little opinion of those who sentimentalize over other people's husbands and wives. Whilst refraining from expressing this feeling, she supposed it to be fairly evident, and had a passing hope that it might have a damping effect upon any further confidences. But Meriel merely sighed again.

"It is all terribly sad, and there is nothing that anyone can do. Because, you see, there is no money. I do feel—don't you—that if people are not happy together, it is better for them to part. Of course divorce is terribly sordid, and it costs more money than any of us have got, so what is the use of thinking about it? I have nothing, literally nothing, except my allowance from Adriana, and Geoffrey has only the merest pittance outside of what she gives him—and that is supposed to be for Edna too. You wouldn't think she would have the heart to cut it off if we went away together, but you never can tell. She might, you know, and one couldn't possibly risk it. It's a dreadful situation! And sometimes I have wondered whether it wouldn't be better to put an end to it by letting Ninian take me away."

Janet said, "Does he want to?"

The dark eyes looked first up, and then down with the lashes shading them. The voice thrilled with reproach.

"Need you ask! But can one—ought one—to turn away from one's fullest emotional development? Ninian is terribly in love with me, but I could only give him a second-best. And there is still the question of money. I believe his last book did better, but writing is such an uncertain business. If only—*only* Adriana would let us all know where we stand! But she is so self-centred, she never thinks about it. She may be going to divide everything between the four of us—Geoffrey, and Star, and Ninian, and me. Or if she thinks Star is making enough on her own she may leave her out—or Ninian if his books really begin to sell. You can see how dreadful it is not to know."

Janet began to feel as if she had reached saturation point. She said bluntly,

"I think you should put the whole thing out of your head and get yourself a job. There was an old woman up at Darnach who used to say, 'Dead men's shoes are awfu' fidgety wear'. For all you know, Adriana may have put everything into an annuity."

"Oh, no, she wouldn't do that—she wouldn't!"

"You don't know what people will do until they've done it. She might divide the money, or leave it to just one of you. Or she might leave it all to a theatrical charity."

Meriel looked genuinely horrified.

"Oh, no—she would *never* do that!"

"How do you know?"

Meriel's face changed. One moment it had been registering everything it could, the next it had closed down and was as blank as a whitewashed wall. She said,

"Of course nobody knows, so what is the good of talking about it? I must go. It's rather a mockery to say *good*-night— but perhaps you sleep—"

"Oh, yes."

Meriel said, "How fortunate you are!" She gathered up her crimson shawl and trailed out of the room.

CHAPTER 12

Adriana sent out invitations right and left. There were to be people to lunch, and people to dine. There was to be a cocktail party—"Frightful, but everyone accepts and it gets things going. Meriel, you can ring up all the people on that list. And for the Lord's sake don't use the sort of voice which will make them think they're being invited to my funeral! It will be quite a shock to some of them to realize that I'm not dead and buried, so you had better try and put some pep into it, or half of them will be turning up in black. Mabel Preston will be here. She is due for her autumn visit, and she looks forward to it as much as she does to anything, so I can't put her off, and she will be quite enough of a death's head at the feast without tragedy airs from anyone else."

Ninian looked up from the envelopes he was addressing at top speed in a hand which resembled cuneiform.

"Darling, not that old Mabel! You can't!"

Adriana nodded.

"Of course I can! She'll love every minute, though she would die before she admitted it. So I couldn't possibly put her off."

Meriel said in a fretful voice,

"I can't think why you bother with her. It isn't even as if she was grateful. She just comes here and complains about everything."

Adriana's fine brows rose.

"She happens to be a very old friend. And if it makes her any happier to complain, I'm sure she's welcome. If I'd had her life I'd probably do a bit of complaining myself."

Ninian kissed the tips of his fingers to her.

"You wouldn't. But we'll let that go. Mabel shall come and enjoy herself to the top of her bent. Relays of guests provided to listen to her woes, and a constant supply of clean pocket-handkerchiefs to catch the frequent tear!"

Mrs. Preston arrived next day. Her visits to Ford House were the only breaks in the dullest of dull lives. She inhabited two furnished rooms in one of the cheaper suburbs, and she had very few friends. People had troubles of their own and were disinclined to listen to endless stories of how badly she had been treated by practically everyone with whom she had come in contact. Four times a year she went down to Ford House and poured out the old grievances. Adriana, not given to suffering incompetence gladly, was surprisingly patient under the infliction, but towards the close of the visit the patience was apt to wear thin and she would speak her mind, thereby adding an up-to-date grievance to the old mouldering ones with which poor Mabel Preston's mind was cluttered. After which she would say she was sorry and forget the whole thing.

Ninian was despatched to meet the 11:45 at Ledbury. He came to the nursery, looking for Janet, and found her sorting through Stella's clothes.

"Darling, you've got to save my life. If I meet Mabel alone, I don't suppose I shall survive it. Snatch a coat and come too!"

"I've got to fetch Stella from the Vicarage."

"And you know, and I know, and so does everyone else,

80

that she won't be ready till half past twelve. There's oodles of time."

"Well, I'm sorting these clothes."

"Why?"

"I've just had a cable from Star. She wants to know a whole string of things."

"Why didn't she find them out before she went?"

"It doesn't seem to have occurred to her. She says the children's frocks are entrancing, and she wants to send some over for Stella. I'm to cable measurements."

"I suppose she knows what she'll have to pay in the customs?"

"I don't suppose it has crossed her mind. And she won't have to pay it—Adriana will. I've just been breaking it to her."

"What did she say?"

"Laughed and said she had been getting a good many clothes herself, it was only fair that Stella should have some too. She seems to be fond of Star."

"Everyone is. Even your chilly heart contrives a little warmth."

"I have not got a chilly heart."

He shook his head.

" 'The proof of the pudding is in the eating'—'Deeds before words', and all the rest of it." He began to recite in a melancholy voice:

>" 'A man of words and not of deeds
>Is like a garden full of weeds,
>And when the weeds begin to grow
>It's like a garden full of snow.'

There you have it to a T. And later on there's a line about 'It's like a penknife in your heart', only I can't remember how you get there. Look here, snatch that coat and come, or we'll be late for the train, and that will give Mabel something to talk about for the rest of her visit. Honestly, darling, I can't face her alone. I'd do a lot for Adriana, but there are limits. And we'll go down the back stairs in case Meriel has one of her bright ideas about three being company."

Janet found herself caught up in what felt extraordinarily like one of their old games of hide-and-seek with the grown-ups. They crept out by the back door, skirted the stable yard, and got away to an exhilarating sense of escape. The car was an old Daimler, the faithful servant of many seasons. It ate petrol, but it went on, year in, year out, and it took them to Ledbury station with a good five minutes to spare.

Mrs. Preston got out of a third-class carriage and came drooping towards them. She was a tall, thin woman with a desiccated look. Everything she had on had once been Adriana's, only instead of the effect being dashing there was a general air of having come down in the world and not liking it. The grey checked coat and skirt hung loosely and dipped at the back. The short moleskin coat was rubbed. And nothing could have been less becoming than the hat in a bright emerald shade and the magenta scarf wound twice about a stringy neck. She shook hands and said in what Meeson called her moaning voice,

"Such a dull journey—nothing to look at the whole way down, and no one in the carriage to talk to. Really, English people are most unfriendly! There was quite a nice-looking man with two papers, but did he offer me one? Oh, dear, no! Didn't think me grand enough to be noticed, I suppose.

82

But that's the way wherever you go—if you're not in the swim you might as well be dead. Or better!"

Janet had to give Ninian marks for the way he handled her. He listened in a sympathetic manner with an occasional murmur of assent, and she responded with mournful satisfaction. Her restricted quarters, her landlady's temper, the rise in the cost of living, the incivility in shops, the indifference and neglect of a once enthusiastic public—the stream of complaint flowed on with hardly a pause for breath.

Janet, dropped at the Vicarage gate, could hear the sound of it above the hum of the departing car. She looked at her watch and found that Stella would not be out for another ten minutes. The morning had been hazy, but the sky had cleared, and now the sun was warm. She walked back past the Vicarage to the row of cottages beyond, their gardens gay with autumn flowers. There really was nothing so pretty as an English village. The first cottage belonged to the sexton. His great-grandfather had lived in it and done the same office. It was he who had begun to shape the holly hedge into cock-yolly birds and an arch. The birds sat one on either side of the arch now, very stiff and shiny, and a hundred years old. Mr. Bury was extremely proud of them. Old Mrs. Street next door had a fine show of zinnias, snapdragons, and dahlias. She had a son in the gardening line and he kept her in plants, but she didn't hold with all these things he got out of books. What she planted grew, and you couldn't say better than that.

There was a regular row of gardens on this side. On the other there was a paddock and the long winding drive which led up to Hersham Place, which stood empty because nowadays no one could afford to live in a house with thirty bedrooms. The Lodge was let to Jackie Trent's mother, who was said to be related to the family. She was a goodlooking young woman, and the village talked about her. She spent a good deal of her time making herself look smart, but she didn't mend Jackie's clothes, and there wasn't a cottage in the place that wouldn't have been ashamed of her unweeded garden. It was certainly very untidy—like Jackie.

As Janet passed, Esmé Trent came out. She was bare-headed, and her hair shone in the sun. It had been brightened to something much more decorative than its original shade, and her eyebrows and lashes proportionately darkened. She had chosen a vivid lipstick. Altogether there was more make-up than is usual in the country. For the rest, she wore grey flannel of an admirable cut, and from the fact that she had on nylons and high-heeled shoes, and that she carried a smart grey hand-bag, it seemed unlikely that she was merely going to fetch Jackie. She went down the road, walking briskly, and by the time Janet had turned back and reached the Vicarage she was to be seen getting on to the Ledbury bus.

Mrs. Lenton was out in the front cutting dahlias. She had the same round blue eyes and fair hair as her two little girls, and she had been born with a disposition to laugh and take things easily. In one way it made her very agreeable to live with, but it also involved her in getting behind with the things which she ought to have been doing when she was doing something else. She had meant to do the flowers after break-fast, but there hadn't been time and she was hurrying over them now with half her mind on the milk pudding she had left in the oven. The sight of Esmé Trent disappearing into the bus distracted her. Her fair skin flushed, and she said in quite an angry tone,

"Did you see that, Miss Johnstone? There she goes, and goodness knows for how long—hours very likely! And that

84

poor little boy left to go back to an empty house and eat up anything she can be bothered to leave for him! And he's only six—it's shocking! I've kept him here once or twice, but she doesn't really like it—told me she had made perfectly adequate arrangements—so I don't like to do it any more."

Janet said, "It's too bad."

Mrs. Lenton cut a dahlia fiercely.

"I wouldn't mind what she said, but she takes it out on Jackie! And it's all very well for John to say we must be charitable, but when people do things to children I *can't!*"

The three little girls ran out, Jackie lagging behind them. Ellie Page, the Vicar's cousin who taught them, came as far as the step, but when she saw Janet she turned back. Mary Lenton called to her.

"Ellie, come here and meet Miss Johnstone."

She came with some reluctance. Janet couldn't make her out. She wasn't pretty, but she had a kind of shy grace. The children enjoyed their lessons, and why on earth should she look at Janet as if she was an enemy, or at the very least someone with whom to walk warily. When she spoke her voice had an unusual tone, sweet and rather high. She said without preliminaries,

"I expect Stella will have told you about the dancing-class. It's this afternoon at three. Miss Lane comes out from Ledbury."

Mary Lenton turned round with the gold and orange dahlias in her hand.

"Of course—I knew there was some reason why I had to do the flowers! We get about half a dozen children, and most of them stay to tea. Stella does always. Oh, and perhaps Jackie would like to come in. He doesn't take dancing, but he could watch." She caught at him as he went by scuffing his feet.

85

"Darling, wouldn't you like to come back this afternoon and watch the dancing and have tea?"

Jackie kicked at the gravel and said, "No!"

"But, darling—"

He twisted away from her and ran out of the gate. Ellie Page said in a plaintive tone,

"Oh, dear, he really is a disagreeable child."

CHAPTER 13

Adriana came down to lunch with plans made for all of them. It annoyed her a good deal to find that Geoffrey was not there.

"I shall rest for an hour and then take Mabel for a drive. If Geoffrey intended to go off like this he should have let me know. I suppose he hasn't by any chance taken the Daimler?" She fixed a demanding stare on Edna, who fidgeted with her table-napkin.

"Oh, no—of course not. I mean, how could he, when Ninian had it to meet Mabel?"

Adriana gave her short red hair a toss.

"Implying that nothing else stopped him from taking my car without so much as asking whether I wanted it myself! And don't say he couldn't have known I was going to use it, because that is merely aggravating! If you leave me alone, I shall probably have got over being annoyed by the time he comes home. I suppose he took the Austin. For all he knew,

I might have wanted to let Ninian have it. Where has he gone?"

Edna crumbled the bread beside her plate.

"I really don't know. I didn't ask him."

Adriana laughed.

"Perhaps it was just as well—men hate it. Especially when they're up to mischief. Not, of course, that Geoffrey—" She left the sentence in the air and laughed again.

Ninian struck in with a light "Aren't you being a little severe, darling?" to which she replied, "Probably," and helped herself to salad.

"Anyhow," she continued, "if Geoffrey isn't here he can't drive us. Meriel will have to. No, Ninian—I want you for something else. We will drop you and Janet in Ledbury, and you can change the library books and do some shopping for me. That is to say, Janet will do the shopping and you will carry the parcels."

Janet said,

"I shall have Stella to fetch."

"It's the dancing-class, isn't it? It doesn't matter how long she stays at the Vicarage. We can pick her up on the way back. Now that's all fixed, and I don't want to hear any more about it."

Mabel Preston spoke in a resigned voice.

"I do usually rest in the afternoon, you know."

Adriana said briskly,

"And so do I, but an hour is quite as long as is good for us. One mustn't let oneself get into bad habits. Well then, it's all settled, and everyone must be ready punctually at a quarter to three."

Ninian was allowed to drive the car as far as Ledbury. There was a horrid moment after they got there when Adriana seemed to be in some doubt about letting him go.

"Meriel is such a jerky driver," she said. "Yes, you are, my dear, and it's no good your looking like a thunderstorm about it." She beamed at Janet. "I hope you are grateful to me for letting you have our only young man. Now, Mabel, I'm going to take you round by Rufford's Tower. I shan't attempt the climb myself, but Meriel will go up with you. The view should be perfect today."

Mabel was still protesting that she hated heights, and that nothing would induce her to climb the tower, when with a noisy change of gears they drove away.

Ninian laughed.

"Adriana at her most peremptory! What's the odds the wretched Mabel will be made to toil up to the top?"

They changed the books and worked through a dull list of household shopping. There really seemed to be no good reason why they should be doing it, since with the exception of the books everything could have been ordered by telephone. However, as Ninian said, there wasn't any point about looking the gift-horse in the mouth.

"Actually, you know, I think Adriana is trying to throw us together."

Janet said, "Nonsense!" and was admonished.

"Now there you are being hasty. And not the first time I have had to tell you about it either! A spot of matchmaking would be a diversion for Adriana, and it would have the added attraction of being quite certain to annoy Meriel."

"Why should she want to annoy Meriel?"

"Darling, don't ask me, but it is quite obvious that she does. At a guess I should say that she just plants a dart wherever she can. No real harm intended, but a distinct pleasure in seeing whether she can't make any of us rise. If we do, it's a point to her. If we can ward it off or throw it back, well, that's a point to us. It's a kind of game."

Janet said soberly,

"It's the kind of game that makes people hate you."

Ninian laughed.

"Do you know, I've got an idea she would find that quite exhilarating."

They were to be picked up by the corner of the station approach at a quarter past four, Adriana declaring that five o'clock was quite early enough for tea, and that anyhow they would be home by the quarter to. But at twenty to four Ninian declared that only immediate refreshment would save him from an ingrowing anti-shopping complex which would probably become chronic.

"And just think how inconvenient you are going to find that!"

Janet looked at him in what she meant to be a repressive manner.

"I?"

"Naturally. You wouldn't be able to risk bringing it on. No little shopping-list pressed into my hand with a farewell kiss as I rush off to the office in the morning."

Ignoring all but a single startling word, Janet caught her breath and said,

"The office?"

"Of course. Didn't I mention it? On the first of October I become a wage-slave in a publishing firm. I shall have a pay-packet, and an office desk in a back room looking on to a Mew."

He saw her face change. It became warm and eager. She said,

"Oh, Ringan!" And then in a hurry, "Do you mind dreadfully?"

He slipped a hand inside her arm and gave it a squeeze.

"I wouldn't be doing it if I did. Actually, I think it's going to be quite interesting. It's Firth and Saunders, you know. You remember Andrew Firth. We've always been friends, so when I found there was an opening with his people I thought I'd put in old Cousin Jessie Rutherford's money. Andrew said they'd probably take me, and they did. I've finished another book, so I've got something in hand."

Janet did not say anything for a moment. They walked along past the shop windows. The town was full, people brushed past them. This wasn't public property. He was telling her what he hadn't told Star. He had always told her things, but he had generally told Star too. She said,

"I thought your book did well—the second one?"

"It did. And the next is going to do better, and so forth and so on. But this doesn't mean I'm going to stop writing— I've made quite a good plan about that. Now this is where we turn off and get our cup of tea. It's a good place to talk."

A stone's throw down the narrow crooked street there hung the sign of a golden kettle, very bright and new. The place it advertised could hardly have been much older without falling to pieces. It had windows dim with bottle-glass, interior visibility of no more than a couple of yards, and beams which threatened anyone over six foot with concussion. As they threaded their way across a floor thick with small tables, Ninian bent to whisper,

"Actually, The Kettle is a joke. People come here if they don't want to be recognized, and then find themselves bumping into everyone they most want to avoid. But there are some really good hide-outs down at the far end."

90

They achieved a table in a nook discreetly screened from the public gaze. A faint light smouldered overhead in an orange bulb. Janet wondered how bad the tea would be. In her experience medievalism very often failed to cover a multitude of sins. But when it came, in a squat orange teapot very difficult to pour from, it really wasn't at all bad, and the cakes were good. Ninian ate four, and went on talking about his publishing job.

"You see, I don't want the books to be a matter of bread and butter. I think it's fatal—or it would be for me. I want to be able to say I don't care what the public likes, I'm going to write what I damn well choose. If I choose to hammer at a thing for a year, I don't want there to be anything to stop me. And if I have an urge to do a firework and let it off in everyone's face, I want to be able to do that. The only trouble is that I'm a pretty regular eater, and the sordid soul of commerce does expect to have its bills paid. In fact, darling, there simply has to be something one can use for money. So I thought this publishing idea was rather a brainwave. A life of honest toil doing the fellow author in the eye or giving him a helping hand, according to which end of the stick you are looking at, and quite a reasonable pay-packet. It's a good investment for the money too. I don't suppose anyone is going to bother about nationalizing publishing for quite a long time yet, and meanwhile there will be the pay-packet."

Janet put down her cup. Now that her eyes were getting accustomed to the gloom she could just see where the saucer was. He said,

"No comment? Don't you ask me what I want with a nice regular pay-packet?"

"Am I supposed to?"

"Oh, I think so. But I'll tell you anyway. I'm thinking of

getting married, and all the best statistics go to show that wives prefer a regular income. It saves awkwardness in the fish queue. They don't like waiting until the cod has been tied up in newspaper and then having to ask the fishmonger to let the bill stand over until the next book comes out. It tends to lower the social standing and prevents other people giving you tick."

Janet poured out another cup of tea. The pot burned her finger and she put it down in a hurry. Ninian said,

"Still no comment?"

"No one expects credit for fish. At least not unless you run a weekly or a monthly book, and you've got to be a very good customer for anyone to let you do that."

"Well, I'm not so hot on fish anyhow, so just make a mental note not to give it to me more than twice a week."

There was a pause before she said, "I don't like that way of talking."

"No?"

"No. And the girl you're going to marry wouldn't care about it either."

He said in a laughing voice,

"Well, you ought to know! Let's change the subject. There are more romantic things than fish. Let us consider the question of a flat. I have secret advance information about one that I think would do. The chap who is in it has been offered a job in Scotland, and he has agreed to let me take over his lease. We can't argy-bargy over it—that's why I'm telling you this now. I thought we could run up to town tomorrow and get it clinched."

Janet looked straight in front of her. The screened recess which had seemed so dark when they felt their way into it now appeared to offer her very little shelter. She felt his eyes on her, with just what look she thought she knew or could guess—mocking, teasing, darting here and there in search of a joint in her armour. And even if she could close her face against him, defend eye and lip, breath and colour, he had brought with him from the days before she had known any need to defend herself, a trick of entry, a way to beguile her from her guard. She said in the most matter-of-fact tone she could manage,

"When it comes to taking a flat, it will be for the girl who is going to live in it to say whether she likes it or not."

"Naturally. But I would like you to see it."

"I have Stella to look after."

"She can stay at the Vicarage for lunch. She always does when Nanny has a day off. Star has an arrangement with Mrs. Lenton. We can catch the nine-thirty and be back by half past four. You see, it really is important for you to see if the flat will do. He wants to leave some things like linoleum, and a lot of curtains which haven't got an earthly chance of fitting the place they are going to in Edinburgh. It's part of an aunt's house, and he says the windows are nine foot high."

A heartening flash of anger enabled Janet to face him with colour in her cheeks.

"I told you before I don't like that sort of talk!"

"But, darling, we'll have to have linoleum and curtains, and suppose I got them and you said you couldn't live with them—"

"I have no intention of living with them."

His face changed suddenly. His hand caught hers.

"Haven't you, Janet—haven't you?"

"Why should I?"

His laugh shook a little.

"Part of the worldly goods I'll be endowing you with. No, that's out of date. The last wedding I went to the chap said 'share'. Rather a pity, don't you think? I rather like the sound of that 'I thee endow'. A bit archaic of course, but so is marriage."

"No one was talking about marriage."

"Oh, yes, darling, I was—definitely. I've been laying my pay-packet and the linoleum and things at your feet for at least ten minutes. Hadn't you noticed it?"

She said, "No." At least she went through the right movements for saying no, but they didn't seem to result in any recognizable sound.

Ninian said, "Come again!" still in that laughing, shaking voice. And then all at once his black head was bent down over the hand he was holding and he was kissing it as if he would never let it go.

There was a moment when everything seemed to go round, there was a moment when everything stood still. With the touch of his lips on her hand Janet knew very well that she couldn't go on saying no. But she could at least stop herself from saying yes. It was, in fact, not really possible to say anything at all.

And then someone spoke on the other side of the screen which divided them from the nook on their right. It was Geoffrey Ford, and he could not have been more than a yard away from them. He said comfortably, "Well, no one is going to see us here," and a woman laughed.

Janet snatched away her hand, and Ninian presented the unmistakable appearance of a young man who is saying, "Damn!" Not aloud of course, but with a good deal of feeling. On the other side of the screen two people could be heard settling themselves.

Janet got up, collected her bag, and skirted the table. Ninian followed her, put a hand on her arm, and was shaken off. As they emerged into the general gloom, the woman who had laughed said in a low but perfectly distinct voice,

"I'm not going on like this, and you needn't think so."

CHAPTER 14

Janet woke up in the night. She had been dreaming, and the feel of the dream came with her out of her sleep like water dripping as you come up out of a stream. She sat up in bed and waited for the feeling to go. It was an old dream, but she hadn't had it for a long time now. It came when her mind was troubled, but she did not know what had troubled it tonight. Didn't she? Ninian and his talk of all the things she had told herself she must and would forget! In sober earnest, how much of it did he mean? Nothing—something—anything? And what kind of fool would she be to be lured back into the passionate moments, the light uncertainties, the day-in, day-out companionship which had been between them? She had said, "Never any more," and he had only to look at her and kiss her hand and her heart broke with longing to take him back again.

In the dream she was fording a burn—just a shallow, pleasant thing with the pebbles shining through the brown water and the sun turning them to gold. Only she couldn't get to the other side, and with every step it was deeper. The water was dark and drumly, and the sun was something she had forgotten long ago. Sometimes she woke then, but once she had waded so deep that the water was up to her mouth and the roaring filled her ears. It hadn't been so bad as that tonight. The stream had been no higher than her knees, and here she was awake. It could rise no farther now.

She looked at the windows standing open with the curtains drawn back and the shape of them just discernible against the denser blackness of the walls. She slipped out of bed and went barefoot to the right-hand one of the two, feeling her way past the dressing-table which stood between them. The night was still, and warm, and very dark, with a feeling of low cloud and not a leaf that stirred. She knelt down and leaned out with her elbows on the sill. There was an autumn smell abroad. Someone had had a bonfire. There was just the tang of wood-smoke on the air, and there was the scent of all the ripe and ripening things that were coming on to their harvest time. The softness and the silence touched her thought and stilled it. The dream wouldn't come again. She could stay here for a little while longer and then go back to bed and sleep.

Quite suddenly there was a streak of light across the gravel under the window—a long, thin streak lying crookedly across the path and slanting over the tall musk roses in the bed beyond. It was there, but it did not stay. It moved, ran backwards, and was gone. And then a moment later there it was again, but much farther to the right. The curtains in the room below didn't quite meet, and someone had just walked across that room with a light. Whoever it was had now gone on through the connecting door to Edna's own little sitting-room. There chintz curtains veiled the light, and it was no longer a streak but a dull glow upon the path.

Janet got up and went through to the nursery. The windows here were shut, but since they were casements they could be opened without making any sound. She leaned out, and the glow was still there. She looked over her shoulder at the nursery clock with its luminous face. It was between ten minutes and a quarter to two. Edna might have gone down—to get a book—or because she couldn't sleep. Or Geoffrey. Or Meriel. Or Adriana, for the matter of that, only it really didn't seem at all likely. No, quite definitely, if Adriana wanted anything in the middle of the night she would send Meeson down for it, and Meeson would expect to be sent. Only Meeson would have everything she wanted for making tea or coffee in the little pantry which was part of Adriana's suite of rooms. Of course it might be any of the others—or it might be someone who hadn't any business to be there. She couldn't just go back to bed and leave it uncertain. Suppose she were to come down in the morning and find that all the silver had been stolen. But it didn't seem very sensible just to walk in on a burglar by herself. She would have to call Ninian.

As the thought went through her mind, the window below her was opened. It was one of those long glass doors with a handle which controls the bolt. It made a faint sound as it swung wide, and at the same moment the light went out. There was a sound of footsteps on the gravel and a sound of whispering voices. She leaned out over the sill, and she strained to hear what the whispering voices said.

But they were just a rustling murmur. She could not tell whether it was man or woman who was whispering there below. And then the rustlings ran together into the syllables of a single sentence, and still she didn't know whether it was man or woman who had spoken. First Adriana's name— suddenly, like water splashing in her face. And then the

97

sentence which she was to go over and over in her mind—and at the end know no more what it meant than she did at the beginning:

"There's nothing for anyone as long as she keeps hanging on."

Someone went away along the path. Janet could hear the footsteps getting fainter, until in the end she could not hear them at all. The flicker of a torch receded with them. When it was quite gone someone stepped back over the sill into Edna's sitting-room and shut the door. She got up on to her feet and went out into the passage and along to the landing at the head of the stairs. There was a light in the hall below, just a weak bulb, but coming out of the dark like this it seemed much brighter than it really was.

Janet looked over the stairs and saw Edna Ford in a grey flannel dressing-gown with her hair scraped back and done up in aluminum curlers. The light shone on her, on the tears that were running down her face. Janet had heard about people wringing their hands, but she had never thought of it as a thing that anyone really ever did. But Edna was wringing her hands as she walked and wept. The thin fingers clung and twisted, the hands were twined together and strained apart. She had the look of a woman who has been stripped of everything and left in a desolate wilderness.

Whatever had happened or was happening, Janet felt that it was not for her to see. She drew back into the dark passage from which she had come.

She had not reached the nursery door, when she heard a sound that brought her running back. It wasn't loud, but there was no mistaking it. Edna had given a kind of choking gasp and come down. She could have tripped on the stair, or she could have turned giddy and lost her balance, but there she was, about five or six steps up, with an arm thrown out and her face hidden against it.

Janet ran down barefoot.

"Mrs. Ford—are you hurt?"

Edna lifted up her head and stared at her. Her face had a naked look, the pale eyes reddened, the sallow skin stained with tears.

"Mrs. Ford—are you hurt?"

There was a faint negative movement of the head.

"Let me help you up."

The movement was repeated.

"But you can't stay here!"

Edna said in an extinguished voice,

"What does it matter?"

Janet had to guess at the words. She said firmly,

"You can't stay here. Let me help you to your room. I'll make you a cup of tea. You are like ice."

After a minute or two Edna began to draw long sobbing breaths and to sit up. Her room faced the top of the stairs. Janet managed to get her there and into her bed again. All the household knew that Mr. and Mrs. Ford did not share a room. He had a good large dressing-room separated from his wife's by a bathroom. When Janet asked if she should call him Edna caught her hand and held it in an icy grip.

"No—no! Promise you won't do that!"

"Then I'll just get you a cup of tea and a hot water-bottle. I have everything in the nursery."

When she came back in her green dressing-gown with the tray and the hot water-bottle, Edna Ford had stopped weeping. She thanked Janet, and she drank the tea. When she put down the cup she said,

"I was upset. I hope you won't speak of it."

"Of course I won't. Are you warmer now?"

"Yes, thank you."

There was a long pause, after which she said,

"It was nothing. I thought I heard a sound. I went down, but of course there was no one there. It was just that something startled me. I'm rather a nervous person, I'm afraid. It suddenly came over me that I had done a very dangerous thing going down like that, and I had one of my giddy attacks. I wouldn't like anyone to know about it."

Janet left the bedside light burning and took away the tray. As she came to the nursery passage, Geoffrey Ford was crossing the hall below. He was in his pyjamas with a handsome black and gold dressing-gown belted over them. She made haste to get back to her own room.

CHAPTER 15

Janet gave Stella her breakfast next morning and took her to the Vicarage without seeing any of the others. When she returned they were all in the dining-room, Edna pouring out the tea and Geoffrey dispensing fishcakes as if there had been no midnight excursions. Edna looked a little more run-in-the-wash than usual, but her manner had not changed. She found small fidgeting faults with the service, the weather, and in fact with everything. The toast was not fresh—"Mrs. Simmons will make it too soon. It is incredible how often one has to say a thing before one can get it done."

Geoffrey gave his pleasant easy laugh.

"Perhaps, my dear, if you didn't say it quite so often—"

Her eyes were still reddened with last night's weeping. They dwelt on him for a moment.

"There are always things that have to be said, Geoffrey."

He looked back at her, handsome and good-humoured.

"Well, my dear, I can't see the use of worrying yourself to skin and bone. You wear yourself out, and people mostly go on taking their own way. You can't change human nature. Live and let live—but I suppose you'll tell me to take my own advice and let you do as you wish. How many people are coming to this do of Adriana's tomorrow?"

Meriel gave a scornful laugh.

"Half the county, I should think! We shan't be able to hear ourselves speak, and everyone will hate it like poison. But Adriana will have staged her come-back, which is all that matters—to her!"

Mabel Preston wanted to know who was coming.

"It really is tomorrow, isn't it? Will the Duchess come— did Adriana ask her? I saw her in the distance once, opening a bazaar. She was very distinguished-looking, but I wouldn't have called her pretty. Of course you don't need looks if you are a duchess. My goodness! I don't suppose I've got anything half smart enough to wear! Not that these high-up people are always smart—not by any means. Why, I saw the old Duchess of Hochstein once at a charity bazaar, and she was really what you would call *dowdy*. Very stout, you know, and miles behind the fashion. And she was Royalty!"

Janet went up to the nursery. Ninian followed her.

"We've missed the nine-thirty, but there's the ten-twenty-nine. You'd better hurry up and dress."

She turned on him, her eyes bright with anger.

"Ninian, have done with this! It's nonsense!"

101

He propped himself against the mantelpiece.

"A serious expedition to town to take a flat is not my idea of nonsense."

"I have no intention of taking a flat!"

"Haven't you then? That's very interesting. I'd better make a note of it in case I forget. Aren't you making it a bit difficult? It's not so easy to get anything done if you won't let yourself have any intentions."

"Ninian!"

"All right, all right, if you won't come you won't, but don't say I didn't ask you. And when I've taken the flat without anyone to help me, don't tell me the linoleum is foul and you can't live with the curtains—that's all. I must rush for the bus."

It was about an hour later that Meriel burst into the room. There was an unusual amount of colour in her cheeks and her voice was angry.

"Really, Adriana is the limit!"

Janet finished writing, "Two blue smocks—won't let down any more—"

Meriel stamped her foot.

"Why don't you answer me? What are you doing?"

"There didn't seem to be anything to answer. I'm making out a list of Stella's clothes."

"Why?"

"Star wants it."

Meriel threw back her head and laughed.

"Clothes! There's no getting away from them! I've just come from Adriana's room, and what do you suppose she's doing? The place looks like a jumble sale—it's got clothes laid out everywhere! And do you know what she's doing

102

with them? She is giving most of them away to that damned Mabel!"

"Why shouldn't she?"

Meriel made a dramatic gesture.

"Because they are all perfectly good clothes! Because she might have asked me if I wanted any of them! Because all she cares about is putting herself over big and having that silly old fool gawping at her and saying how marvellous she is! Do you know, there's a coat there I've wanted ever since she got it! I'd look wonderful in it, and Mabel makes everything look as if it had come out of a rag-bag."

"Why didn't you ask Adriana to give it to you?"

"I did—I did! And what do you suppose she said? I'll swear she was just going to give it to Mabel, but when I asked for it she said oh, no, she didn't think she could spare it! It was so nice for the garden, and she thought she would keep it in the cloakroom so as to have it handy if she just wanted to go out for a little!"

"Well, that seems reasonable."

"It's not—it's not! She's doing it to spite me! I tell you she got herself a new coat in town the other day—big soft checks of rust and brown! And this one is much more my style—bold squares of black and white with an emerald stripe! I tell you it's *me!* And as soon as my back is turned she'll give it to Mabel—I know she will! Unless—Oh, Janet, couldn't you say something—couldn't you stop her?"

"No, I don't think I could."

"You mean you won't! You don't care—nobody does!"

Janet controlled herself. She found it difficult to carry on a conversation with Meriel for more than five minutes without wanting to shake her. She thought regretfully that her moral character must be deteriorating. She made a real effort.

103

"Now look here—why don't you wait until Adriana is alone, and then ask her quietly about the coat? If she has said she wants to keep it for a bit she won't have given it to Mabel, and you can't very well ask for it now. But you could tell her how much you liked it and say you hope she won't give it to anyone else."

Meriel went into a pose.

"And you think that would stop her? How little you know about us! If she thought I had set my heart on anything, it would just make her determined to keep it from me—yes, it would! And have me there to look on while she gave it away to somebody else! It is the sort of thing she would enjoy. You see, you have the ordinary commonplace mind—no, don't be offended. It must be wonderful to take the everyday things as they come and never look beneath the surface or long to walk among the stars! I wish I could be like that, but it's no use. And you can't begin to understand Adriana or me, so it is no good your trying. But we see clearly enough about each other. She knows just what will hurt me, and I can see her enjoying it. It isn't a happy thing to be able to see into someone else's mind. Be thankful that you were not born that way. I see too much, and sometimes I shudder at what I see!" She passed a hand across her eyes and went trailing out of the room.

When Janet had finished with Stella's clothes she made her way to Adriana's room. She found a scene which resembled a dress shop. Clothes of every description trailed from the chairs, hung over the back of the couch, and were piled wherever there was room to pile them. The coat described by Meriel was very much to the fore. Adriana was, in fact, in the act of slipping it off.

It was certainly striking. The sharp black and white of the

two-foot checks, the vivid green of the stripe which crossed them, made Janet blink and reflect that it would certainly be a trying garment for poor old Mabel Preston. Much more suitable for Meriel really. She could see her looking dramatic and rather handsome in it.

Adriana waved it at her.

"Just take this down when you go, and hang it in the cloakroom. I'm giving it to Mabel, and Meriel has been throwing a fit of the sulks about it, so I thought the best thing was to put it downstairs and go on wearing it once or twice myself. Mabel can use it too if she wants to, and then she can just take it with her when she goes and there won't be any fuss. Meriel is the end when she sets her mind on anything!"

Janet made her voice soft and coaxing.

"She really does want it very badly."

Adriana gave a dry laugh.

"Did she send you to ask me for it?"

"Well, I said I wouldn't."

Adriana tapped her on the cheek.

"Don't let people make use of you, or you'll end up somewhere under foot. You can have no idea what Meriel is like when she wants something she can't have."

"And she really can't have the coat?"

Adriana frowned.

"No, she can't, and I'll tell you why. It's much too marked, and I've worn it too much myself. I don't choose to have people say I keep Meriel so short she has to wear my cast-off clothes. And they would, you know. Everyone within a ten-mile radius has seen me in that coat, and you must admit that it's once-seen-never-forgotten—now, isn't it?"

As Janet turned to the door with the coat on her arm, Mabel Preston came in from the bedroom in a black and yellow cocktail dress which imparted a most unfortunate resemblance to a wasp. She had pulled her dry red hair into rather wild-looking puffs, and she had been experimenting with Adriana's rouge and lipstick. The result had to be seen to be believed, but it was obvious that she was extremely pleased with it. She came into the room with quite a good imitation of the mannequin's glide.

"There!" she said. "How's that? Pretty good, don't you think? And nobody remembers black, so it will be all right if I wear it to your party tomorrow—won't it darling? And shan't I feel smart! Quite new too! No one would think it had ever been worn—at least not unless you looked right into it, and nobody is going to do that."

Janet made her escape. She took the coat along to the nursery, and when she went to fetch Stella from the Vicarage she carried it downstairs with her and hung it in the cloakroom.

CHAPTER 16

Ninian stayed the night in town. He rang up at seven, demanded Janet on the nursery extension, and was rather lavish with the time.

"Is the child in bed? . . . Good! I thought I had calculated rather neatly. Now listen! The linoleum is quite a pleasing shade—wear and tear negligible. And the curtains are a bit of all right. How good will you be at visualizing them from a description? Just turn on the imagination."

"Meriel told me this morning that I haven't got any. I'm

the fortunate possessor of a perfectly commonplace mind, with none of the perceptions which are such a burden to sensitive people."

She heard him laugh.

"Never mind, I'll come back tomorrow and protect you. Now do your best about the curtains. The bedroom is northeast, and the ones there are a nice creamy yellow with a pattern of hollyhocks. Calculated to give the illusion that the sun is shining even if it hasn't let out a blink for days. Quite nice to wake up to, don't you think?"

"Ninian—"

"Darling, don't interrupt. You are supposed to be listening. I was rather taken with the living-room curtains. A pleasing shade of green, and lined, so they oughtn't to fade. They really are a good colour—very restful to the eye. So I've taken the plunge and told Hemming we'll have the lot. I hope you approve?"

"Ninian—"

"It will be your fault if you don't, because I wanted you to come up with me, and you could have managed quite easily. So when—or shall we say if—you wake up and hate the hollyhock curtains, you will just have to remind yourself that you rushed upon your doom."

"Ninian—"

"Woman, let be! This is my show, and I want to talk. It is your part to listen—resign yourself to it! I have also said I will take over—" He proceeded to waste time in enumerating things like a front door mat, a kitchen cupboard. "His aunt has things like that built in—superiority of Scottish houses! Also a rack for drying clothes, and two more or less fitted book-cases."

As he described all these things in minute detail with comments and interjections obviously designed to draw her fire, Janet considered that she would really be thwarting him better if she just held her tongue. There is nothing quite so damping as to let off fireworks with no one to scream or say "Oh!" when they go up. He had been talking for quite a time before he checked to say,

"Darling, you're still there?"

Janet said, "Just."

"I thought you might have swooned with ecstasy."

"At hearing you talk a lot of nonsense? There's nothing so very new about that."

"Darling, that came out pure Scots.

> 'The accents of the Doric tongue
> Upon her lightest murmur hung—'

I believe those beautiful lines to be original, but I won't swear they were not written by Sir Walter Scott in one of his more exalted moments."

"I shouldn't think it at all likely!"

"Darling, I could listen to you all night, but the pips are mounting up. Oh, by the way, I see in the evening paper that the leading man in Star's play has been rushed to hospital with a broken leg and the opening is put off. They're going to fill in with a revival of something or other until he is all right again. Rather a knock for Star—she was building a good deal on this show. I wonder if she'll come back."

"Won't she be in the thing they are putting on?"

"Oh, no, not her line—it's a Josefa Clark play. Darling, this is a most expensive call. Good-night! Dream about me!"

The house next day took on all the more trying features of the pre-party rush. Mrs. Simmons displayed the temperament upon which great cooking rests as surely as do the other major forms of art. It is sad to reflect that the hand so light upon pastry and soufflé should drag so heavily upon the reins of office. There is a certain flush which when it reaches the forehead may be regarded as a danger signal. There is a tone in the voice at which the boldest of domestic helps hastens upon the errand assigned and does not dream of answering back. Simmons, a husband of many prudent years standing, knew better than to be what his wife would have stigmatized as "under foot." He returned to his pantry, where he marshalled drinks and polished the cocktail glasses until they shone like crystal.

It was left to Edna Ford to precipitate a storm which might otherwise have been averted. Constitutionally unable to let well alone, she came fretting into the kitchen at a delicate moment in the creation of the cheese straws which were Mrs. Simmons' pride. Undeterred by a portentous frown, she burst into fluttered speech.

"Oh, Mrs. Simmons, I hope you are not doing too much. Miss Ford was particularly anxious—I understood she had made it quite clear—those *are* cheese straws you are making, are they not?"

In a voice that matched the frown Mrs. Simmons said, "They are."

Edna pushed at a wisp of hair that had straggled down on to her cheek.

"Oh dear," she said, "I quite understood that Miss Ford had ordered all the savouries from Ledbury. I know she was most anxious you should not be overburdened."

Mrs. Simmons' fingers paused on the pastry knot she was twisting.

"Bought cheese straws is what we've never had, not since

I've been in this house, and if they come in, I tell you fair and square, Mrs. Ford, that I go out! Now, if you don't *mind* letting me go on with my work—"

"Oh, no—no—of course not. I just came to see if there was anything I could do."

"Nothing except to let me get *on*, Mrs. Ford, if you *don't* mind."

Edna transferred her attentions to Mrs. Bell who was doing the drawing-room, and succeeded in making her so nervous that she broke a Dresden figure which had been the gift of an archduke in those distant days when there was still an Austrian Empire.

Over her elevenses Mrs. Bell bewailed the tragedy.

"Enough to upset anyone's nerves, her coming right up behind you and saying, 'Oh, do be careful!' And I'm sure there isn't anyone in the world carefuller with china than what I am. Why, I've got my great-grandmother's tea-set that she had for a wedding present a hundred years ago this spring, and there isn't a piece so much as chipped. And I'm still using a frying-pan what my grandmother had."

"Then it's time you had a new one," said Mrs. Simmons.

Janet, asking Adriana whether she could be of any use, was advised to choose the lesser of two evils.

"If you offer to help Meriel with the flowers, she'll probably stab you with the gardening-scissors. If you don't help her, the worst she can say is that no one ever gives her a hand. I should advise you to play for safety."

Janet looked unhappy.

"Why is she like that?"

Adriana shrugged.

"Why is anyone like anything? You can pick and choose

among the answers. It's written in your forehead, or in your hand, or in the stars. Or someone thwarted you when you were in your cradle and it struck you crooked. I think I really prefer Shakespeare—

'The fault, dear Brutus, is not in our stars,
But in ourselves, that we are underlings.'

Of course, what's wrong with Meriel is that I've never been able to lead her aside and tell her she is the romantically illegitimate offshoot of a royal house. If she tries me too high, I shall probably some day tell her what she really is!"

Janet said, "Oh—" on a caught breath, because the door behind Adriana had swung open. Meriel stood there, her face white, her eyes wide and blazing. She came forward slowly, a hand at her throat, and did not speak.

Adriana made an embarrassed movement.

"Now, Meriel—"

"Adriana!"

"My dear, there's really nothing to make a scene about. I don't know what you think you heard."

Meriel's voice came in a whisper.

"You said if I tried you too high you would one day probably tell me what I really was! I ask you to tell me now!"

Adriana put out a hand.

"My dear, there is nothing much to tell. I have told you that often enough, but you don't believe me because it doesn't fit in with your romantic fancies."

"I demand that you should tell me the truth!"

Adriana was making an unusual effort at control. She said, "We have had all this out before. You come of quite ordinary people. Your father and mother were dead, and I said I would look after you. Well, I have done it, haven't I?"

Meriel flared.

"I don't believe you! I don't believe I come of ordinary people! I believe I'm your daughter, and you've never had the courage to own me! If you had, I might have respected you!"

Adriana said in a quiet voice,

"No, I am not your mother. If I had had a child I should have owned it. You must believe me when I tell you that."

"Well then, I don't! You're lying just to spite me!" Her voice had risen to a scream. "I'll never believe you—never—never—*never!*" She ran out of the room and banged the door behind her.

Adriana spoke in a voice of cold rage.

"Her father was a Spanish muleteer. He stabbed her mother and himself. The baby was a pretty little black-eyed thing. I took it—and trouble enough with it."

Janet stood there, shocked and silent. After a minute Adriana reached out and touched her.

"I've never told anyone. You won't speak of it?"

Janet said, "No."

CHAPTER 17

Stella talked about the party all the way home from the Vicarage.

"I can wear my new dress that Star got me just before she went away. It's a sort of yellow. I like it because it hasn't got frills. I hate frills. Miss Page has got a dress with frills—she's going to wear it this evening. It makes her look all fluffy like a doll on a Christmas tree, only black. She put it on, and Mrs. Lenton pinned up the hem, and she said, 'Oh, Ellie, you look like a picture!' I think that was a silly thing to say—don't you? Because there are all sorts of pictures, and some of them are ever so ugly."

Janet laughed.

"Mrs. Lenton meant that Miss Page looked nice."

Stella made a face.

"I don't like black dresses. I won't wear one ever. I've told Star I won't. I don't know why Miss Page has one."

"Fair people look nice in black."

"Miss Page doesn't. It makes her look like that pink dress I had which the colour all washed out of and Nanny said it would have been better if Star had tried a bit of the stuff first and washed it. Joan Cuttle says Miss Page has gone off something dreadfully."

"Stella, it isn't very nice to repeat things about people."

"No—Star says so too. But Miss Page used to be much prettier and nicer than she is now. Jenny Lenton says she cries in the night. She told Mrs. Lenton, and she put her and Molly into another room. They used to sleep with Miss Page, but they don't any more because it kept them awake. Isn't it nice it's such a fine warm day? Jenny said you wouldn't know it wasn't summer, but I told her that's silly because of the flowers. You don't have dahlias and michaelmas daisies in the summer, do you?"

By dint of encouraging these horticultural speculations it was possible to get home without any more embarrassing confidences on the subject of Ellie Page.

It was indeed one of those early autumn days which are sometimes hotter than anything conceded by July. Edna Ford, under the necessity of having something to worry about, now concentrated upon the unseasonable temperature.

"Adriana never makes proper lists of who has accepted and who has refused, but I believe she has asked about two hundred people, and if even half of them come the drawing-room will be unbearably hot, because she won't have the windows open—at least I suppose she won't. She always says she had enough draughts when she was on the stage and she means to be comfortable now. Only once the curtains are drawn, perhaps she wouldn't notice if a window was opened behind them. I could ask Geoffrey to see about it. But of course if she did notice, it might make her very angry. You see, as soon as the lights are on inside, the curtains will have to be drawn. There is nothing she dislikes so much as being in a lighted room with the curtains open. It's quite a *thing* with her. So really I think I shall have to speak to Geoffrey and see what he can do."

By a little after six the drawing-room was beginning to fill. The day was still warm, but it was clouding. Adriana stood to receive her guests, her head high, her pose gracious. Behind her the fine old fireplace was banked with flowers, and an antique carved chair stood ready to support her when she should feel in need of rest. She wore a grey dress of great elegance, with a diamond flower on her shoulder and three rows of exquisite pearls. As the light faded and the great chandeliers were turned on, her hair caught the glow and reflected it. The colour was certainly a work of art, as was the flawless tinting of her skin.

Poor Mabel Preston came off a very bad second. Since her last visit she had reduced her straw-coloured locks to a messy imitation of Adriana's deep copper-beech red, and she had been unwisely lavish with powder, rouge and lipstick. The black and yellow dress was a disaster. Ninian, penetrating the crowd and arriving by dint of perseverance at Janet's side, gave one glance at her and murmured,

"Queen wasp! They should all be destroyed quite early in the year."

"Ninian, she is pathetic."

He laughed.

"She is enjoying herself like mad. You look very handsome, my sweet."

"Star didn't think so. She said I was like a brown mouse in this dress."

"I like brown mice. Nice companionable little things."

Janet ignored this.

"It's useful, because no one remembers it," she said.

He was looking across the crowd.

"Hullo, Esmé Trent is very smart! I wonder whether Adriana asked her, or whether she gate-crashed."

"Why should she?"

"Up-and-coming sort of girl—she might think it a joke."

"I mean, why shouldn't Adriana ask her?"

115

He cocked an eyebrow.

"Dear Geoffrey might be led astray. Or dear Edna might have issued an ultimatum. Someday, you know, she'll go right off the deep end, and Adriana will be bored stiff. Geoffrey amuses her, but she expects him to keep within bounds. What are the odds he slips into the garden with Esmé as soon as it's dark enough to be safe?"

It was later on, when Simmons had drawn the long grey velvet curtains and the dusk was deepening outside, that Janet was making her way back to the table at the end of the room with a tray in her hand. The cheese straws and small savouries she had been offering had run low, and she was coming back to renew the supply. The easiest way to get along was by the wall on the window side. The three recesses afforded elbow-room, and at any rate you could only be bumped into from one direction. But just by the last of the windows she became hemmed in and could get no farther. A solid block of people was pressed against the table beyond her, all talking at the top of their voices and forming an impenetrable barrier. She was forced up against the curtain, the thick velvet touching her cheek, and beyond it from the window recess voices came to her.

By some trick of acoustics these voices did not merge with the babel in the room. They were detached and clear. Ellie Page said, "Oh, Geoffrey *darling!*" and Geoffrey Ford said, "My dear girl, do take care!"

Janet went hot and cold. She couldn't move away. She couldn't even put her fingers in her ears because of the tray she was holding. If she coughed or shook the curtain, they would know that they had been overheard.

Ellie said, "Couldn't we slip out? I heard her asking you to open a window. No one would miss us."

116

"I can't possibly. It would be madness."

"I must see you!"

"You saw me last night."

So it had been Ellie Page down there in Edna's sitting-room at two in the morning—*Ellie Page.*

Ellie said on a sob,

"You sent me away—"

"Well, if you want to ruin us both—"

"Oh, I don't!"

"Then you've got to be patient."

There was another sob.

"How long is it going on?"

He said in an exasperated tone,

"What is the good of asking me that? If I leave Edna, Adriana will cut off supplies—she has told me so right out. Well, we can't live on nothing, can we?"

Someone moved on Janet's left and she stepped into the gap. That poor wretched girl—what a mess! She pushed and prodded her way up to the table and set down the tray.

CHAPTER 18

Mabel Preston was enjoying herself. All those nice little savouries and any amount to drink. Every time she took another glass she felt more convinced that she was right on the top of her form. After the third or fourth she had no hesitation in talking to anyone. And why not, if you please? Most of the women's clothes were not half so smart as hers. Adriana always did go to good houses, and there was one thing about black and yellow, it showed up well in a crowd. Right from the beginning she had noticed people looking at her, which made it quite easy to get into conversation and let them know who they had been looking at.

"Mabel Prestayne. That was my stage name—I expect you'll remember it. It's some years since I retired—on my marriage of course. But the public doesn't forget. Now I always think Adriana stayed on too long. I believe in being remembered at one's best."

She did not really notice that the people to whom she addressed these remarks had nothing very much to say to her and soon detached themselves. She continued to sip from one little glass after another and to confide more and more frankly in the total stranger. It was disappointing that the Duchess shouldn't be here, but she heard Lady Isabel Warren announced, and she was the Duke's sister, which would do very nearly as well to talk about afterwards. She ought perhaps to make the next drink her last. The bother was she was out of practise, and the room was so hot. She thought perhaps she would go out into the hall and cool down. It wouldn't do if she came over queer in a crowd like this.

Meriel edged her way between two chattering groups and skirted old Lady Bontine, who took up as much room as two other people and was a great deal harder to shift. It brought her to the point she was aiming at. Ninian was simply bound to come back this way. He set down the tray he was carrying, turned, found her at his elbow, and said, "Hello!" She gave him the smile which she had spent some time practising before her looking-glass.

"Oh, you're back! Did you have a good time?"

"Quite a successful one, thank you."

"I wish I had known you were going up. I would have come too. I have quite a lot to do in town, but I do so hate travelling alone. It would have been delightful if we could have gone together."

"Well, I had to meet a man, and I was a bit rushed."

"A friend?"

"Oh, just a man I know."

She tried the smile again.

"That sounds mysterious—and interesting. Do tell me all about it! Only it's so hot in here—couldn't we open one of those windows behind the curtains and slip out? We could go down into the garden and sit by the pool. It would be lovely, and you could tell me all about everything. Oh, Ninian, *do!*"

He had begun to wonder what she was up to. There was just one thing you could always be sure of with Meriel, and that was that she was playing a part. He thought she was being the sweet and sympathetic friend, in which case her get-up was a mistake. That slinky magenta dress and the matching lipstick! Sweet sympathy flows oddly from magenta lips. Definitely the wrong note to strike. He thought what an ass she was, and he was hanged if he was going to pour confidences into her ear in a dark garden. He shook his head and said,

"Adriana expects me to be on duty—you too, I imagine. We shall both have black marks if we don't get on with it. I must go and pay my respects to Lady Isabel."

Meriel stood where she was. Why should Adriana have what she wanted? They were all at her beck and call. And why? Just because she had the money. It was no use having beauty and youth and genius unless you had the money to back them up! And why should Adriana have it and go on

119

keeping it away from everyone else! She saw Ninian laughing and talking with Lady Isabel, and thought angrily that if she wasn't a duke's daughter nobody would look at her twice. The anger reached her eyes as she saw Ninian move on and find his way to Janet and Stella.

Stella caught at him.

"She says it's my bedtime, but it isn't. Say it isn't!"

"Darling, I only wish it was mine."

"You can go to bed instead of me. Why should I go when I don't want to? What would Janet do if I was to scream?"

"You had better ask her."

Stella swung round.

"Janet—what would you do?"

"I don't know."

Stella jigged up and down.

"Think—think quick!"

"There's no need to think about things that won't happen."

"Why won't they happen?"

"Because you have too much sense. Only a very stupid person would want to be remembered for ever and ever as the child who screamed at Adriana's party and had lemonade poured over its head."

Stella's eyes became immense.

"Would you pour lemonade on me?"

"I might, but I'm sure I shan't have to."

Stella looked down at a brief yellow skirt.

"It would spoil my dress," she said.

Mabel Preston stared at the little group. She saw them hazily. She began to make her way towards the door.

Esmé Trent stood with her back to the room talking to Geoffrey Ford. She said,

"Where have you been hiding yourself? I thought you were never coming near me."

"Oh, there are always plenty of duty people to talk to at a show like this. I have to play host for Adriana."

"Getting into training for doing it for yourself?"

"My dear girl!"

She laughed.

"No one can hear in this uproar. It's as good as being on a desert island. By the way, who is that ghastly Mabel creature who buttonholed me? She seems to be staying here."

"Mabel Preston? Oh, she's just an old stage acquaintance of Adriana's—a bit of a down-and-out. Adriana has her here, gives her clothes—all that kind of thing."

Esmé Trent was explicitly profane.

"Well, I call it cruelty to guests. The most ghastly bore I've ever come across, and the most ghastly sight. Like one of those wasps you find crawling about the house after there's been a frost and it ought to have died. By the way, where is Adriana?"

He said,

"She was over by the fireplace. Didn't you see her? Very good stage effect—one of those carved Spanish chairs set back against greenery and chrysanthemums—other lesser chairs for the favoured few."

"Yes, I saw her." She gave a hard little laugh. "How she adores the limelight! But she isn't there now."

Geoffrey frowned.

"It's frightfully hot in here—she may have found it too much for her. Edna wanted me to open a window behind those curtains some time ago. I expect I had better do it."

They began to push their way into the crowd.

They had not seen Mabel Preston between them and the

121

door. When they moved, she managed to get it open and slip out. Esmé Trent's words rang in her head—her false, cruel words. How could she say such dreadful wicked things? They weren't true—they couldn't be true! They were just spite and envy! But her head was throbbing and the tears were running down over her face and spoiling her make-up. She couldn't go back, and she couldn't stay here for anyone to see her like this. Someone was coming from the direction of the hall.

She began to walk the other way until she came to the end of the corridor and the glass door which led into the garden. Fresh air—that was what she wanted, and to get away quietly by herself until she had got over the insulting things that horrible woman had said. But she had better have a wrap. The black and yellow dress was only crêpe-de-chine. There was a cloakroom here by the garden door, and the very first thing she saw when she looked inside was the coat Adriana was giving her—the one that girl Meriel had made all the fuss about. But Adriana wasn't giving it to Meriel, she was giving it to *her*! There it hung, with its great black and white checks and the emerald stripe which had taken her fancy. She didn't know when she had seen anything smarter. She slipped it on and went out into the dusk.

The air felt fresh after the heated house. She walked waveringly and without conscious aim. She really had overdone those drinks. Or perhaps it was just the room being so hot and that Mrs. Trent insulting her. She had asked who she was, because she looked as if she might be somebody. Mabel Preston shook her head. Smart looks aren't everything. She wasn't a lady. No lady would have used such an insulting expression. The words ran together into a blur. When she tried saying them aloud they sounded exactly as if she was

122

tight. Hot room and too many drinks—never do to go back until she was all right again.

She lifted the latch of a small gate and passed into the flower-garden. Wandering on in the half light, she saw that she had come to a place where there was a pool and a seat. Nice quiet place with hedges round it. She went and sat down on the seat and shut her eyes.

It was much darker when she opened them again, and at first she didn't know where she was. She just woke up in the dusk with the black hedges round her and a glimmer of light on the pool. It was frightening to wake like that. She got to her feet and stood for a little remembering. It had been hot—she had had a drink too many—and that Mrs. Trent had insulted her—but she was all right now—she wasn't hot any more. A shiver went over her. Silly going to sleep like that.

She moved towards the pool and stood looking down into it. Her legs felt stiff. A small bright light came flicking through an arch in the hedge. The arch was behind her and to her left. The light slid over the black and white of her coat and the emerald stripe. It startled her, but she had no time to turn or cry out.

CHAPTER 19

The last car having gone off down the drive, Sam Bolton followed it in the direction of the lodge. He was the under gardener and he had been helping to get the cars away. He was now about the unlawful business of courting Mary Robertson with whom he had an assignation which would have been strictly forbidden by her father if he had known anything about it. Mr. Robertson was head gardener, and an autocrat. His notions of parental authority might, as Mary declared, be fifty years out of date, but she wouldn't have dared to flout them openly, and he looked higher for her than Sam, whom he admitted to be a steady, hard-working lad but "withoot sae much ambeetion as ye could lay on a saxpence." He had a distressing homily which he was only too willing to deliver as to the extent to which he himself had burned the midnight oil in the pursuit of knowledge. Sam and Mary were therefore in the habit of waiting until he had departed to the White Hart for a moderate glass and game of darts before, with the connivance of Mrs. Robertson, they snatched an hour together.

He came whistling down the drive and she slipped out of the bushes to meet him. Then arm-in-arm they went back towards the house, cut through the shrubbery by a path which came out at the bottom of the lawn, and so to the gate which led into the enclosed flower-garden. Mary had brought a torch, but they knew the way too well to need it. The place might have been made for courting couples—perhaps it had. On a warm evening there were the seats beside the pool, and if it was colder there was the summerhouse.

They came through the arch in the hedge and saw at their feet the faint mysterious glimmer of the cloudy sky reflected from the water of the pool. There was a light air moving and the clouds moved with it—up there in the arch of the sky and here within the round of the low stone parapet. But the circle was broken by a shadow. Mary pressed closer.

"Sam—there's something there!"

"Where?" His arm had tightened.

"There! Oh, Sam, there's something in the pool! There's something—oh!"

"Give us your torch!"

She fumbled for it, her fingers shaking on the catch, and when he took it from her and a faint beam trembled on what lay across the parapet and fallen down into the water, she screamed. The light showed a black square and a white square and an emerald stripe that crossed them. To both it was a perfectly familiar sight. Sam felt his insides turn over. The torch fell out of his hand and rolled.

"It's Madam! Oh, my lord!"

He made a movement and Mary clutched him.

"Don't you touch her! Don't you dare to touch her! Oh, Sam!"

There was stuff in Sam Bolton. He said doggedly,

"I'm bound to get her out of the water."

Mary went on clutching him.

"We've got to get away—we don't want anyone to see us!"

He said, "We can't do that."

She hadn't known how strong he was. Her hold was broken and she was pushed aside. She slipped on a patch of moss and fetched up against the wooden seat, catching at it. Her foot touched the fallen torch. She picked it up, but it had gone out. The catch clicked, but whichever way she pushed it the light was dead. The word in her own mind frightened her. She stared into the darkness for Sam. He had gone down into the pool. She could just see him there, stooping, lifting, and she could hear the water running from what he lifted and a horrid soft thud as he set it down. That was when she screamed again. She hadn't meant to—it just happened. She screamed and she ran, with the nightmare sound of her own voice and of that dripping water in her ears.

No one had locked the front door. Sam found it open when he came running and out of breath. He had held a drowned woman in his arms and he was soaking wet. His feet squelched on the floor of the hall and left great muddy tracks. He came upon Simmons carrying a tray of drinks, and said on a gasp,

"Madam's dead!"

Simmons stood there, ghastly. He told Mrs. Simmons afterwards that he felt as if someone had hit him over the head. He heard himself say something, but he didn't know what it was. But he heard what Sam said,

"Madam's dead! She's drowned in the pool—and she's dead!"

His hands stopped feeling the tray, and it fell, tilting first and then going down with a crash. And that brought everyone running.

Joan Cuttle with her mouth open and her eyes popping, Mrs. Geoffrey with a confusion of cries and questions, Miss Meriel, Mr. Geoffrey, Mr. Ninian—they were all there, and all he could say was to be careful of the broken glass, and all he could do was to point at Sam who stood and dripped in

126

the middle of the hall with his face like tallow and his big hands shaking.

Sam said his piece all over again.

"Madam's dead! I found her in the pool!"

And with them all standing there struck for the moment into a paralysed silence, Adriana Ford came out on the landing above and set her foot upon the stair. The light shone down on the gleaming dark red hair, on the dress of pleated grey chiffon, on the three rows of pearls which fell from throat to waist, on the diamond flower at her shoulder.

The silence broke to the sound of an approaching car. The door stood wide as Sam had left it, and there came in Star Somers in a grey travelling coat with a little winged cap on her pale gold hair. She came running, holding out her hands, her colour high and her eyes bright.

"Darlings, I'm back! Where's Stella? Aren't you surprised—" And then she checked. She looked at Sam standing there muddy and dripping, at Simmons with the smashed glass at his feet, at all the shocked faces and staring eyes, at Adriana high on the stair above. Her colour failed. "What's the matter? What's wrong? Can't any of you speak?"

Adriana came composedly down the stairs. It was a good entrance, and she got the last ounce out of it.

"Sam has just been telling them he has found me drowned in the pool. Geoffrey—Ninian—don't you think you had better go back with him and find out who it is?"

127

CHAPTER 20

Miss Silver, glancing at the Monday morning paper, found her eye caught by a small paragraph.

FATALITY AT FORD HOUSE

"Playgoers of thirty years ago may remember Mabel Prestayne. Amongst other parts, she played Nerissa to the Portia of Adriana Ford, and it was at the home of this great actress that she met with the accident which has caused her death. A cocktail party was in progress, and it is surmised that she wandered into the garden in the dusk and tripped over a low parapet guarding the pool in which her body was found. She had been living in retirement for a good many years."

Miss Silver read the paragraph twice, and permitted herself to say, "Dear me!" It was now ten days since Miss Ford's visit, but the circumstances were all quite fresh in her mind. When she presently put down the paper and took up her knitting, she did not find herself entirely able to dismiss the topic.

It was two days later when she lifted the telephone receiver and heard a deep voice say,

"This is Mrs. Smith speaking. You will remember that I wrote and afterwards telephoned and came to see you."

Miss Silver said, "I remember perfectly." She paused slightly before adding—"Mrs. Smith."

"You remember the subject of our conversation?"

"Certainly."

The voice hardened.

"There has been a development. I don't feel that I can discuss it on the telephone, but I should like you to come down here." There was a moment's silence, and then, "As soon as possible."

It was about seven o'clock in the evening. Miss Silver said in her temperate voice,

"If the matter is not immediate, perhaps you will suggest a morning train."

"The ten-thirty will get you down by half past eleven. You will be met at Ledbury. Since you are an old friend whom I have not seen for some time, it will seem quite natural if I am at the station. Those are the arrangements I should suggest. I hope they suit you."

Miss Silver said, "Perfectly," and the receiver was replaced with a click.

Since speculation without fact upon which to exercise itself can hardly be considered profitable, Miss Silver did not permit herself to indulge in it. She wrote informing her niece Ethel Burkett that she was going into the country and provided her with the address, and she packed her modest requirements for an autumn visit. Country houses, and especially old ones, were sadly apt to be draughty, and the weather at this or indeed any time of the year very little to be depended upon. She would therefore wear her black coat and fur tippet, trusted friend of many years, over the dress of light wool appropriate to the season. Since it was her invariable practise to use a last year's flowered silk for evening wear, this was also packed, together with an aged velvet coatee, so warm, so cozy, which had on many previous oc-

129

casions fortified her against such idiosyncrasies as a passion for open windows or a determined economy in the matter of fuel. She could remember large dining-rooms where the draught poured in through an ever open service door, and drawing-rooms where the windows remained fixed in an open position and were far too heavy to be moved. Inspector Frank Abbott of Scotland Yard, that devoted but irreverent young man, might declare the coatee to be a museum piece, its origin shrouded in a Victorian past, but nothing would have induced her to visit in the country without it, and it was in her opinion both suitable and becoming.

When she alighted from the train at Ledbury wearing the black coat, the yellow fur tippet, and the hat which had been her best last year brought up to date with a small bunch of shaded pansies mixed with sprigs of mignonette, she was at once, and in the most agreeable manner, approached by a tall, dark young man. He smiled, and said,

"I am sure you must be Miss Silver. My name is Ninian Rutherford. Adriana is waiting in the car."

Adriana acted the part of an old friend in the most artistic manner.

"So very nice that you were able to come. After—let me see—how many years is it? Well, perhaps we had better not say. Time does not stand still for any of us. We must just pick up the threads."

When she was settled beside her in the back of the car and Ninian was driving them through the narrow Ledbury streets, Miss Silver was able to observe the vast difference between the Mrs. Smith who had visited her at Montague Mansions and Adriana Ford with her gleaming hair, her delicate make-up, the handsome fur wrap over a beautifully cut coat and skirt, the flashing rings on an ungloved hand.

As they came out of the town and began to thread a number of winding lanes, conversation remained on a pleasantly conventional level. There was an old house or two to be pointed out. "The fifteenth-century staircase is worth seeing, but of course the front is modern . . . And that ridiculous castellated place is Leamington's Folly. He was a wealthy Victorian industrialist who ran himself into the bankruptcy court and finished up in the workhouse. Nobody has lived there for years, and the place is falling to bits."

For the last mile the road ran along by the river, and there was much in the autumn scenery to charm the eye. Miss Silver, whilst duly admiring, could not avoid the conclusion that the neighbourhood of so much water must of necessity increase the tendency to damp so prevalent in country places.

As they entered the grounds of Ford House, she observed them to lie regrettably low, and opined, though not audibly, that the house must be constantly invaded by the river mists. It was a picturesque building in a rambling style, with autumn roses blooming on the walls and a quantity of other creepers. Not really what she considered desirable in view of the fact that so much vegetation was bound to harbour insects.

She was conducted to a room in a wing to the right of the main staircase. It was fresh and bright, with flowered chintzes and comfortable chairs. There was also, she was pleased to notice, an electric fire, Adriana informing her that they made their own electricity and were very well served.

"You are next to Janet Johnstone and little Stella, with Meriel and Star Somers across the way. When you are ready, come back to the landing and across it to the west wing. My sitting-room is at the end."

It took Miss Silver a very short time to remove her outdoor things, put them neatly away, and unpack her modest suit-case. She washed in the adjoining bathroom, and then, knitting-bag in hand, betook herself to the west wing. She met no one, but as she crossed the landing a young woman in a red jumper passed through the hall below. Glancing at her with interest, Miss Silver observed the dark good looks, the smouldering eyes, the restless step. It was her first sight of Meriel Ford, and it gave her food for thought.

She found Adriana on her couch. She had changed into a flowing house-coat in a shade of purple so deep as to be almost black. She looked tired in spite of the careful make-up, but the note in her voice was one of exasperation.

"Sit down and make yourself comfortable. Well, I suppose you want to know why I've dragged you down here in all this hurry."

Miss Silver coughed.

"I imagine that it has something to do with the death of Miss Mabel Prestayne."

Adriana gave a short laugh.

"I suppose you saw the notice in the papers. Poor Mabel—how she would have hated to think she would be remembered because she had played Nerissa to my Portia!"

Miss Silver was opening her knitting-bag. Having taken out of it a pair of needles and a ball of fine fleecy white wool, she addressed herself to the warm shawl destined for Dorothy Silver's unexpected twin. The bootees and a little coat had been completed and despatched, and she considered that the shawl should now take precedence of the second coat. About two inches of the ornamental border showed like a frill on the wooden needles. She looked over them and said,

"She met with an accident?"

Adriana looked back frowning.

"I don't know—we must call it that, I suppose. Look here,

I had better tell you what has happened. After I came to see you I decided that I had been making a fool of myself. I thought I had been dead long enough, and that it was time I got up and showed them it was a bit soon to think about burying me. I went to a specialist, and he told me to go ahead, so I did. I bought a lot of new clothes and started coming down to meals, and I sent out invitations to a big cocktail party just to show people I was still there. Mabel Preston came to stay for it—that's her real name you know—Prestayne was just for the stage. Sounded silly to me, but she was like that. I used to have her here every so often. She adored a party. Well, here she was, and so were about a hundred and fifty other people. It went with a bang. Whenever I saw Mabel she was enjoying herself—having lots of drinks and going up and talking to people as if she had known them for years. She was *enjoying* herself. When everyone had gone I came up here. I tidied up my face, and I thought I would go down for a bit and see what the others thought of the party. But when I got out on the landing something had happened. The first I knew about it, there was a crash. I came to the top of the stairs and looked over. Simmons had just dropped a tray full of glasses and drinks. The front door was wide open, and Sam Bolton, the under gardener, was standing in the middle of the hall dripping wet. Everyone in the house seemed to be there, all looking at him. And no wonder, because just as I came to the head of the stairs I heard him say, 'Madam's dead! She's drowned in the pool—and she's dead!'"

Adriana paused. She gave that short hard laugh again.

"And he meant me!" she said.

CHAPTER 21

Miss Silver employed her strongest comment.

"Dear me!"

Adriana Ford regarded her with a touch of impatience.

"When I walked down on them they all got the fright of their lives. Sam went the colour of melted tallow."

"Pray, what made him think the drowned person was yourself?"

"She was wearing my coat."

"But if it was dark—I gather it must have been, since your guests had left—"

Adriana said impatiently,

"He had a torch, a wretched weak little thing, but enough to show up the pattern of the coat. I have had it for some time, and it is—pretty noticeable—big squares of black and white with an emerald stripe running across them. Quite unmistakable, and everyone knows it. Sam will have seen me in it for years."

"And how did Miss Preston come to be wearing it?"

"It was hanging in the cloakroom, just by the garden door." She hesitated for a moment, and then went on. "I don't know why she went out, but her dress was thin—she would have needed a wrap. And in a way, I suppose, she thought of the coat as her own. You see, I had half given it to her."

Miss Silver looked at her in a questioning manner.

"Half?"

Adriana moved impatiently.

"Meriel made a fuss. She had set her heart on the coat. But it was too marked—I couldn't have people saying I let her go about in my cast-offs. It's just the sort of thing she might make a handle of herself! It wouldn't have done. But she threw a scene, so I thought the best way was to hang it downstairs, wear it a few times more myself, and just let Mabel take it away with her when she went. I didn't want Meriel to upset her—she was rather easily upset."

Miss Silver asked another question.

"Had you worn the coat lately yourself?"

Adriana looked away.

"The day before."

"You mean the day before Miss Preston was drowned?"

"Yes."

"Who saw you in it?"

Adriana's hand lifted and fell.

"Everyone," she said.

"You mean everyone in the house?"

"Oh, yes. You see I went for a turn in the garden just before lunch, and it was so fine that I went on into the village. I've been walking a little farther every day. It's only about a quarter of a mile, really."

"Did you meet anyone you knew?"

Adriana laughed without amusement.

"I could hardly go into the village without doing that! Why are you asking me all this?" Her voice had risen suddenly.

"Because I think the answers may be interesting."

Their eyes met. Miss Silver's were kind and steady. It was Adriana who turned her head.

"Oh, very well, then—here you are. The Vicar passed me on his bicycle, and I saw his wife and her cousin Ellie Page

135

in their front garden. Ellie Page has a class for children—my little niece Stella goes to it. I stopped and said a few words to them. Whilst I was doing so Esmé Trent went by—I imagine on her way to catch the bus into Ledbury, as she seems to spend most of her time there and she was made up to the nines. She is a young widow with a little boy whom she neglects, and there is no love lost between her and Ellie Page."

"Is the little boy in Miss Page's class?"

"Oh, yes. Anything to get him off his mother's hands! By the way, you had better not mention her to Edna."

"Indeed?"

Adriana nodded.

"I gather that Geoffrey and she have been seen together often enough to prompt the usual kind friend to let Edna know. Very stupid, and it probably means nothing at all, but Edna has no philosophy where Geoffrey is concerned. She's a fool of course, because he's like that and she'll never change him so she had much better make the best of it."

"Did you see anyone else?"

"Old Mrs. Potts was calling her cat in. Her husband is the sexton. I think that was all . . . Oh, Mary Robertson was in the Lodge garden as I came back. She is the head gardener's daughter. She and Sam Bolton are courting, and she was with him when he found poor Mabel. She had to give evidence at the inquest, and her father is furious because he doesn't approve of the affair with Sam."

Miss Silver gave the slight cough with which she was accustomed to lend emphasis to a remark.

"The inquest has taken place?"

"Yesterday. The funeral was this morning."

"And the verdict?"

"Accidental death." There was a pause, after which she continued in rather a strained manner. "She had had a good many drinks. The idea is that she wasn't any too steady, and that she tripped over the parapet and fell into the pool."

"Was there any sign that she had struggled or tried to save herself?"

"The Coroner wanted to know about that, but you see Sam had got her out of the pool. The moss and plants on the edge were all dragged and crushed, and there was no telling whether she had done any of it herself."

"She was drowned?"

"Yes."

"Were there any bruises?"

"They didn't say so."

"There was no suggestion that it could have been anything but an accident?"

Adriana made a sharp movement.

"Who in the world would want to kill Mabel Preston?"

Miss Silver's look was stern and compassionate.

"Miss Preston was bareheaded? Miss Ford—what shade was her hair?"

All the natural colour left Adriana's face. She said in a cold, flat voice,

"It used to be fair—but this time—she had copied the colour of mine."

CHAPTER 22

A gong sounded, and they went down to lunch. The family was introduced—Geoffrey Ford and Mrs. Geoffrey; the dark girl Miss Silver had seen crossing the hall; Miss Janet Johnstone and the little girl Stella. Star Somers, it appeared, was up in London on business—"She is just over from America and has so much to attend to." A rather daring flight on the part of Adriana, because everyone in the room except Miss Silver knew perfectly well that Star's "business" was to avoid being dragooned into attending poor Mabel Preston's funeral. Simmons, serving the meal with dignity, had heard her say as much in the high, sweet voice which carried so—"No, darling, I won't, and that's flat! I haven't any black down here, and if you are going to suggest that I trail round in some archaic garment of Edna's you have just got to think again. I will admire you all doing your noble duty, but you know, actually, I have got to see Rothstein, just in case anything goes wrong about the New York production—I mean, no one can be quite certain about how soon Audrey will be able to play."

Miss Silver found herself with quite enough people to study. Whilst conversing in her usual amiable and fluent manner she was able to observe a number of points of interest. Mr. Geoffrey Ford made himself very agreeable. From what she had heard of him, and from his general air of handsome well-being, she concluded that this was his usual manner. It went smoothly and well, but just once or twice it occurred to her that the pace was a little forced, and the pleasant laugh a shade too frequent. There had, after all, been a funeral from the house that morning. He drank whisky and water, and filled his glass a second time. Mrs. Geoffrey on her right was still in the old black coat and skirt she had worn for the ceremony. It hung on her, suggesting that she had lost weight, and it could never have been either smart or becoming. With a dingy grey blouse, it reduced eyes, hair, and skin to a colourless uniformity. The eyes looked as if they had not slept, and the lids were reddened. There are women who always weep at a wedding or a funeral, but they are of an easier and more emotional type than Edna Ford.

On her other side Meriel's scarlet jumper struck a defiant note. It emphasised the dark clustering hair, the smouldering eyes, the ivory pallor. She had used a jarring shade of lipstick with the most discordant effect. Miss Silver could readily believe in the selfishness and temper which would make a scene if things did not go just as she wished. She sat helping herself from every dish and leaving most of what she took upon her plate. Sitting beside her, she was aware of resentment and a fretting impatience to have the meal and her proximity done with.

Across the way Janet Johnstone and Ninian Rutherford sat on either side of the little girl with the fine eyes who was Stella Somers. Miss Silver regarded them with interest. Miss Johnstone had a very good way with the child, and her brown skirt and fawn jumper struck the happy mean between Mrs. Geoffrey's mourning black and Meriel's scarlet. Her features were pleasing, her eyes of an unusual and very charming shade, and her whole air that of a sensible and dependable person. With Miss Silver's experience, it was impossible for her to mistake the fact that Mr. Ninian Rutherford was attracted. He took no pains to hide it, and it was equally plain that at least some part of Meriel's annoyance proceeded from this cause. Adriana, facing Geoffrey down the length of the table, ate little and only spoke occasionally. She looked tired, and the purple house-dress gave her a sombre air.

For once, no one checked Stella's flow of conversation. After rehearsing for Miss Silver's benefit every detail of the six dresses which Star had brought her from New York— "and it was very, very good of her, because it meant she had to leave a lot of her own things behind"—she was brightly informative on the subject of her lessons.

"I read better than Jenny and Molly, and much better than Jackie Trent, but Jenny is better at sums. I don't like sums, but Jackie says he is going to be an engineer, and Miss Page says they have to know them. She says everyone has to know them, but I can't see why. I heard Mrs. Lenton say she was rotten at sums."

Edna Ford said reprovingly, "Oh, Stella! Not a nice word at all! I'm sure Mrs. Lenton never said it!"

Stella gazed calmly back across the table.

"Well then, she did. I heard her. She said it to the Vicar. She was sort of laughing, and he kissed her and said, 'Darling, what does it matter?'"

Janet said, "Stella, finish up your meat! It's horrid when it's cold."

Meriel laughed in a manner which Miss Silver found far from pleasant.

"So next time the Clothing Club accounts are wrong we shall all know why!"

Stella swallowed three pieces of meat in rapid succession, took a hasty drink of water, and continued.

"Mrs. Lenton laughs a lot when she talks to the Vicar. He laughs a lot too. I like him. But Miss Page doesn't laugh. She used to, but she doesn't now."

Janet said,

"Tell Miss Silver about your dancing-class. You can do a foxtrot and a waltz, can't you?"

Stella looked indignant.

"Oh, we're past waltzes!"

It did not escape Miss Silver that everyone was relieved, and that the conversation was not permitted to return to Ellie Page. The pudding which Simmons now brought in proving to be of special interest to Stella, she talked much less, and when she had finished Janet took her away.

CHAPTER 23

Down at the Vicarage the Lentons were finishing lunch. As soon as it was over it would be the Vicar's part to stack everything together and carry it through to the pantry, where Mrs. Lenton would wash and Ellie Page would dry. But when he arrived with a deftly balanced pile of plates Ellie was nowhere to be seen. His abrupt demand as to where she had got to having been met with a rather over ready, "I'm afraid she has another of her headaches", he frowned at Molly and Jenny and told them to go and play in the garden.

As soon as they had gone he shut the pantry door with some force.

"Mary, what is the matter with that girl?"

Mary Lenton was running the hot tap—a noisy business, because the pipes were old and made strange hiccupping sounds. He understood her to be repeating what he had begun to find a maddening remark.

"She isn't strong."

"Has she seen Dr. Stokes?"

She turned off the tap and said,

"Not lately. But he always says the same thing—she's delicate and she needs care."

"Well, she's getting it, isn't she? She couldn't have an easier job, and she scrimshanks out of half the things she ought to do to help you. Washing-up, for instance. Headache or no headache, it wouldn't hurt her to stand here and dry."

She threw him a laughing glance over her shoulder.

"It won't hurt *you*, darling! There's a nice dry cloth on that hook."

He took it, but he had no answering smile for her.

"The girl eats nothing—no wonder she has headaches. I shall talk to her."

Mary Lenton looked round again, this time in some alarm.

"Oh, no! Darling, you mustn't do that—you really mustn't!"

"And why mustn't I?"

"Oh, because—John, that's one of the old spoons, if you rub it like that it will break!"

His frown deepened.

"Never mind about the spoon. I want to know why I mustn't speak to Ellie."

She said, half laughing,

"But, darling, I do mind about the spoon. It's one of your great-grandmother's, and they are thin."

"I said why mustn't I speak to Ellie?"

142

Mary Lenton stopped laughing. She caught her breath and said,

"John, she's unhappy."

"What has she got to be unhappy about?"

"I don't know—she doesn't tell me. Oh, darling, don't be stupid! What are girls generally unhappy about? I suppose it's that, and I suppose things have gone wrong."

"You mean it's some love affair?"

"I suppose so. And it's no good asking, because if she wanted to tell me she would, and if she doesn't want to it would only make things worse. She'll get over it. One does!" She laughed again.

"Are you going to tell me you—I don't believe it!"

"Of course, darling! Dozens! When I was sixteen it was a film star. I was much too fat, and I took off about a stone and a half gazing at his photograph and pining. I was thrilled! And if anyone had told me I should marry a person and settle down in a country vicarage, I should have screamed!"

His arm came round her.

"Are you sorry you did it? Are you? Are you?"

"I'm bearing up. No, John—let me go! Oh, darling, you are a fool!"

This time they both laughed.

At Ford House, Adriana having gone upstairs to rest, Miss Silver, who had declined this indulgence, put on coat, hat, and gloves and went out into the garden. The air was mild and the sun shone, but it would not have occurred to her to go out bareheaded or without the neat black woollen gloves which she considered appropriate to the country. Strolling down the lawn in the direction of the river, she observed undoubted evidence of recent flooding. It was obvious that after heavy rain such as they had had during the early part of the month the winding walk along the bank would tend to be submerged. Even now, after three days of fine weather, it was damp under foot.

She turned back towards the higher ground, and coming to a gate in the hedge which skirted the lawn, she raised the latch and found herself in a garden bright with autumn flowers. At its centre she came upon the pool. A second hedge surrounded it, with arches cut in the green. There were two seats of weathered oak, and a small summerhouse which broke the hedge. A pleasant place when the days were drawing in, and admirably sheltered. It was a pity that the shadow of a fatality should have fallen upon it.

She came and stood above the pool and looked at it. It would be easy enough to trip over that low parapet in the dusk and fall into the water. But it was surely not so very deep—two feet, or two and a half. She found a stick in the summerhouse and made it nearly three. People have drowned in less than that. She recalled what Adriana had told her of the evidence at the inquest. Sam Bolton had deposed to finding the body half in and half out of the water—in fact not much more than the head and shoulders had been submerged. Mabel Preston had tripped, fallen forward, and so drowned. A dummy tilted over that low stone wall would have remained like that, but a living woman would only do so if she were stunned by the fall or held beneath the water till she drowned.

Miss Silver explored with the stick. There was nearly three foot of water, and there was no stone upon which Mabel Preston could have hit her head. Cocktails are extremely insidious. She had taken a considerable number of them, but she had not been too much under the influence of alcohol to make her way to this place, and though she may not have

144

been quite steady on her feet, yet the sudden shock of falling head foremost into cold water should certainly have produced some reaction. Her hands would have been able to reach the bottom. There should have been a struggle, an attempt to save herself. How, in that case, was it possible to believe that the lower limbs would remain in the position assumed at the moment of the fall? Adriana had questioned Sam Bolton, and questioned him shrewdly. The dead woman's knees were still on the parapet when he was trying to get her out of the pool. She had repeated his words—"I'd never have done it else, not if it was ever so. What I did, I got down in the pool and I pushed her up, and hard work it was and no mistake."

It would have been hard work to move that dead dripping thing weighed down by the soaking coat, but when Mabel Preston fell she was alive and the stuff was dry. It would take time for the heavy material to become sodden. Then why had there been no struggle, no reaction to the shock of the cold water? Why did a living, breathing woman just lie as she had fallen and let the water drown her? Try as she would, Miss Silver could find only one explanation. Mabel Preston had been pushed, and the person who pushed her had held her under the water until its work was done.

It was a shocking conclusion, but she could come to no other. She considered whether it would be possible to kneel upon the parapet, or behind it, and carry out this dreadful act. The low wall was some eighteen inches above the paving which surrounded it, but on the pool side the water rose to within three or four inches of the top, a circumstance no doubt due to the recent heavy rains. If the author of the murderous attack had leaned over the parapet or kneeled upon it, it would have been perfectly possible to ensure that the woman who had fallen should not rise again.

She wore her gravest expression as she turned to go. Here, on this warm afternoon with the blue of the sky reflected in the pool and the sun bright upon the water, it was a pleasant place. There would be sunshine and blue skies in the time to come, but she wondered how long it would be before anyone would sit here alone for his pleasure, or without remembering that here murder had been done. She was as sure about it as that.

But there was no one who had any reason to wish Mabel Preston dead. If she had been murdered, it was because she had been taken for someone else. She had dyed her hair in imitation of Adriana Ford's. She went to her death in Adriana's coat. Adriana's own description of it came to her mind—great black and white squares and an emerald stripe. Even in the dusk, or by the faltering light of an electric torch, such a pattern would leap to the eye. And Adriana had worn the coat so long that she would not let Meriel have it. "Too well known, and people would say I made her wear out my old clothes. She might even come to saying it herself. Meriel is like that." Was not that what Adriana had said—that or something like it?

As she passed under the arch in the hedge, the sun picked up a point of colour and she stopped. Caught between one twig and another was a wisp of stuff. It was the merest shred, and if the sun had not shone directly on it, she would have passed it by. When she had disentangled it, she had a few silky threads of the colour known as cyclamen. She put them carefully into the palm of her glove and returned to the house.

Invited to tea with Adriana in her own sitting-room, she displayed the shred.

"Has anyone in the house a dress of this colour?"

Adriana looked at it with disfavour.

146

"Meriel has—and quite horribly unbecoming. You've got to have white hair, a good skin, and perfect make-up, before you can look at magenta. Meriel isn't nearly smart enough, and she doesn't take enough trouble. She wore the dress for the party, and she looked ghastly. Her lipstick clashed by about three shades! But it's no use telling her anything like that—she just flies into a temper. Where did you get these threads? I shan't be sorry if she's torn the dress and can't wear it any more. Well, where did you get them?"

"They were caught on the hedge which surrounds the pool."

Adriana said sharply,

"On the hedge?"

"On the inner side of one of the arches. I saw them as I was coming away. I should not have noticed them if the sun had not happened to pick them out."

Adriana said nothing. Her face became a mask. Before she could speak Meeson came in with the tea. Just as she was going out again Adriana called to her.

"Gertie, take a look at this!" She held out the scrap of stuff.

Meeson made a clicking sound with her tongue.

"Well now, isn't that Meriel all over! Pays twenty guineas for a dress, and I know she did that, for I saw the bill—left it lying about in her room and the wind blew it down on the floor! And then goes and mucks it up first time she wears it!"

"Oh, she mucked it up, did she? On Saturday?"

Meeson nodded.

"Can't say I was struck on the dress, but she mucked it up properly! Coffee all down the front of it, and cleaners or no cleaners, it's never going to come out!"

"So she spilt coffee on it?"

"Said someone jogged her elbow. 'Lord!' I said. 'What have you been doing to yourself?' And she said someone had jogged her elbow. 'Well,' I said, 'you're never going to get that out this side of kingdom come—not coffee, you can take my word for it!' And she goes pushing past me as if I wasn't there! But that's Meriel all over! What she's done herself, well, it's always got to be somebody else's fault. That's her from a baby!"

She might have gone on, but she was interrupted sharply.

"When was all this?"

"When was what, ducks?"

Adriana made an impatient gesture.

"This coffee-spilling business."

"How do I know?"

"You know when you saw Meriel's dress with the coffee on it."

Meeson cast up her eyes.

"Oh, *that?* Let's see—it would be somewhere about the time everyone was getting a move on, for I thought to myself, 'Well, anyhow the party's as good as over, which is better than if it had happened earlier on.'"

"What has she done with the dress?"

"Took it off to the cleaners on the Monday. But they'll never get those stains out, and so I told her. 'Have it dyed,' I said, 'and make a job of it—black, or brown, or a good navy. Always very ladylike, a good navy is.' And for once in a way she hadn't got anything to say."

When Meeson was gone Adriana looked defiantly at Miss Silver and said,

"Well?"

Miss Silver had been knitting in a very thoughtful manner. She was, in fact, engaged in the process known as putting

148

two and two together. They added up to an ugly four. She said,

"What do you make of it yourself, Miss Ford?"

Adriana lifted the teapot and began to pour out. Her hand was perfectly steady.

"She went down to the pool at some time when she was wearing the dress."

"Yes."

"She was in the drawing-room during all the time that people were arriving, but after the room got very full I can't say whether she was there or not. She could have slipped out—only why should she?"

"She had not worn that dress before?"

"No."

"Then she did go out, since I found a torn shred from it caught on the hedge by the pool."

Adriana said, "Do you take milk and sugar?"

Miss Silver gave her slight formal cough.

"Milk, if you please, but no sugar." She laid down her knitting, took the cup, and continued as if there had been no interruption. "We have, then, two certain facts. Miss Meriel went down to the pool, and at some time towards the end of the party she told Meeson that she had spilt coffee on her dress. Did you notice the stains yourself? Either during the party or afterwards?"

Adriana looked startled. She finished pouring out her own cup of tea and set down the teapot. Then she said,

"But she had changed—when I came out on the landing and they were all in the hall, she had changed!"

"You are sure about that?"

"Of course I am sure. She had put on her old green crape. A hideous garment—I can't think why she ever bought it,

149

but she has no clothes-sense." She added milk to the cup and lifted it to her lips, but she did not drink from it. Her hand jerked suddenly and she set it down again.

"Look here, where is this getting us? Are you asking me to believe that Meriel—*Meriel*—went down to that pool in the dusk and pushed Mabel in? Because she was wearing my coat—because she took her for me? Is that what you are asking me to believe?"

Miss Silver looked at her compassionately.

"It is not I who am saying these things, Miss Ford. It is you."

"What does it matter who says them? Do you think them? Do you believe that Meriel pushed poor Mabel Preston into the pool and held her down there, thinking she was me? And that she then came back into the house and spilt coffee on her dress to hide the stains? There's moss on the parapet, you know, and the water from the pool would leave a dirty mark, but coffee—coffee would hide anything."

Miss Silver said firmly,

"Miss Ford, I have not said any of these things. It is you who are saying them. They exist as a possibility, but a thing that is possible should not necessarily be accepted as a fact. Circumstantial evidence can be extremely misleading. Miss Meriel seems to have been in the neighbourhood of the pool in that cyclamen dress, and she subsequently changed it as it had become stained with coffee. There is a possibility that it was stained deliberately, and for the purpose of concealing other and more compromising stains, but there is no proof that this was so."

Adriana lifted her cup, and this time she drank from it, a long steady draught. When she had set it down again she said,

150

"She is in a state of resentment against me. It has been going on for a long time. She thinks I could use my influence to push her on to the stage. But she isn't willing to be trained. She thinks she can stroll in at the top with all the hard work cut out. She thinks I could make that possible. Well, I couldn't if I would, and I wouldn't if I could. I said that to her once, and she hated me for saying it. And these last few days she has been very angry with me about that damned coat. She is like that, you know. She sets her heart on something, and she has got to have it. But if she gets it, nine times out of ten she doesn't care about it any more. There you are—that's Meriel! But still I don't think—"

Her voice did not choke, it stopped. There was no colour under the careful make-up. She took a long breath and went on as if there had been no broken sentence.

"I don't think she would try to kill me."

Miss Silver said,

"She is a very uncontrolled person."

Adriana nodded.

"She blows off steam. I have spent my life among people like that. They fly into a temper and get it off the chest. It sounds like a lot more than it really is. The artistic temperament—and a bit of a curse if you have it without the talent which makes it go down!"

When Meeson came up presently for the tray she was in no great hurry to take it.

"What price me being a spying, tale-tattling old devil?" she said with the air of one who has received a mortal affront and is determined to rise above it.

Adriana, not unaccustomed to this mood, supplied the question for which Meeson was waiting.

"And who has been calling you a tale-tattling spy?"

Meeson tossed her head.

"Tale-tattling, spying devil is what it was—and twenty years ago I'd have turned her up and spanked her for it! Spoilt her—that's what you've done! And not the first time I've told you what would come of it! *Spying! Me!* And tale-tattling, which my worst enemy couldn't throw up at me! 'Now look here, Meriel', I said, 'that's enough and a bit too much! There's Miss Ford showing me that bit of stuff off of the dress you tore, and all I said was, 'Torn it was—and what's a tear more or less, for it's neither here nor there!' I said. And she come back on me like a fury and said she'd take her dying oath she never tore it! And 'Oh, yes, you did!' I said. 'And what you were doing down by that horrid pool in a brand new dress—it isn't for me to say!' Well, ducks, you'd have thought I'd hit her. 'I wasn't down by the pool', she said. And I said, 'Oh, yes, you were, my lady! And that's where you tore your dress, because that's where Miss Silver found the scrap from it! Just outside the door I was, getting it open, when she told Miss Ford about finding it caught in the hedge!' "

"Gertie—you listened!"

Meeson bridled.

"Well, I'd got to get the door open, hadn't I? And if you're going to start and have secrets from me, what's the good? Which is what I told that Meriel, and that's when she had the cheek to call me what she did! Tale-tattling spy! I was clean ashamed of her, and so I told her! With Mr. and Mrs. Geoffrey coming out of their rooms, and Mr. Ninian and Simmons down in the hall! What they could have thought!"

When she had gone, Miss Silver spoke in a tone of extreme gravity.

"Miss Ford, you came to me for advice, but when I offered

it you were not disposed to give it any consideration. Since then there has been a tragedy. You have summoned me with great urgency, and I am here. After only a few hours in the house I am not in a position to offer a solution of the events which have occurred, or to dogmatize upon the situation, but I do feel obliged to offer you a warning. There are elements which may produce or precipitate some further explosion."

Adriana directed a hard stare upon her.

"What elements?"

"Do I need to point them out to you?"

"Yes."

Miss Silver complied.

"You have in your household three persons in a state of mental conflict. One of them displays considerable emotional instability. Miss Preston's death occurred at some time between, shall we say, six o'clock and shortly after eight. You have told me that you saw her yourself certainly as late as six o'clock. You have also told me that Miss Meriel was in evidence until about the same time."

Adriana said in her deep voice,

"You can put it as late as half past six for both of them. I spoke to Meriel myself at about twenty past, and poor Mabel—well, she was making herself heard, even in all that din. One of those high metallic voices."

"Then that narrows the time to something under an hour and a half. During that period Miss Preston and Miss Meriel were both down by the pool. We do not know what took either of them there, but it is certain that they were both within that enclosing hedge. There is, of course, no evidence to prove that Miss Meriel's visit coincided with that of Miss Preston. It may have done so, or it may not. Whether it did, or whether it did not, she is now aware that her presence

153

there is known, and other members of your household are also in possession of this fact."

"What other members?"

"You heard what Meeson said—Mr. and Mrs. Geoffrey Ford were on the landing when Miss Meriel was accusing her of telling tales. The fact that a piece of stuff torn from her dress had been found caught up in the hedge which surrounds the pool was clearly mentioned. They must have heard what was said. Mr. Ninian Rutherford and Simmons were in the hall below. They also must have heard. Meeson, in fact, intimated that they had done so. Do you suppose that by tomorrow there will be anyone under this roof who will not be aware of Miss Meriel's presence at the pool? Or can you believe that the knowledge will remain confined to this household?"

Adriana said, "What do you mean?"

"Do you wish me to tell you?"

"Certainly."

Miss Silver spoke in a quiet, level voice.

"It is entirely possible that Miss Meriel's visit to the pool had nothing to do with Miss Preston's presence there, or with her death. She could have come and gone without seeing her. It is also possible that she did see Miss Preston and witnessed the fatality which caused her death. It is possible that she participated in it. It is possible that, herself unseen, she witnessed the participation of another person. I need not point out to you that, in such a case, she might be in a position of considerable danger."

Adriana said abruptly, "Isn't all this a little intense?"

Miss Silver gave a slight reproving cough.

"There is sometimes such an intensification of the emotions of fear and resentment as to precipitate a tragic event."

Adriana said harshly, "I should like to say 'Rubbish!'"

"But you cannot?"

"Not quite. What do you want me to do?"

Miss Silver said soberly,

"Send Miss Meriel away on a visit and go away yourself. Let all this strain and emotion die down."

There was a silence between them. When it had lasted a long time Adriana said,

"I don't think I'm very good at running away."

CHAPTER 24

A pleasant evening could hardly be expected. There was too much that was discordant, apprehensive, and resentful in the thoughts of the six people who sat round the dinner-table and presently adjourned to the drawing-room. With the grey velvet curtains drawn and the grey carpet under foot, it was rather like being enclosed in a fog. Not the kind which steals close and takes your breath, but the watching kind which stands a little way off and waits. Time was when Adriana could have warmed and lighted it, but not tonight. She wore grey velvet with some dark fur on it, and matched the room too nearly. Silent during dinner, she remained throughout the evening without words to waste, a book on her knee which she did not appear to be reading, though every now and then she turned a page. When spoken to she made some brief reply and went back again into an abstracted silence.

Meriel had changed into what Miss Silver took to be the

old green crape referred to slightingly by Adriana. In this artificial light it certainly had a dingy effect and did nothing to mitigate its wearer's air of gloom. She herself was wearing the neat dark blue crêpe-de-chine which her niece Ethel Burkett had induced her to buy during that summer holiday a year ago. It had cost a great deal more than she was accustomed to pay, but Ethel had urged her, and Ethel had been right. "You really never will regret it, Auntie. Such good stuff and such good style. It will last you for years, and you will always feel and look well dressed." Brightened by the large gold locket which displayed a monogram of her parents' initials in high relief and contained the treasured locks of their hair, she admitted to herself that it looked extremely well. She had sustained a gentle flow of conversation all through dinner. Now in the drawing-room she opened her knitting-bag and took out the large needles from which depended some three or four inches of the shawl designed for Dorothy Silver's extra twin.

She had placed herself next to Mrs. Geoffrey, who sat with an embroidery frame on her lap and plied a mechanical needle. When the coffee came in she drank two cups of it without milk and went back to her embroidery again. Her old black dress hung upon her and was unrelieved by so much as a brooch or a string of pearls. Her feet were placed side by side in a pair of old frayed shoes with a single strap. They had rather large steel buckles, and they were very much worn. One of the buckles was loose and moved whenever she did. It was evidently not her habit to use make-up. It would in fact have done very little, if anything, to mitigate that look of fatigue and strain. But she could still talk, and continued to do so. The small trivial details of day-to-day

156

housekeeping in the country flowed from her pale, pinched lips.

"Of course we grow our own vegetables, or I do not know what we should do. But it is no economy. On the contrary, Geoffrey worked it out once—and was it half-a-crown or three shillings that you reckoned every cabbage came to? Which was it, Geoffrey?"

Geoffrey Ford, on his feet by the coffee-tray, glanced over his shoulder and smiled.

"My dear, I haven't the slightest idea what you are talking about."

Edna's voice sharpened.

"The cabbages—you worked it out once how much they cost—and of course the cauliflowers and all the other things as well. It was either half-a-crown or three-and-sixpence."

He laughed.

"I don't think I ever got as far as working it out to the last pea! Naturally, home-grown vegetables are an extravagance, but what a pleasant one." He set down his cup. "Well, I must write some letters."

Edna Ford put a stitch into the formal pattern of her embroidery and said,

"Who are you writing to?" Then, as he looked at her with a momentary flash of something very near dislike, she added quickly, "I was just thinking that if it was to Cousin William, you had better give him my love."

"And what makes you think I should be writing to William Turvey?"

Her hand shook.

"I—just thought—"

"It's a bad habit."

He went out of the room and shut the door. Meriel laughed.

157

"Geoffrey and his letters!" she said, and left it at that. Edna began to talk about the price of fish.

Janet and Ninian came in together. Their arrival distracted Meriel's attention.

"Your coffee will be cold. Where on earth have you been?"

It was Ninian who answered her.

"We went up to say good-night to Stella."

She said rudely, "She ought to be asleep!"

"Oh, she was. So what?" His voice was gay.

Janet had coloured a little. She looked young and rather sweet in her brown frock with the little old-fashioned pearl brooch fastening it. She said,

"Star rang up. She won't be back tonight."

Meriel laughed.

"Well, now you're here, let's do something! I'll put on some records and we can dance."

Ninian looked at Adriana. She lifted her eyes to his for a moment and turned a page. Oh, well, if that was the way she wanted it—But if Meriel thought he was going to dance with her all the time and leave Janet odd man out, she could think again.

Meriel had other ideas. She put down the record she had taken and turned to the door.

"I'll get Geoffrey back. It's nonsense his going off to write letters. Besides, does anyone believe in them? I don't! Or perhaps Esmé Trent gives him a hand!"

She went out too quickly to see the displeased look which Adriana turned upon her.

Edna neither moved nor spoke. Her hands rested upon her embroidery frame, and just for a moment she closed her eyes. When she opened them again Miss Silver was addressing her.

158

"How fortunate it is for Stella that there is this class at the Vicarage. The little girls there are about her own age?"

"Jenny is a little older, and Molly a little younger."

"There is a little boy too, is there not?"

"Not at the Vicarage."

"Indeed? But he lives quite near?"

"Quite near."

Adriana looked up from her book and said in her decided way,

"He lives with his mother in the Lodge of that big empty house nearly opposite the Vicarage. She is a widow—a Mrs. Trent. She neglects the child, and we don't care for her very much."

If this was meant to save Edna Ford it had the opposite effect. She spoke in a shaking voice.

"She is a wicked woman—a horribly wicked woman. We ought not to have her in the house." Her pale eyes stared at Adriana. "You shouldn't have asked her to your party. It was quite, quite wrong. She is an immoral woman."

Adriana shrugged.

"My dear Edna, I'm not a censor of morals!"

The extreme dryness of her tone reminded Miss Silver of some of the things which had been said about Adriana Ford some forty years ago. But Edna was beyond consideration or tact.

"She's bad through and through. She doesn't care for any-one except herself. She doesn't mind what she does so long as she gets what she wants."

Adriana threw her a contemptuous glance and said,

"Really, Edna! Need you be quite such a fool?"

Over by the gramophone cabinet at the other end of the room Ninian spoke under his breath.

"It looks as if the peace of the morgue was being rudely disturbed. Do we keep out, or do we butt in?"

Janet looked up at him gravely. With the light shining down into them her eyes were of exactly the same brown as her hair. He considered it an agreeable shade. He didn't really hear all she said, because his thoughts were otherwise engaged, but he gathered that she was in favour of keeping out. The last words registered.

"It really hasn't got anything to do with us."

It was absurdly pleasant to have her bracketing them together like that. For a young man who had been taking things so very much for granted the pleasure was surprising. It even surprised himself. He had a horrid feeling that his colour had risen, and he found himself with nothing to say. Janet felt some satisfaction. It was years since she had seen Ninian out of countenance, and she found it heartening.

Meriel took her way to the study and walked in. She found Geoffrey in the act of opening the glass door to the terrace and immediately enquired where he was going, to which his laconic reply was, "Out."

"I thought you were going to write letters!"

He laughed angrily.

"The well known formula for getting away from the family circle! Have you never used it yourself?"

She put on her tragic look.

"I've got no one to write to."

"You might try a pen-friend."

"Geoffrey—how can you! I suppose you are going to see Esmé Trent?"

"What if I am?"

"Only that I know why." As he turned away with a frown

160

she repeated the words with emphasis. "I tell you, I know why."

He was arrested.

"My dear girl, I haven't got time for a scene."

"Haven't you? What a pity! Wouldn't you like to have a towering row, and then kiss and be friends? . . . No? Well then, you'd better run along to Esmé. You won't forget to give her my love, will you, and tell her I saw you both down by the pool on Saturday evening?"

His hand was on the door. He turned abruptly.

"What do you mean?"

"What I said. You went behind the curtains and out through the window. Well, I followed you. It was frightfully hot, and I thought I would see what you were up to. Who knows, Edna might want to get rid of you some day, and a spot of evidence would come in useful! So I followed you, and you went through to the pool and into the summerhouse. And I tore my dress on the hedge as I came away. You knew that, didn't you? You and Edna came out on the landing when I was telling Meeson off. She'd been tattling to Adriana about my dress, and you must have heard what I said—both of you! What about my telling Edna about the summerhouse? Or Adriana? Or both of them? It might be quite amusing, don't you think? Or perhaps not so amusing—for you! People might think you had given poor old Mabel Preston a push in the dark!"

"And why should I have done that?" His voice was rough. She laughed.

"Oh, darling, don't be dull! You don't know why you should have pushed her? Because she was wearing Adriana's coat, and you thought she was Adriana. That's why!"

"What a foul thing to say!"

161

She nodded.

"You mean, what a foul thing to do. But clever, darling, clever—if you had chosen the right person to push! With Adriana gone, we would all have been in clover. You could have snapped your fingers at Edna and gone off with anyone you chose—couldn't you?"

He said in a sudden flat tone of bewilderment,

"You're mad! Or else you did it yourself—I don't know which."

Back in the drawing-room Ninian found a gramophone record which was not jazz. Turned down low, it made a good excuse for staying at this end of the room and was no serious bar to conversation. After that moment of confusion he was himself again, and he had plenty to say. He always did have plenty to say to Janet. He had just had a very good idea for a book, and as a listener she was both inspired and inspiring. If she had no sparks of her own, she presented a surface from which he could produce them in showers. He was developing this theme, when the record came to an end and he had to find another one.

> "A nice soft sugary tune beneath the bough
> A cup of Mrs. Simmons' coffee and thou
> Beside me listening in the wilderness,
> And wilderness were solitude enow!

As Omar didn't say. You really are the goods, you know, darling."

The brown eyes sparkled.

"And what do I say to that?"

"You show a proper appreciation, and you go on listening."

162

"I don't say anything?"

"Well, it would depend on what you wanted to say."

He kept on telling her about his idea.

Adriana sat in her carved chair. It had cushions of a deep violet colour. In spite of Meeson's careful make-up the grey of her dress and of the room appeared to have invaded her skin. Her book lay on her knee. The hand which turned an occasional page had a bloodless look. The quite discreet red of the nail-polish was too apparent. The places of her mind were full of images. They came up out of the past and went by in a wan light which took from them all the colour and brightness which they had had for her. Some of them had brought her a flaming joy, and some of them had brought her bitter pain, and she had taken the joy and the pain and fed her art with them. She looked at the images and let them go. They belonged to something she had left behind. What she had to consider was, not the past, but this present now. A verse from the Bible came into her mind and stayed there—"A man's foes shall be they of his own household." She had had enemies in her time. She had gone on her way without heeding them. They had never done her any lasting harm because she had never really let them touch her. She had not stooped to fight back, she had not let herself hate. She had held her head high, and she had gone on her chosen way. But the foes of one's household were too near to be ignored. They sat at your table, they compassed your path. They could slip death into your cup, they could set a snare for your feet or strike a blow in the dark.

She considered the people who were under her roof.

Geoffrey—whom she had known since he was four, and the typical angel child with golden curls and a rosy smile. It was Shakespeare that came into her head this time—"One may smile, and smile, and be a villain." Geoffrey still had that very charming smile. Impossible to believe that there was murder behind it. He loved ease and comfort, he liked women and the flattering incense which they burned before his vanity, he liked the good things of life and to have them come to him without effort. In all these easy ways murder would be a most uneasy ghost.

Edna—sitting there with her embroidery, her mind, or what passed for it, a clutter of the trivial. What a life, what a fate, what monotony, what dullness! Days made up of the smallest of small things, months and years submerged in futility! Why had Geoffrey married her? She had a mental shrug for that. They had been thrown together. Edna, like all the other women, had burned her incense, and Geoffrey's vanity and the conventions had snared him. She recalled that Edna's father was a solicitor, and her mother a formidable person who sat on committees and would certainly stand no nonsense. She had four plain, penniless daughters, and she had married them all. If Edna had been like her, Geoffrey would have been managed for his good. But Edna couldn't have managed a mouse, let alone a man. Poor Edna!

Meriel—why had she ever taken the creature into her life? She went back to the first sight of her—six months old in the arms of a frightful old woman with a glib tongue and greedy eyes. And the baby had looked at her through its long dark lashes with the strange unwinking stare of all very young things. Puppies, kittens, babies—they stare at you, and you have no idea of what may lie behind the look which does not see. The child's mother lay dead with her lover's knife in her heart. And the baby stared.

Adriana turned a page mechanically. If she had known, would she still have taken the child? She thought probably.

She looked back at Meriel emerging from a stormy, passionate babyhood into the moody and still passionate little girl—the hysterical, passionate schoolgirl—the unstable neurotic woman. She made her thought cold and quiet. Here, if anywhere, must be the enemy. Only you couldn't really believe a thing like that about the creature who had grown up beside you, and who, for all its tempers, was a part of your life.

She went on with her list.

Star—oh, no, not Star. There was nothing in Star that hated or would strike. Star loved Star, but she loved other people too. She would have neither use nor time for murder.

Ninian—her mind refused the thought. Janet's judgment of him marched with her own. He could be selfish certainly, light perhaps—she thought there were depths below. But there wasn't any hatred, or the cold ruthlessness which can strike where it does not hate.

The staff—She wearied suddenly. What, after all, did you know of any other human being? The Simmonses—they had served her for twenty years. The daily woman—respectable to her backbone, with crime of any sort a social taboo. That irritating girl Joan Cuttle who was Edna's pet. . . . She let them go, and shut her book, addressing Miss Silver.

"Well, it is only half past nine, but I suppose most of us have had enough of today. Speaking for myself, I am going up to my room. How about you? And Edna?"

Miss Silver smiled and began to put away her knitting. Edna Ford finished the stitch she was taking and folded up her embroidery. She had not spoken for quite a long time. She said now in a thin, tired voice,

"Oh, yes, I shall be very glad. I haven't been sleeping at all well. One can't go on without sleep. I must take something tonight."

165

CHAPTER 25

John Lenton had come in late to his supper. He was tired, and out of the common grave. Mary Lenton was a good wife. She set food before him, and she asked no questions. If he wanted to eat in silence, well, he could. And if he wanted to talk, she was here. She thought he looked dreadfully tired, but she thought there was more in his silence than fatigue. She kept her thoughts to herself, changed his plate, and presently cleared away. As she went out with the tray, he said,

"Come to the study when you've finished. I want to talk to you."

She put the used china in a bowl of water and went to him.

He was walking up and down with a face of perplexity and anger. She said, "What is it, John?" and he paced the room twice before he answered her.

"You know I had a sick call—old Mrs. Dunn over at Folding—"

"Is she very bad?"

"No—no—she always thinks she's dying—there's nothing much wrong with her. But as I was there, I thought I would go on and see Mrs. Collen about that girl of hers, Olive. You know she's at Ledbury with Mrs. Ridley, helping with the children, and she hasn't been behaving at all well—staying out late at night and making friends who are not much good to her. She's only just sixteen, and Mrs. Ridley is a good deal worried about it. She rang up this morning and asked me if

166

I would say a word to Mrs. Collen, so I thought as I was so near I had better get it over."

Mary Lenton was wondering what all this was leading up to. John would be sorry and concerned about Olive Collen, but it wouldn't be on her account that he would look as he was looking now. She said,

"Yes?"

He made an odd abrupt movement.

"I went to the Collens', and I got more than I bargained for."

She was gazing up at him, her fair hair catching the light, her face sweetly serious.

"John, what is it?"

His hand came down on her shoulder.

"I spoke to her about Olive. I wasn't looking forward to it. She is the type of woman who can be disagreeable."

"And she was?"

"She told me to look to my own household. 'What about what's going on under your own roof?' she said."

"Oh, *John!*"

"She said that Ellie was carrying on with Geoffrey Ford. She said everyone knew about it except me. And she said I had better put things right in my own house before I started taking away her daughter's character—" He stopped, took his hands off her, and walked to the window and back. "I won't tell you all the things she said. She's a foul-tongued woman and I couldn't bring myself to repeat them. She said Ellie had been going up to Ford House in the night. She said it was common talk. She said Ellie had been seen coming back here at two in the morning! I want the truth! Is it all lies, or is there anything in it? If you know anything, you've got to tell me!"

Mary Lenton's blue eyes were steady.

"John, I don't know. She has been very unhappy. I moved the children into a room of their own because Jenny said she cried in the night. And she locks her door—"

"Since when?"

"Since I moved the children."

He said with a hard anger in his voice,

"I won't have it in my house! It's a most dangerous thing! There's no reason—there's no reason at all!"

But in both their minds a reason stood out plain. If a girl was getting out at night she wouldn't want to run any risk of her room being found empty while she was away.

He said, "I'll have to see her."

"No, John—no!"

He turned a darker look upon her than she had ever had from him.

"This can't be covered up!"

The tears had come into her eyes.

"John, let me see her first. She isn't strong, and she has been terribly unhappy. It may not be nearly so bad as you think. Let me see her first."

There was a moment of suspense. Then he said harshly,

"Very well, but it must be now."

"She will have gone to bed."

He looked at his wrist-watch.

"At half past nine?"

"She often goes at half past eight—you know she does."

"She won't be asleep, or if she is you must wake her. I won't have this thing put off or glossed over! You can see her first since you make such a point of it, but in the last resort the responsibility is mine, and I neither can nor will hand it over to anyone else."

168

Mary Lenton had not been married for eight years without knowing when she had come up against an immovable barrier. In this case it was John's conscience. She stood aghast at the thought that it might some day arise between them. Her own was of a less unyielding type. It could speak with no uncertain voice, but it did, and always would, listen to the promptings of kindness. In theory she could condemn the sinner, but in practise she found it only too easy to forgive.

She went upstairs with a heavy heart and knocked upon Ellie's door. There was no answer, and she knocked again. After a third time she tried the handle.

The door was locked.

CHAPTER 26

The Vicarage was an old house. There were old creepers on the walls, old fruit trees spread to take the sun. When Ellie had a mind to be out of the house by night there was no need for her to risk the stairs or to meddle with a bolted door. She had only to lock her own and step from the window-ledge to the laddered boughs of a pear-tree. It had been easy—too easy for the heart and conscience which now tormented her. At first there was the glow of a romantic love. She had warmed herself at its brightness and asked no more than to hold out distant hands to the flame. And then he had begun to notice her, to look, to touch, to kiss, and the flame had turned to this torment. There had been the struggle with her conscience, the building up of Edna as the unwanted wife who held him against his will, and in the end the manifest fact that he was in retreat. He couldn't leave Edna, because if he did, Adriana Ford would cut off his allowance. He wouldn't leave her, because he loved his easy way of life much better than he would ever love any woman. Little by little he emerged from the mists of her fancy as he really was. He took what she offered as long as it was easy and safe to take it, but if it stopped being easy and safe, why, then it was time to say good-bye.

On this day, which had begun with the funeral of poor Mabel Preston, Ellie Page had gone about in a daze of misery. She did not go to the funeral. Mary Lenton had gone—"John says it would be nice if I did. The poor thing is a stranger, and there are no relations." But Ellie had her class as an excuse, and somehow—somehow she had got through the day. Up in her room that evening she locked the door, put out the light, and sat down by the window. She did this every night now, because after a while her eyes got accustomed to the darkness and she could see as far as the Lodge of Bourne Hall and beyond it. Esmé Trent lived in the Lodge.

Ellie had reached the point where she could not lie down and sleep until she was sure that no one came down the road from Ford House and turned in at the Lodge. Sometimes nobody did. Then towards midnight she would fall on her bed and sleep her exhausted sleep. Sometimes it was too dark to be sure if anyone came or not. Then she would hope, and believe, and pray, and know that she had no right to pray, and sink into a state that was neither sleeping nor waking. But sometimes she would see a shadow that she knew was Geoffrey Ford come down the road and turn in at the drive. And then she would lie awake until the dawn.

Tonight the time of waiting was shortened. She had sat

there for no more than half an hour when she saw that someone was coming along the road. At first it was just that the darkness was stirred. Something moved in it, or it moved within itself, as water moves, or mist. Then, as she pushed open the two sides of the casement window and leaned out, there was a walking shadow and the sound of a footfall faint and far away. The night was still. The footsteps came on. Perhaps it wasn't Geoffrey at all. Perhaps he wouldn't come tonight. She leaned right out, holding on to the central bar of the window. The footsteps slackened and turned in at the entrance to the drive.

Then it was Geoffrey. Because Bourne Hall was empty, and no one came and went between it and the road. The Lodge had a little wicket gate which opened no more than a dozen feet inside the crumbling stone pillars of the entrance. The shadow passed between the pillars and was lost to her sight. But there came to her straining sense the click of a lifted latch, and a moment later the sound of the closing door that shut him in with Esmé Trent. He did not need to knock or ring. The door stood ready for him. He came and went as he pleased.

She drew back into the room and stood there, still holding to the bar of the window. It had happened before—many times. It was never any easier to bear. Rather, like the pressure upon a bruised place, it became less endurable with each recurrence. Tonight it reached the point when it was no longer to be endured, when this pent-up agony must find release in action.

She was wearing a dark skirt and a light-coloured jumper. She crossed the room, opened a drawer, and took out the navy cardigan which matched the skirt. She did not need a light to find it. Everything in the drawer was in order, and she could lay her hand upon what she wanted in the dark. Just the movement, just putting the cardigan on and buttoning it up to the neck, gave her a little relief. She went back to the window, kneeled on the sill, and began to climb down the pear-tree. By the time she had to let go of the bar there were the espaliered branches to hold on to. It was quite easy and she had done it many times before, at first with a sense of tremulous adventure, then with a half-frightened, half-joyful expectancy, and in the end with fear, and doubt, and pain.

Her foot touched the ground, felt for the grass verge, and followed it. When she was out on the road she could hurry.

It was when she had nearly reached the drive that she was aware of someone coming in the opposite direction—a second shadowy figure, but walking soft-foot without sound. She stood where a tree leaned over the nearer pillar, and a woman went by her. The light of a torch flickered briefly on the wicket gate, on the scrap of path between it and a little hooded porch. And then the torch clicked off, the latch was lifted, and the woman went up the path and into the Lodge. Ellie stood where she was and watched her go. She did not know who the woman was. She thought it would be Edna Ford. Following Geoffrey. If she found him there with Esmé Trent, what would come of it? She didn't know. But she had to know—she had to know.

She went in through the wicket gate, but she did not go up to the door. She kept to the right, passing between a holly and a great bush of rosemary which sprawled against the house. The strong smell of it came up as she brushed past it, and the holly pricked her. There was a neglected garden on this side. The living-room windows looked out upon it— casement windows, with the curtains drawn across. There

172

was a light in the room. It turned the curtains to a glowing amber. Ellie came up close to the glow and saw that the nearer window was open a handsbreadth. The rooms in the Lodge were small, and the night was warm and still. Esmé Trent was one of the people who thought you were stuffy if you sat in a room with the windows shut. All these casement windows opened outwards. Very slowly, very carefully, Ellie lifted the metal bar and pulled the window towards her. Now there was nothing between her and the voices in the room but the bare thickness of a curtain. She heard Geoffrey Ford say,

"I tell you she saw us there."

Esmé Trent made an impatient sound.

"I don't suppose she saw anything of the sort! You know perfectly well that she couldn't speak the truth if she tried!"

There was a wood fire in the room. The faint smell of it came to Ellie. She heard Geoffrey push it with his foot.

"How did she know we were down by the pool if she didn't see us there?"

"I think she's chancing it. She was keeping her eye on us, you know. She may have seen us slip behind the curtain, and have guessed that we had gone out. She couldn't *know* we were anywhere near the pool. She just wants to be awkward. She's as jealous as hell."

"I don't know—"

Esmé Trent laughed.

"It sticks out a mile! I don't know if you ever made a pass at her, but she would certainly adore it if you did."

Ellie had a bewildered feeling. She had thought they were talking about Geoffrey's wife, but it must be somebody else. She heard him say,

"Meriel would like anyone to make a pass at her. That's not what I meant."

"What did you mean?"

"I meant she's out to make trouble, and she can do it."

"My dear Geoffrey, be your age! Who cares if we took a stroll in the garden?"

From behind the curtain there came the sound of a door flung back.

CHAPTER 27

Meriel could not have wished for a more dramatic entrance. Everything was going her way. Without any foreknowledge, she had had the impulse to wear her old green dress, then when she had made up her mind to follow Geoffrey there was no need for her to do anything but pick up a torch. The soft clinging stuff, the dark colour, were perfect for the role she was going to play, and when she reached the Lodge she had only to walk in and very gently and cautiously set the living-room door ajar. It was not the first time she had played that trick when she wanted to listen, and no one had ever tumbled to it. It was just a matter of a steady hand and taking your time to turn the handle and free the catch.

And now she had her cue. Pat on Esmé's "Who cares if we took a stroll in the garden?" she flung the door wide and stood on the threshold, saying in her deepest voice, "The police might be interested, don't you think?"

Esmé Trent had a cigarette in her hand. The smoke rose faintly. She lifted her brows and said in a cool, sarcastic voice,

"Play-acting, Meriel?"

Geoffrey Ford's colour deepened. There was going to be a row, and there was nothing he hated so much. And both these girls had tempers. He had a fleeting thought of Ellie Page, gentle and clinging as a woman ought to be—only the worst of it was that kind took everything so hard.

Meriel came into the room, thrusting the door to behind her. She said, quick and angry,

"The police won't think so when I tell them you were down by the pool just about the time someone pushed Mabel Preston into it!"

Esmé Trent drew at her cigarette and let out the smoke with slow deliberation. Her brightly painted lips were steady, her hand was steady. She said with the same sarcastic intonation,

"You seem to know rather a lot about it, don't you? How she was drowned. When she was drowned. You might wish you hadn't started putting ideas into the heads of the police. After all, you tore your dress on the hedge, which proves that you were there. Whereas with regard to Geoffrey and me it's just your word against ours. You say we were there, and we say not. And that makes two to one." She blew out another little cloud of smoke. "The room was hot. We went out for a breath of air and strolled on the lawn. We were never anywhere near the pool. That's the way it goes, isn't it, Geoffrey?"

She looked up at him over her shoulder and saw his uneasy eyes. He had got to his feet and stood there in front of the chair from which he had risen, the hand with the cigarette hanging down, ash dropping from it on the carpet. Contempt for him came up in her. He looked like a horse that is going to shy. She wasn't scrupulous, but she would always take her fences.

Her look stung him into speech.

"Yes—yes—of course."

Meriel laughed.

"Not much good as a liar, are you, Geoffrey? I should have thought you would have had plenty of practise. Or do you always tell Edna just where you've been and with whom? But I suppose this is a little bit different. You don't push someone into a pool and drown them every day, and I suppose it's rather unnerving to find that you were seen."

The angry colour rushed into his face.

"Have you gone mad? Mabel Preston was drunk, and she tumbled into the pool and was drowned! Why should I— why should anyone want to drown her?"

"Oh, not her—not poor old Mabel. It was Adriana you thought you were doing in. But as it turned out, it wasn't. It was only Adriana's coat—the one she wouldn't give me when I asked her for it. It would have served her right if she had been wearing it—wouldn't it? And we should all have been free and with enough money to do what we liked. It's a pity you didn't bring it off, isn't it? But I'll say you tried! I'll not only say it, I'll swear it! You were there in the summerhouse—I could hear you whispering. And when I came away, there was Mabel Preston coming across the lawn full of cocktails and talking to herself. You see, I really have got something to tell the police—" she paused and added, "if I choose."

Esmé Trent's alert gaze had gone from one to the other. She said now in a cool, drawling voice,

"And what do you expect to get out of going to the police? You had really better think it over. You say we were in the summerhouse, and we say no. And we say—listen carefully, Meriel!—we say you came down here and tried to blackmail us because you knew that Geoffrey and I were friends and you were jealous. We could also tell Adriana some of the amiable things you have just been saying about her. She would be interested to know you thought it was a pity that it wasn't she who was drowned!" Her eyes were bright and hard on Meriel. She gave a short laugh and went on speaking. "You know, really you had better not stick out your neck. Geoffrey says there was something about your spilling coffee all down the front of that cyclamen dress you wore on Saturday. Now I wonder how you came to do that—or shall I say why you did it? Yes, that's nearer the mark, isn't it? And I think I can give you the answer. Coffee would be a very convenient thing to hide the sort of stains you might get on a light-coloured dress if you pushed someone into a pond and held them down. By the way, what have you done with the dress? If you can't produce it, that will look a bit odd, won't it? And if you've been stupid enough to take it to the cleaners, the police will be able to get their evidence as to just what stains there were. I don't suppose the coffee would have covered everything exactly. No, my dear Meriel, you had really better hold your tongue. And if you will stop dramatizing yourself and put your mind to it, you will begin to think so too."

Meriel's natural pallor had become ghastly. Her eyes blazed. She was caught up in a rush of fury. She went back until she could feel the door behind her. She groped for the handle and pulled on it until there was a gap that was wide enough to let her through. It gave her confidence to stand like that on the threshold, dominating the room. She stared at Geoffrey, angry and embarrassed, at Esmé Trent whom she hated with all her heart, and she said,

"Supposing I was to swear I saw you push her in?"

Esmé said, "They wouldn't believe you."

Meriel said, "Shall we try?" Then she turned round and went away across the little hall, and down the flagged path, and through the wicket gate.

CHAPTER 28

Ellie heard her go. After all the other things, she heard Meriel's footsteps dying away. At first it was a relief to hear them go. And then drowning the relief, drowning everything else, there was the memory of what she had heard Meriel say. It came on her with a rush, and it brought fear with it—terrible, heart-shaking fear. She had to lean upon the windowsill because of the fear that was shaking her. Her whole body trembled with it, and her thoughts too. If she had not had something to lean on she would have fallen. And then perhaps they would have come out and found her there. . . .

At the thought of being found by Esmé Trent a cold mist came up between her and the amber glow from the lighted room. There were voices beyond the mist. Esmé Trent said sharply,

"She's dangerous." And Geoffrey said on a low, troubled note, "What did she mean, Esmé—what did she mean?"

"She said she saw you push her in."

"Me—or you?"

"She said 'You'."

"She could have meant either of us."

"Or both." Her voice was taut and hard.

He said, "I don't know what you mean."

"Well, we didn't do it together—we both know that. But—we separated. You thought you heard someone coming. If you did, it was probably Mabel Preston. I went one way, and you went the other. The question is, did you come back?"

"Esmé, I swear—"

"Well, did you?"

He said, "My God, no!" And then, after a choking pause, "Did *you*?"

Her carefully darkened eyebrows lifted.

"Really, Geoffrey! What do you expect me to say? I suggest that you cut out the hysteria and get going! I suppose you don't want Meriel's trick of showing off to take her as far as ringing up the County police! I should say she was capable of it in her present mood, and however silly the whole thing is, it would raise the most appalling stink. I suggest that you go after her and call it off."

His ruddy colour had faded. He stood and looked at her.

"What can I do?"

She laughed.

"My dear Geoffrey! Are you going to tell me you can't talk a woman round? She has always wanted you to make love to her. Run along and give a good performance!"

The colour came back into his face with a rush. Just for a moment he could have struck her. But the moment passed. He caught at his control.

"I'll do what I can to talk her round."

Outside the unlatched window Ellie heard Esmé Trent say

179

something, but she couldn't wait to hear what it was. She had got to get away before Geoffrey came out. As soon as she stopped looking at the glow through the curtains it was difficult for her to see. The orange dazzle made her three parts blind. She had to feel her way along the narrow path which skirted the house. With arms stretched out before her she was no more than a yard from the porch, when the door opened. There was a light in the little hall. It shone out on to the stones and showed her the gate. Geoffrey Ford would have seen her if he had not turned on the threshold. She heard him say, "Esmé—" and, "You can't really think—" And then he was coming down the path.

Esmé Trent stood where she was to see him go. The gate swung to behind him and his footsteps went away down the drive and on to the road. Ellie stood there frozen. If Esmé looked this way, she would be seen. The light from the passage shone out upon the stones. Esmé went on standing there, but she looked in the direction in which Geoffrey had gone. The time just went on. It seemed endless, but it did come to an end. Esmé stepped back, the door shut, and the light was gone. And with that the frightened life came back into Ellie Page. She reached the gate, the drive, and was running like some frightened woodland thing out between the broken pillars and on to the road. She did not know then, and she was never to know afterwards, just what made her turn to the right instead of to the left as she ran. They say that, other things being equal, a right-handed man will tend to take a right-hand turn. But in this case there was no equality of choice, since a turn to the left would have brought her almost immediately to the shelter of the Vicarage garden, whereas by turning to the right she committed herself to the stretch of road between the Lodge and the entrance to Ford

180

House. It may have been that in the panic which had taken her she was incapable of thought, and so that slight preference for the right-hand turn asserted itself. However that may be, she ran with a desperate urgency, and came to the darkened drive which led to Ford House.

Meriel and Geoffrey were before her. Meriel did not run. She had no need to do so. She was very well pleased with herself. She wanted to go over the scene at the Lodge and think how clever she had been, and how she would be able to score off that horrid Esmé Trent. She might let Geoffrey off if he was properly humble and devoted. She began to make up another and even more satisfactory scene in which he told her that it was she whom he had always loved—Esmé had enticed him for a time, but when he saw them together just now he had realized the difference between them, and knew that she, Meriel, was the only one in the world for him. Yes, if Geoffrey played his part, she would save him. She could always say that he had said good-bye to Esmé and left her down by the pool before Mabel Preston came across the lawn. It would all fit in very well if she told it like that, and then Esmé would be out of the way for good and all. The more she thought about it, the better pleased she was. And with her own cleverness down at the Lodge. She had seen Esmé's silly little wisp of a handkerchief lying on the floor between the sofa and the door. She had seen it at once, but from where she sat Esmé couldn't see it at all. Meriel had seen it, and when Esmé turned away from her to look round at Geoffrey she had picked it up as quick as a flash and pushed it down the neck of her dress. If that handkerchief was dropped in the summerhouse and found by the police, it would prove that Esmé had been there. She had said there wasn't any proof, but the handkerchief would be a very good proof indeed. Esmé had a dozen of these silly little squares with her name embroidered across the corner. They were of four different colours, green, blue, amber, and buff. This was one of the amber ones. Nobody but Esmé had a handkerchief like that. Nobody could have picked it up and dropped it in the summerhouse by mistake. It would be quite a good enough proof to give Esmé a lot of trouble. Even if it didn't hang her or get her into prison, it would be quite enough to drive her away from Ford.

She was still very pleasantly occupied with these thoughts when she came up to the house. Anyone who was following her might have seen her hesitate for a moment and then abruptly turn and take the path which ran through a shrubbery to the lawn. Her thoughts went on pleasing her. There was no time like the present. The sooner the handkerchief was in the summerhouse, the better. It would be properly limp and damp after lying there through the night, and it would take just no time at all. She had her torch in her hand, but she used it as little as possible. There was a moon behind the clouds, and she knew every step of the way.

When she came to the summerhouse she put the torch on so as to choose the best place for dropping the handkerchief. It must be where it would be found, but it must not be too conspicuous. When she had placed it to her satisfaction she switched off the light and came to stand by the pool. It reflected a sky which seemed brighter than it really was. The light of the unseen moon was heightened by the water. The black hedges shut it in. There was a plane coming up out of the distance. She hardly noticed it, because with the airfield at Ledbury they came over so often. This one was flying low. The noise it made was there in her mind as an accustomed sound. She gave it no conscious thought, but it prevented her from hearing any movement behind her. There was a movement, and there were footsteps. She might not have heard them in any case, since the paving was damp and soft with moss. Her thoughts were full of triumph.

The blow fell without any warning at all.

CHAPTER 29

Mary Lenton sat in the dark and waited. It had not been very difficult to open Ellie's door. There were at least three other keys which fitted it. She went in, switched on the light, and saw that the bed had not been stripped of its counterpane. The curtains had been drawn back from the open window. She at once turned out the light. Since they had already made a thorough search of the rest of the house, it was now quite certain that Ellie had left it, and since the outer doors were locked and the ground floor windows latched, there could be very little doubt that she had climbed out of this window. When she came back there must be no light in the room to frighten her away. She went out on to the landing and spoke to John.

"She isn't there. She hasn't undressed. She must have climbed down the pear-tree."

He said in a voice she would hardly have known, it was so full of a hard anger,

"Then she will find us waiting for her when she comes back."

"Not you, John."

"And why not?"

"Because she will be—very much ashamed."

"I hope so. This is no time for softness."

They spoke in undertones, as if there was someone who might hear them in the empty room. In the end Mary got her way.

John Lenton went back to the study at the other side of the house and sat there writing letters, clearing up his desk, with anger in his mind and an urge to vent it. He had left the bedroom to Mary, but she need not think he would forbear to speak his mind when Ellie came home.

Mary Lenton sat there in the dark. The thing was unbelievable, but it had to be believed. She looked back through all the years of Ellie's life. She was five years the younger. Mary remembered her very small and pretty in her pram. She remembered the gentle little girl who was always good, the delicate girl in her teens who was never quite strong enough to play games or take long walks. That it should be Ellie who had climbed out of her window to meet a man just did not seem as if it could be true.

She pushed a chair up level with the window and to one side of it, so that when Ellie came back she would not see her until she had climbed right into the room. She did not have to push it far, because it was the chair in which Ellie had sat to watch the road from Ford House. Mary's mind was so full of unhappiness that she had no sense of the passing of time. She had never seen John in such anger. His household, which should have been a pattern, to become a byword! His home with Mary and his children in it to be the setting for a sordid intrigue! For this time at least there was no room for mercy, and Ellie would get none.

Mary could think of no way out. John would make her

send Ellie away. There would be no one to help with the children. He wouldn't let Ellie teach them any more, he wouldn't let her be with them. And where were they to send her? There was no one but old Aunt Annabel, and she would want to know why they couldn't keep her themselves. The longer she went on thinking about it, the more dreadfully difficult it was. If John would only help instead of piling up his anger on the top of everything else. Of course Ellie must be talked to and got to see how wrong she had been. And she must give up meeting Geoffrey Ford, who ought to be ashamed of himself. If she did that, the talk would die down. Mrs. Collen was a coarse-tongued woman who thought she could stick up for her daughter by accusing somebody else. It was silly of John to think that he could do any good by going to her about Olive. She would have tried to stop him if she had known, but it probably wouldn't have been any good. Men were so headstrong, and they always thought they knew best.

Soft as it was, she heard Ellie's footstep as it came round the side of the house. She had run till there was no more breath in her. She had not known when there was grass under her feet, or when there was gravel. She had scarcely known that it was dark. She had been driven by terror, as a leaf is driven before the wind. She ran from the pool—through the gap in the hedge, and across the lawn, and through the shrubbery, and down the drive of Ford House. She ran out upon the road and along it. But when she came to the Vicarage gate the pace slackened. She came in past the tall shapes of the dahlias—black leaves, black sculptured flowers in a thicket of darkness—and she came, slow and dragging, to the pear-tree under her window. She took hold of it and stood there panting, straining for breath. It had been easy enough to climb down, but how was she going to get up again? There was no strength in her, no breath. She leaned forward over her hands and held on to the pear-tree.

Mary Lenton was on her feet, pressed back against the wall. What had happened—what could possibly have happened? She had not thought that anything could be worse than to sit here waiting for Ellie to come back. But this was worse, far worse. She was afraid to call out, to move, to do anything.

And then, very slowly and with sobbing breath, Ellie set a foot on the lowest branch of the pear-tree and began to climb. Mary moved then. The dressing-table stood across the corner just beyond her. There was a light switch there. She moved until she could reach it. And waited. Ellie's hands groped and clung to the stretched boughs, her feet stumbled and slipped, her breath caught in her throat. It was terrible to listen and not help her, but if she were startled Ellie might fall. It came to Mary Lenton then that you can't always help the people you love—they must help themselves. It came to her that Ellie must find her own way back.

Painfully and very, very slowly Ellie was finding this part of her way. A shadow rose beyond the sill, the laboured breathing was in the room. There was a moment when the dark shape at the window seemed to hang there motionless, there was another moment when it moved again. With the last of her strength Ellie put a knee on the windowsill and dragged herself over it. She caught at the drawn-back curtain and stood there swaying.

And then the light came on. She saw the room, and Mary, her hand dropping from the switch. Her lips parted, but no sound came from them. Mary looked at her, aghast. Her

186

jumper, her cardigan, all the front of her skirt, was soaked and dripping. She said,

"Ellie!"

Ellie Page stared at her blankly. Her hands slipped from the curtain. The floor in front of her tilted and she went down—down—down.

It took so long to revive her, and the consciousness to which she did eventually return was of so precarious a nature, that John Lenton's righteous indignation failed him and he agreed without demur to whatever Mary suggested.

"I can't leave her, John—she isn't fit to be left."

He looked down at the strained white face on the pillow. They had lifted her on to the bed and covered her. She was deathly cold. He had filled hot water-bottles and heated milk. Until this moment there had been no time for anything but fear and haste. Now quite suddenly he said,

"Why had you taken off her things?" And then, more sharply, "She hadn't been out like that?"

Mary did not know just what prompted her answer. She was the most candid of women, but—you don't tell a man everything where another woman is concerned. She didn't know just why she had taken off the soaked jumper, the cardigan and skirt, and the wet shoes and stockings before she ran for John. There was, perhaps, some vague idea that Ellie might have tried to drown herself, and that there was no need for him to know. She had stripped the wet things off and pushed them out of sight. When John was asleep she could put them down in the kitchen to dry. She looked at him by the light of the candle which she had shaded from Ellie's eyes and said without a tremor,

"I thought she would be more comfortable without them."

187

CHAPTER 30

It was not Sam Bolton who found the body this time, but the head gardener himself. There was nothing special to take him to the pool, but it was a fine morning after the cloudy night and he was taking what he called a bit of daunder round the garden before getting on with his autumn seeds. The sun shone out of a blue sky with no more than a streak or two of grey in the west. The sunrise had been too red to promise any continuance of this pleasant state of things. As far as Mr. Robertson was concerned, he didn't trust it a yard, and if Maggie had no more sense than to come telling him what the B.B.C. said about it, he would just have the one word to say to her, and that was, "Blethers!" He hadn't come to his time of life without having his own ideas.

He passed through one of the arches of the yew hedge and saw the body in the pool. It lay as the other one had lain, tilted forward over the parapet with the head and shoulders under water. It was Meriel Ford, and there was no doubt in his mind that she was dead. It wouldn't be any business of his to be touching her. He went up to the house and told Simmons without any fuss.

The news spread like a spark in a dry field. It reached Janet when Joan Cuttle came up with her morning cup of tea. It took her all she knew to muzzle Joan and get her out of earshot of Stella. She was whimpering and catching her breath as she went, but not daring to raise her voice.

Janet went to the telephone and rang up Star. She emerged from the nursery half an hour later with her plans made, and ran into Ninian. He said, "You've heard?" and she nodded.

"Look, I've got to get Stella away. I've just been on to Star about it."

He gave a slight shrug.

"And what did Star say? She won't be keen on having Stella in town."

Janet had her determined look, brows very straight, eyes very steady.

"It's all arranged. Star's friend Sibylla Maxwell will take them in. She has a nursery, and children about the same age. The Maxwells have a big house at Sunningdale. She has been asking Star to take Stella there, so it fits in beautifully. We're catching the nine-fifteen from Ledbury."

He stood there frowning.

"Stella ought to be out of it—you're right about that. But I don't know about you. The police will want to see every-one."

She nodded.

"Star is meeting us. I'll take the next train back."

"That would be the eleven-thirty. I'll meet it. How are you getting to Ledbury? I don't know that I can get away."

"I've ordered a taxi. I'm going down now for Stella's break-fast. Could you possibly stay with her till I get back? I'm not letting her out of the nursery till the taxi comes."

All the way up in the train Stella chattered about the Max-wells. They had a garden with a wall round it, they had a swimming-pool, they had a swing. They had two ponies, and they had guineapigs, as well as rabbits. Janet had never seen her so animated.

Star, meeting them at the terminus, looked at Janet over

189

Stella's head with frightened eyes. They said, "What is happening?"

Janet had no answer to give. All her energies had been concentrated upon getting Stella away. When they had got the luggage out of the van Star pulled her aside.

"Janet—what does Stella know?"

"Nothing so far. I watched her like a dragon."

"I shall have to tell her something."

"Yes. Why don't you just say there has been an accident? She doesn't like Meriel, and I don't believe she'll take a lot of notice—not with swimming-pools and ponies and guineapigs to think about. She has been talking about them all the way up."

Star held her arm so tightly that she left a bruise.

"I told you something dreadful was going to happen. I had a feeling about it. That is really why I came back. I could have stayed in New York and had a marvellous time, but I just *couldn't!* I kept on being frightened about Stella!"

Janet detached the clutching fingers.

"Star, you're making a hole in my arm. And there's nothing the matter with Stella. Take her away and have a good time with her."

The return train got into Ledbury at just after half past twelve, and Ninian was on the platform. When they were clear of the traffic he said abruptly,

"They've found a handkerchief belonging to Esmé Trent in the summerhouse."

Janet made no comment. She watched his dark unsmiling profile.

"They don't know why she should have dropped it there, and they don't know when, but it wasn't there after the first business, because the police say they went through every-

190

thing in the summerhouse. And it wasn't there as late as four o'clock yesterday afternoon, because Robertson didn't like the way the police had left the chairs and he was in there putting them right. According to him, 'There was nae handkerchiefs nor other fancy goods tae be seen then.'"

Janet said,

"How do they know it is Esmé Trent's handkerchief?"

"Oh, rather a conspicuous article—what Robertson would call kenspeckle. Getting on towards orange in colour, with Esmé all across one corner."

"And what does Esmé Trent say to that?"

"I don't know. They've been asking us all a lot of questions. You'll be for it as soon as you get back—or as soon as they do. You wouldn't believe how difficult it can be to account for one's simplest actions. Why, for instance, did Adriana and Edna go up to bed at half past nine? Very suspicious for Adriana to be tired of Edna's exhilarating company, or for Edna to have had enough of that interminable embroidery of hers! And who is Miss Silver, and what is she doing down here? Geoffrey will have to admit that he went to see the girl friend and stayed there for an indefinite period. Not in itself an offence against the law. And, as we know, Meriel was last seen leaving the drawing-room with the avowed intention of following him to the study. The police naturally wonder whether she followed him farther than that. He says she didn't. That leaves you and me to give each other an alibi. It is, of course, highly suspicious to have an alibi at all. And why did we sit up until the riotous hour of half past ten, when as far as we knew, the rest of the virtuous household had gone to bed? Also, why didn't we hear Geoffrey come in? I did point out that this is a big house, and that the study is well away on the other side of it. I also intimated that we were having quite an interesting conversation, but it didn't seem to cut a lot of official ice. By the way, I furnished them with a brief biography of you and told them we were engaged, so don't do anything stupid like shaking my credibility as a witness."

"You shouldn't have said we were engaged."

"Darling, I've been telling you so for days. Hasn't it penetrated? It really will be a Suspicious Circumstance if you start cavilling at what I've said. Honestly, you'd better let it ride."

Janet was pale and frowning. She said nothing for a minute or two, and then came out suddenly with,

"What is all this about? Do they think—do the police think—it wasn't an accident?"

His eyebrows rose.

"How many coincidences do you expect a policeman to swallow before breakfast? Do you suppose there was a hope that they would get this one down? Even if there had been nothing more, there wouldn't have been an earthly."

She said, "Is there anything more?"

"Oh, yes, I'm afraid there is. You see, Meriel didn't just fall into the pool. She was struck on the back of the head with our old friend the blunt instrument."

CHAPTER 31

The news had come to the Vicarage whilst Jenny and Molly were eating bread-and-milk out of brightly coloured bowls with a pattern of cherries, their fair hair smoothly brushed, their rosy faces newly washed, and their blue eyes intent on the business of breakfast. They made a pleasant picture. Mary Lenton's colour was not as fresh as theirs. She had slept and waked, and slept and waked again through what had seemed like double the number of hours the night should hold.

Ellie Page did not wake at all. She lay in a deep exhausted sleep with the sheet drawn up to her chin. Her breathing made no sound, and the sheet did not move. Mary had set a night-light in the wash-basin. It made a faint steady light in the room. Every time she waked and saw Ellie lying so still she felt a cold touch of fear. Sleep should not look so terribly like death. But each time, rising and tiptoeing to the bed, she knew that this was not death, but sleep.

She was pouring milk into the children's cups, when John called her out of the room. He put a hand on her arm and took her into the study.

"The baker has just been—I took two loaves. Mary, he says there has been another accident up at Ford House. It doesn't seem possible, but he has just come from there. He says they found Meriel Ford in that pool—drowned in the same way as Miss Preston. He says the police are there now."

Mary Lenton turned very pale indeed.

"She was drowned—in the pool?"

"That is what he says. I don't know if I ought to go up there."

"Not just now—not while the police are there."

He said, "How is Ellie? Isn't she getting up? I shall have to see her about last night. Isn't she awake?"

"I gave her some hot milk, and she went to sleep again. You can't talk to her yet."

The look on his face was not encouraging. Men must always do things the hard way. He said coldly,

"If she is ill, you had better send for the doctor. If she isn't ill, she can see me."

She said, "Wait. . . . No, John, I think you must. Don't you see we've got to be careful?"

"Careful!"

"Yes, John. You can't have a scene with Ellie—not now. You really can't! Mrs. Marsh will be here any minute to do the cleaning. I shall tell her Ellie isn't well and I'm keeping her in bed. Nobody—nobody must know that she was out of the house last night."

He gave an angry laugh.

"You're locking the door after the horse is stolen, aren't you? Half the neighbourhood seems to know she was getting out at night!"

"But not last night. There mustn't be any talk about that."

He said in a horrified voice,

"What are you suggesting?"

She took hold of his arm and shook it.

"I'm not suggesting anything. I'm telling you no one must know that Ellie went out last night."

"We're to cover up for her—tell a lot of lies?"

"I'm not telling lies, I'm telling the truth. She isn't well, and I'm keeping her in bed."

He pulled away from her and went to the window, staring out. Presently he said without turning round,

"The police say Meriel was murdered."

"John!"

"He says he had it from Robertson. She was struck on the back of the head and pushed into the pool."

CHAPTER 32

Adriana Ford was waiting for the family to assemble. She sat in an upright chair with the folds of her purple house-gown falling to her feet. Her hair was as carefully ordered, her face as carefully made up, as if this was just any day with everything running smoothly and no shadow of tragedy resting upon the house. She had lunched in her room, and it was there she awaited the people whom she had summoned. Miss Silver sat on her right, the white shawl she was knitting making quite a little heap on her lap, her needles moving swiftly. The door into the bedroom was ajar and Meeson came and went. The chairs had been placed conveniently. The business might have been any family gathering.

Ninian and Janet came in together. She had not seen Adriana before going up to London, or since her return. She got a brief "Good-morning," and the remark that for once Star was showing some sense, and at least one of her friends doing a hand's turn. After which no one spoke again till Geoffrey

Ford came in. His florid colour was mottled, and he looked like a man who has had a shock. He had seen Adriana already, and sat down without speaking.

Edna came in last, with her work-bag on her arm and her embroidery-frame in her hand. She had on the black coat and skirt and grey blouse which she had worn for Mabel Preston's funeral, and she looked very much as she had done on that occasion, but her hair less wispy than usual and her face less strained. As she seated herself she remarked that it was all very trying, but that she had had a rather better night.

"I don't like taking anything to make me sleep, but there really does come a time when you feel as if you can't go on. So I went up early last night and took one of those tablets Dr. Fielding prescribed, and I had quite a good night."

Adriana drummed on the arm of her chair.

"I am sure we are all very glad to hear it. And now perhaps we can begin."

Geoffrey said, "Begin what?"

"If I am allowed to speak, I will tell you."

She sat with her back to the windows. Her hair took the light. The folds of her dress looked black where the shadows lay. She wore her rings, but no other jewelry—a big claw-set amethyst on her left hand, and a blaze of diamonds on the right. She still had very beautiful hands.

"Now!" she said. "I've asked you to come here because I think we may all have something we can contribute towards clearing up the things that have been happening. It goes back farther than last night, but I think we will begin with last night, because it is still quite fresh in everybody's mind. I know we have all made statements to the police, but what you say to the police is one thing, and what may come back

196

to you when you are talking in your own family circle is another—Yes, Geoffrey?"

He said in a forced voice,

"There are at least three people here who can hardly be said to belong to the family circle. If you want to talk to Edna and myself, we are most willing that you should do so at any time. To Ninian too, if you think he can be of any use. I must confess I don't see the need of this formality."

Rather to his surprise, she showed no temper.

"Thank you, Geoffrey. A little formality is quite a help in ordering one's thoughts. As to the people whom I have invited to be present, Meeson has been with me for more than forty years, and I regard her as a member of the family—Sit down, Gertie, and stop fidgeting! I find Miss Silver's presence a support, and I particularly desire her to be present. And Janet will stay because it is my wish. You may perhaps be interested to know that I rang up Mrs. Trent and invited her to come. She refused on the somewhat surprising grounds that she would be looking after her little boy. She said he couldn't go to school because Ellie Page wasn't well. It was naturally impossible to leave him alone for half an hour!" Her voice had a cutting edge.

Since the spectacle of Jackie Trent left on his own for hour after hour of almost every day was perfectly familiar to everyone in the room, it was not surprising that Geoffrey should look embarrassed, or that Meeson should sniff and toss her head in the background. Edna Ford made no sign and she did not look up. She took a stitch in her embroidery, knotted it, and went on to another.

When the silence had lasted for what she considered an appropriate time, Adriana spoke.

"I will begin with myself and with what came under my

197

own observation. Miss Silver, Edna, Meriel, Geoffrey and I went straight from the dining-room into the drawing-room. Simmons brought in the coffee. Ninian and Janet came in after that. When he had drunk his coffee Geoffrey left the room, saying that he was going to write letters. Meriel suggested dancing. She said they would need Geoffrey for a fourth, and she said she would go after him and bring him back. She left the room, and that is the last occasion on which anyone admits to seeing her alive. Miss Silver, Edna and I remained where we were until half past nine, when we went upstairs together. We separated on the landing. I came to my room, where Meeson was waiting for me, and I went to bed. Edna, what did you do?"

Edna Ford looked up from the pale, dreary flower on which she was working. It might have been intended for a poppy if the colouring had not been a sickly mauve shading into grey. She said in her rather high, plaintive voice,

"I went across the landing and into my room. I undressed and washed and did my hair, and took the tablet I was telling you about. No, let me see—I think I took the tablet before I brushed my hair, because I thought it would be a good thing to give it a little time, if you know what I mean. I thought if I got sleepy before I actually got into bed it would give me a better chance of getting off. It is so disagreeable to lie in the dark and wonder whether you are going to sleep."

Miss Silver had been knitting rapidly. She looked across the fleecy wool and said,

"Yes, indeed, there is nothing more trying. But you slept?" Her tone was pleasant and sympathetic.

Edna Ford responded with a rehearsal of the number of nights during which she had been unable to sleep at all.

"And of course I have felt good for nothing during the

day—and with so much to be done. A big house does not run itself. The staff need constant supervision, and I had really begun to feel as if I could not go on. But the effect of the tablet was very satisfactory—I had several hours of most refreshing sleep. In fact I did not wake until Joan came into my room with the dreadful news this morning."

Adriana had been showing signs of impatience. She turned her head and said sharply,

"Janet and Ninian, you stayed behind in the drawing-room. Were you together all the time?"

Ninian nodded.

"Until half past ten, when we went up. Janet went into her room, and I went along to mine. I slept all night."

"And you, Janet?"

"Yes, I slept too."

Adriana looked over her shoulder.

"Gertie?"

Meeson bridled.

"I don't know what you want to ask me about, but I'm sure anyone is welcome. I had my supper, and I came up here and laid everything out for you, thinking you would be glad enough to go to your bed. Then I put on the wireless and had a good laugh over someone telling her grandmother how to suck eggs, which always gives the young ones a lot of pleasure and no harm done. And thank God for a sense of humour, for where would we all be without it! Then up you came, and when I'd got you settled I went off to my own bed, and glad enough to get there."

"And what was the last time you saw Meriel?"

Meeson tossed her head.

"As if you'd any need to ask me that, when I came straight along after it to take your tray! Out on the landing she was,

199

and flew at me like a fury! Said I'd been tale-tattling about her because I told you she'd spilt coffee down that new dress she wore Saturday for the party! And that's something I'll not take from anyone! Tale-tattling indeed! And what was the secret about it I'd like to know! Coffee all down the front of your dress isn't what you can hide, no matter how hard you try! And what's the good anyhow? I wasn't taking it from her, and we had a regular set-to, with Mr. Geoffrey and Mrs. Geoffrey coming out of their rooms, and Mr. Ninian and Simmons down in the hall! She ought to have had more control of herself, and so I told her! And the dress torn anyhow! Coffee stain or no, she'd torn it on the hedge down by the pool! And what was she doing there, I'd like to know! I asked her that, and she faced it out she'd never been near the place! But she had, for Miss Silver found the torn piece of her dress that was caught in the hedge, and so I told her! And what took her to the horrid place nor poor old Mabel either the Lord knows! But for the both of them it was once too often!"

She stopped, and there was a silence until Miss Silver said,

"Mr. Ford, did you hear all this?"

He said in a heavy voice,

"They were quarrelling. That wasn't anything new. I heard some of it."

"And you, Mrs. Geoffrey?"

"Oh, yes. Meriel had so little control. It didn't mean a great deal, you know. She was excitable."

"But you heard all this about her having torn her dress down by the pool?"

"There was something about her having spilt coffee on it. Such a pity—it was quite a new dress."

200

"But you heard Meeson say that the dress had been torn down by the pool, did you not?"

"Oh, yes, I think so. They were quarrelling, you know, and talking very loud. I can't remember everything they said."

"No, of course not." She turned to Ninian. "Mr. Ninian, you were in the hall. Did you hear all this about Miss Meriel having torn her dress down by the pool on Saturday evening?"

She got a very straight look back.

"Yes, I did."

"Will you tell us what you heard?"

"Meeson said you had found a piece of Meriel's dress caught in the hedge by the pool. Meriel was very angry indeed and said she had never been near the place, and Meeson went on saying she must have been, or how did the piece of her dress get there?"

"Anyone on the landing could have heard what you heard?"

"I should think so, unless they were deaf."

Adriana lifted the hand with the amethyst ring.

"Well, Geoffrey, you are the only one left to tell us just what you did after you left the drawing-room last night."

His head jerked back. Their eyes met.

"Really—I don't see—"

The hand fell again.

"No, I don't think you do. My dear Geoffrey, this is the day of judgment. What the police haven't asked you already, what they haven't asked all of us, has only been put off until next time. And they will ask everything all over again at the inquest, so we might just as well get it all straight and have done with it. Where did you go when you left the drawing-room?"

He looked past her to the right-hand window. The old-fashioned pink rose which clambered about it was in bloom. It had a very sweet scent, but the window was shut and the air of the room held no hint of it. He said in a stubborn voice, "I can see no use in all this. If you must know, I went for a stroll."

Edna held the eye of her embroidery needle to the light. She threaded it with a strand of lime-green silk and said, "He went to see Esmé Trent."

CHAPTER 33

It was at this moment that the door was opened by Simmons. He came a little way into the room and said in a low voice, "It's the police, madam—Superintendent Martin and Inspector Dean. They are asking for Mr. Geoffrey."

Adriana said, "Ask them to come up here!"

Geoffrey turned, protest in voice and manner.

"No—no—I'll go down."

"I think not. I would like to see them. Show them up, Simmons! And everyone will please stay here until they come!"

Geoffrey got up out of his chair and came to bend over her, speaking urgently. Edna took her slow stitches and never looked up. Miss Silver pulled on her fleecy ball. Heavy steps came down the corridor. Simmons opened the door and announced the names. The two men passed him, and he shut them in.

Adriana knew them both by sight—the Superintendent, a big fair man with a ruddy face, and the Inspector with a dash of ginger in his hair, and a quick way of talking. She said, "How do you do?" And then, "We were having what I suppose you might call a family consultation—pooling our ideas about this tragedy. Won't you both sit down?"

It had been the Superintendent's intention to interview Mr. Geoffrey Ford alone, but perceiving that this was Mr. Ford's own strong desire, it occurred to him that not only his reactions but those of the family circle might be worthy of some attention. He cast a quick glance at them, concluded that they were a mixed lot, and decided that it would do no harm to stir the mixture up a bit. He accordingly took the chair which Adriana had indicated and pointed the Inspector to another.

"Well, madam," he said, "since you are all here, there are just one or two things I might want to put to you, though it really was Mr. Geoffrey Ford I was intending to see. . . . Perhaps you will sit down again, sir."

Caught between Adriana's look of command and the Superintendent's air of authority, Geoffrey Ford sat down. Martin looked across at Janet and enquired, "Is this the lady who went up to town with the little girl—Miss Johnstone, wasn't it?" And when Janet said, "Yes," he took her briefly through what she knew of the events of the previous evening, finishing up with,

"And you had known the deceased how long?"

"Just a few days—since I came down here."

"Had any disagreement with her—any quarrel?"

"No."

He nodded.

"Just one question more. Do you play golf?"

"I haven't played for a year or two."

"Why was that?"

"I have been working in London."

"Bring any clubs down here?"

"Oh, no."

"Any talk of your playing down here—with the deceased or anyone else? Any suggestion of lending you clubs?"

Her look was candid and surprised.

"Oh, no."

He swung round on Geoffrey.

"You play golf, Mr. Ford?"

Geoffrey shrugged.

"I'm not much of a player."

"But you do play?"

"Oh, once in a way."

"Then I take it you have a set of clubs."'

"Well, yes."

"Where are they kept?"

"In the cloakroom, by the garden door."

The Superintendent turned his look on Edna.

"Do you play, Mrs. Ford?"

She rested her hand upon the embroidery-frame.

"Well, I used to play a little, but I haven't for a long time now. There is so much to do in a big house like this, and my health isn't what it was. I'm afraid the idea of going out for a long tramp over rough ground doesn't appeal to me any longer." She took up her needle again.

Martin said, "Does anyone else in the household play? Oh yes, you, Mr. Rutherford—I remember. You have a pretty low handicap, haven't you?"

Ninian laughed.

"They put me up a stroke last year. Horrid result of London."

"Have you got your clubs down here?"

"No, as a matter of fact I didn't bring them. I didn't expect to have time to play."

Adriana said in her deep voice,

"Why are you asking all these questions about golfclubs?"

His face was set in grave and heavy lines.

"Because Miss Meriel Ford was killed by a blow from a golfclub."

It is probable that everyone in the room drew in a quicker breath. Adriana, sitting up straight in her purple gown with the light on her dark red hair, spoke for all the rest.

"What makes you think that?"

"Because the club has been found, pushed in between the summerhouse and the hedge. It was a heavy niblick. It shows unmistakable signs of having been used as the weapon of attack. The fact that it has been wiped free of fingerprints points to the deliberate nature of the crime."

Janet found herself trembling. The picture came up in her mind so suddenly, so horribly. The pool with the sky reflected in it—a sky of clouds—a sky of stars? No knowing which it had been. Meriel with her tormenting jealousies, and the dark thought of murder sweeping into action with one appalling blow. She heard the Superintendent say, "She was dead before she touched the water," and it was not only she that was shaking now, but the room.

Ninian put his arm round her, and she put her head down on his shoulder and shut her eyes.

When everything had steadied again, Geoffrey Ford was saying,

"I told you before—I went out for a stroll."

"Did you call in on anyone?"

Edna's pale eyes were lifted. They looked at him, they looked at Superintendent Martin. She said,

"He went to see Mrs. Trent at the Lodge."

"Is that so, Mr. Ford?"

"Well, yes."

"May I ask how long you were there?"

"Well, really, Superintendent, I don't know. I suppose I smoked a couple of cigarettes—"

"Would you say you were there for something over half an hour?"

"Well, something like that—perhaps a little longer. I really couldn't say."

"It would take you about ten minutes each way, coming and going?"

"Oh, scarcely so much as that. I've never timed it."

"Nearer five or six minutes?"

"Something like that."

"And you left this house when?"

"I'm afraid I didn't look at the time."

Adriana said, "It was about twenty past eight when you left the drawing-room, and about half past when Meriel went after you."

The Superintendent nodded.

"At that rate, Mr. Ford, you should have been back at Ford House by half past nine. Is that what you say?"

Geoffrey's colour had deepened considerably.

"It's really no good pressing me about either the time I went out or came in. Hang it all, man, one doesn't go about with one's eye on one's watch! It was a mild evening—I strolled down to see a friend—we got talking about this and that—I really haven't any idea how long I stayed. I said I

206

smoked a couple of cigarettes, but it may quite easily have been more. I can't tell you when I got back here. All I know is it wasn't late."

Edna's hands had been resting idly on her work. She said now without any expression at all,

"The time does go so fast when you are—talking."

No one could have failed to notice the pause before the final word. She picked up her needle as soon as it was spoken. Martin said,

"So it might have been as much as ten o'clock when you got back. Was there a light on in the drawing-room?"

"I have no idea. I went out, as I came in, by the study window, and I went straight to my room."

"You did not look at a clock, then?"

"No, I did not."

The Superintendent turned to Adriana.

"I think you stated that you, and Mrs. Ford, and this lady—" he indicated Miss Silver—"went up to bed at half past nine. That was very early."

"We had had a tiring day."

"Did any of you come down again?"

"I certainly did not."

"You, Mrs. Ford?"

Edna said in her dreary voice, "Oh, no. I had been having such bad nights. I took the sleeping-tablet Dr. Fielding had prescribed for me and went to bed."

"And you, Miss Silver?"

She looked across her knitting and said,

"No, I did not go down again."

He turned back to Geoffrey Ford.

"Miss Meriel Ford followed you out of the drawing-room

at about half past eight. She had avowed her intention of fetching you back from the study. Did she find you there?"

They had asked him that before, and he had said no. Why did they ask him again? It looked as if they didn't believe him. Perhaps it would have been better to say that Meriel had found him, and that he had told her he was going out. But then they would have wanted to know where she had been, what she was doing—how she came to fetch up in the pool. He oughtn't to have hesitated—he should have said something at once. He spoke now in a hurry.

"No—no—of course not. I don't know if she came to the study or not, but if she did, I wasn't there."

The Superintendent got up. Behind him his Inspector pushed back his chair and rose. Martin walked towards the door, but just before he got to it he turned and spoke to Geoffrey.

"I have been seeing Mrs. Trent. She seems as uncertain about the times as you are. I went there early to ask her about the handkerchief which was found in the summerhouse—a yellow handkerchief with the name Esmé embroidered across the corner."

Edna Ford's hand was arrested in the act of taking a stitch. She said,

"Mrs. Trent's name is Esmé."

Martin nodded.

"That is why I went to see her. She says she is quite unable to explain how her handkerchief could have got there. Can you throw any light upon the subject, Mr. Ford?"

"Of course I can't!"

"Miss Meriel Ford did not by any chance accompany you to the Lodge? If she did, she might have picked up the handkerchief by mistake."

"Of course she didn't!"

"Why of course, Mr. Ford?"

"She was not on those terms with Mrs. Trent."

He knew as soon as he had said it that it was the wrong thing to say. There shouldn't be any suggestion that Meriel and Esmé didn't get on. It was the suggestion that Meriel might have followed him to the Lodge or gone there with him which had stampeded him into saying a thing like that. He didn't really make it any better by going on to say,

"They weren't on those informal terms. She wouldn't just drop in without being asked."

Edna said in a plaintive voice,

"Esmé Trent is Geoffrey's friend."

Superintendent Martin found himself with considerable food for thought. He was left with the very decided impression that Geoffrey Ford had not been speaking the truth. He might or might not be as uncertain about his comings and goings as he appeared to be, but there was certainly something he was anxious to conceal, and it might or might not be something germane to the murder of Meriel Ford. There was, quite plainly, a husband-and-wife situation with Esmé Trent as the disturbing third party. Geoffrey Ford's embarrassment could proceed from his wife's jealousy, in which case it might have nothing to do with the murder.

He did not speak until he reached the hall, when he sent Inspector Dean along to the cloakroom to have a look at the golfclubs which were said to be kept there. He went on turning things over in his mind until his attention was distracted by the sight of Miss Silver descending the stair. Not that he thought of her by her name, although it had been given to him. She appeared among his thoughts as "the little visiting

209

lady," and he was not best pleased when she came directly up to him and said,

"Forgive me, Superintendent, but I should appreciate the opportunity of a few words with you."

He gave her a little more of his attention than he had done so far. The primly netted hair, the dress of sage-green wool, the gaily flowered knitting-bag—these were of a not uncommon type among the elderly ladies who frequent a less expensive kind of boarding-house. But the expression of alert intelligence was more uncommon. When she opened the door of a small room and preceded him into it he had no hesitation in following her.

The place was obviously not in the way of being used. There was a desk, and some book-cases, but it had a cold, unlived-in feeling. When Martin turned from shutting the door Miss Silver was standing by the empty hearth. She spoke as he came towards her.

"Since this is a case of murder, there are things which I think you ought to know." Her voice was so grave, her air so much that of a serious and responsible person, that he found himself regarding her with attention. He had up to now considered her merely in the light of the casual friend who happened to be visiting Adriana Ford at the time of the second tragedy. The fact that she had only been a little over twenty-four hours in the house seemed to relegate her to comparative unimportance and to detach her from any possible connection with the death of Miss Preston. Now he was not so sure. At his slight frown she moved in the direction of a chair and indicated that he also should sit. He found himself complying with a slight sense of surprise that the conduct of the interview should have passed out of his hands.

Miss Silver settled herself and said,

210

"I think it is right that you should know that I am here in the capacity of a private enquiry agent."

If she had announced that she was there in the capacity of a Fairy Godmother or of First Murderer, she could hardly have surprised him more. In fact the Fairy Godmother would have seemed quite appropriate by comparison. Under his incredulous stare she opened her knitting-bag, extracted a mass of fleecy white wool, and began to knit.

He said, "You surprise me," and she smiled gravely.

"Miss Adriana Ford approached me in my professional capacity about a fortnight ago. She was in considerable anxiety and distress because she had some reason to believe that her life was being attempted."

"What!"

Miss Silver inclined her head.

"There have been three incidents. In the early spring she fell down the stairs and broke her leg. She believed that she was pushed. During the intervening months she was an invalid in her own room. Two more incidents occurred. Some soup which was served to her had a strange burning taste, and she ordered it to be thrown away. The third incident, which occurred not so very long ago, concerned a bottle of sleeping-tablets. Tipping them out into her hand in order to select the proper dose, she saw that one of the tablets was of a different size and shape to the others. She threw it out of the window. You will naturally remark, as I did, that both the soup and the tablets should have been analysed."

"Certainly—if she suspected that they had been tampered with."

Miss Silver gave her slight prim cough.

"I do not know whether you are well acquainted with Miss Adriana Ford, but a student of human nature such as yourself

211

cannot have failed to remark that she is a person of impulsive and determined character. In the matter of the soup and the tablets she acted on impulse. In her interview with me she showed a good deal of determination."

"What did she want you to do?"

"Nothing, Superintendent. Having told me of these three incidents, they ceased to trouble her. She said what was of course obvious, that the whole thing might have grown up out of very little. As far as she knew, there was no one beyond her on the landing when she fell from the top of the stairs. The soup was mushroom soup, and it was possible that some non-edible kind had been introduced by accident. The different sized tablet could have been a misshapen one. She said her mind was completely relieved, and that there was nothing she now wished me to do. I advised her to give up her invalid ways, take her meals with the family, and be on her guard. This advice I believe she followed."

He nodded.

"And when did she communicate with you again?"

"On the Wednesday evening. I had seen a brief notice of Miss Preston's death on the Monday, but it was not until Wednesday that Miss Ford rang me up. She asked me to come down by the ten-thirty next day, which I did. That was yesterday. On my arrival Miss Ford informed me that the inquest on Miss Preston had resulted in a verdict of accidental death, but from a circumstance which she communicated to me, and which had not been communicated to the police, there seemed to be some doubt about this."

"What circumstance, Miss Silver?"

She laid her knitting down and rested her hands upon it.

"She told me that Miss Preston was wearing a coat of a very striking and decided pattern—great black and white squares with an emerald stripe. This coat belonged to Miss Adriana Ford herself. She had proposed giving it to Miss Preston, but Miss Meriel Ford objected. In fact she made a scene about it, and Miss Adriana thought it would be best not to insist for the moment. She had it hung in the downstairs cloakroom, and was intending to give it to Miss Preston at the close of her visit. Miss Preston probably regarded it as her own already, but Miss Adriana continued to wear it."

The Superintendent leaned forward.

"Are you suggesting that Miss Preston met with foul play because she was wearing a coat that belonged to Adriana Ford?"

Miss Silver looked at him steadily.

"I think that Miss Ford draws that inference."

He said, "There's no evidence."

She took up her knitting again.

"None, Superintendent. But there might have been if Miss Meriel Ford had lived."

"And what do you mean by that?"

"Miss Preston fell or was pushed into the pool at some time after half past six whilst a cocktail party was going on. Adriana Ford saw both her and Meriel in the drawing-room up to that time. Meriel Ford was wearing a dress of a pinkish mauve shade. I found a piece of this dress caught in the hedge which surrounds the pool."

"It might have caught there at any time."

"I believe not. It was a new dress, and she was wearing it for the first time. For some time after half past six no one seems to have seen her. Later, Meeson, Adriana Ford's maid, saw Meriel Ford with coffee stains all down the front of this dress. Later still, when the guests had gone away, she had changed it."

213

"And what do you want to make of that?"

"I think she was certainly down by the pool between half past six and the time that Meeson saw her. She had never worn the dress before, and she packed it off to the cleaners on the Monday. In no other way and at no other time could that shred of her dress have got caught in the hedge. The spilled coffee suggests that the dress had become stained as well as torn, and that the stains were of such a nature that she thought it necessary to camouflage them with coffee. I believe that she was down by the pool, and that she either heard or saw something which made her dangerous to the person who pushed Miss Preston in. I believe there was such a person, and that Meriel Ford had some clue to this person's identity. It is significant that her own death occurred very shortly after a violent quarrel between Meeson and herself. This quarrel took place on the landing at the top of the stairs. It was certainly overheard by Mr. and Mrs. Geoffrey Ford, by Mr. Ninian Rutherford, and by the butler Simmons. It could have been heard by almost anyone in the house. In the course of it Meeson stated that I had found a torn piece of Meriel's dress in the hedge by the pool, and Meriel loudly accused her of telling tales. I find it difficult to believe that this scene has no connection with what followed."

Superintendent Martin was in two minds. He was impressed, and he had no desire to be impressed. He felt like a man who is doing a jigsaw puzzle and to whom an intrusive stranger proffers the missing piece. Gratitude is very seldom the reward of the onlooker who sees more of the game than you do yourself. He was, at the same time, a just man and too intelligent not to recognize intelligence in another. He recognized it in Miss Silver, and while not prepared to subscribe to her reasoning, he was prepared to consider it.

As he turned these things over in his mind he became aware that Miss Silver was waiting for him to speak. She did not fidget or show any signs of wishing to interrupt his train of thought. She sat there knitting quietly and maintained an attentive attitude. It occurred to him that he would like to know what impression had been made upon her by the scene in the drawing-room on the previous evening. He said with an effect of abruptness,

"You were in the drawing-room last night when Mr. Ford left the room, and when Meriel Ford followed him. Would you mind telling me just what passed?"

She did so without comment and in her usual careful and accurate manner. When she had finished he said,

"Miss Johnstone and Mr. Rutherford did not come into the drawing-room until after Mr. Ford left it, then?"

"Just a few minutes afterwards."

"And how long was it before Meriel Ford went after him?"

"Not long at all. Not more than five minutes. There was some talk about Mrs. Somers having rung up—the little girl's mother. And then Miss Meriel suggested that they might dance. She took up a record, but put it down again almost at once and said, 'I'll get Geoffrey back. It's nonsense his going off to write letters. Besides, does anyone believe in them? I don't! Or perhaps Esmé Trent gives him a hand!'"

"This was said in front of Mrs. Geoffrey Ford?"

"Yes."

"Did she say anything?"

"Not at the time. But a little later, when I unfortunately made some reference to a little boy who shares the children's class at the Vicarage, Miss Adriana Ford said he was Mrs. Trent's child, and that she neglected him. Mrs. Geoffrey then showed considerable feeling. She said Mrs. Trent was an immoral woman, and told Miss Adriana Ford that she ought not to have her in the house."

"And what did Adriana Ford say to that?"

Miss Silver coughed.

"She said that she was not a censor of morals, and she told Mrs. Geoffrey not to be a fool."

"A pleasant family atmosphere," said Martin drily.

Miss Silver said,

"If I may draw an apposite quotation from the works of the late Lord Tennyson—

'Manners are not idle, but the fruit
Of loyal nature, and of noble mind'."

He gave a short laugh.

"Not much of that here!"

This time she quoted from the book of Common Prayer.

"'Envy, hatred, and malice, and all uncharitableness'. Where these are present, you have the ingredients of a crime."

"Well, I suppose that's true. At least none of these people seem to mind treading on each other's corns. You must have had a pleasant evening—I don't wonder you were ready to go to bed by half past nine. Let us come back to Meriel Ford for a minute. I don't expect a definite answer to this, but if you have any kind of impression on the subject, I shall be interested to know what it is. She went out in pursuit of Geoffrey Ford, and so far as anyone will admit, that was the last time she was seen alive. Did you have any idea from her manner that her following him might have been just an excuse for getting out of the room—like his saying that he was

216

going to write letters? Or did you think she had a serious interest in getting him to come back?"

Miss Silver pulled on her ball of wool. After a moment she said,

"I cannot answer that directly. From what I have been told, and from what I have myself observed, Meriel was one of those people who crave to be the centre of attention. She was noticeably vexed and jealous because of Mr. Rutherford's attentions to Janet Johnstone. Her references to Mrs. Trent suggested a personal resentment. She evinced jealous ill feeling towards Mrs. Geoffrey. She was, I think, anxious to attract and keep the attention of both Mr. Rutherford and Mr. Ford."

He said, "You don't miss much, do you!"

She gave him a grave smile.

"I was for some time engaged in the scholastic profession. Human nature shows itself very plainly in the schoolroom. 'The Child is father of the Man,' as Mr. Wordsworth says."

He nodded.

"Do you think she followed Geoffrey Ford? We know she did go out. He admits that he went to see Mrs. Trent. If she followed him there, what took her to the pool?"

Miss Silver knitted thoughtfully. After a moment she said,

"I walked down to the general shop and post office this morning. It is very nearly opposite to the Lodge occupied by Mrs. Trent. She came out and walked along the road to the bus stop. After the bus had left, the little boy came out and ran off up the road to the Vicarage. I thought it a good opportunity to observe the surroundings of the Lodge. The actual entrance, as you doubtless know, is within the drive. I walked up the flagged path to the front door and afterwards skirted the house. The sitting-room windows look towards the garden. There is a wide bed under them, neglected and

217

full of weeds. There are bushes of lavender and rosemary in sad need of pruning. You will remember that it rained yesterday morning. The streets were still wet when my train got in, but it has been dry since then. The soil in the bed was soft and damp. It retained the clear evidence that a woman had stood outside that window for some little time. The footprints are deep, especially that of the right foot. If you will look at them yourself you will, I think, agree that a woman did stand there at some time after it had rained, and that she was leaning forward on her right foot. Such an attitude would suggest that she was either listening or looking in. To maintain her balance she would have had to rest her hands upon the windowsill. Perhaps a test for fingerprints would determine whether this woman was Meriel Ford."

Martin said suddenly and irrelevantly,

"Have you been in Ledshire before, Miss Silver?"

She smiled.

"Yes, Superintendent."

"Then I think I have heard of you. Inspector Crisp and Inspector Drake have both mentioned your name. I think you met Crisp over the affairs of the Catherine-Wheel and the Brading Collection. And Drake—yes, Drake was on the Brading case too. Your name was mentioned, but it had slipped my memory." He was remembering what he had heard. Crisp had been angry and jealous, but she had been right, and he had been wrong. And Crisp was no fool. "If I may say so, no one would suspect you of being a detective."

Miss Silver began to put her knitting away.

"I have often found that a considerable help," she said.

218

CHAPTER 34

Ellie Page lay in a state of dazed wretchedness. She made no effort to rouse herself. As long as she did not move, perhaps they would leave her alone. She took the bread-and-milk which Mary brought her in the morning, the bowl of soup and the custard pudding at lunch-time. Mary held them to her lips spoonful by spoonful and she swallowed them. If she had refused, they would have sent for the doctor. So she took them, and turned her face into the pillow again. And at tea-time when she had swallowed a cup of hot milk Mary brought water to wash her face, and then sat down by the bedside.

"Ellie, I've got to talk to you."

She looked with imploring eyes.

"If I don't, John will."

She had to say it, because it was the truth. There had to be an explanation between her and Ellie, or John would come up and force one on his own account. It seemed dreadful with Ellie lying there as white as the bed linen, but they couldn't go on like this, and if there was anything to be told it had better be told to her. She said,

"Ellie, it's no use—you'll have to tell me what you have been doing. John came home very much upset last night. Someone had told him you were meeting Geoffrey Ford at night. That was why I came up to your room. He said I must

219

ask you about it, or he would. Then, when I came up, the door was locked and you weren't there."

"How did you get in?"

The trembling words were the first she had spoken, and Mary was thankful to hear them. There is nothing so frustrating as a dumb resistance, and nothing that is harder to break.

"The spare room key fits your lock. When I found the room was empty I had to wait till you came back. And then you fainted."

"You frightened me. Dreadfully."

She could only just catch the words, but at least they were being spoken. Mary steeled herself.

"Ellie, is it true that you have been meeting Geoffrey Ford?"

There was a faint affirmative movement of the head. Ellie's frightened eyes looked, and looked away. Tears brimmed up in them and began to run slowly down over the pale cheeks.

"Oh, Ellie!"

With sudden energy Ellie pushed the bedclothes away from her chin.

"We loved each other!"

Mary Lenton said,

"He had no right to tell you so. He has a wife."

"He doesn't love her! He couldn't! Nobody could!"

"He married her."

"He didn't want to—her father and mother made him!"

"Because he had made love to her and wanted to back out. Suppose it had been you. Suppose he hadn't a wife now and John made him marry you. Would you feel it was quite all right for him to run after the next girl he fancied?"

Ellie choked on a sob.

"You're cruel!"

220

"I've got to be. I've got to know. Ellie, how far has this gone? You're not—you're not—you didn't faint because—"

A pale blush ran up to the roots of Ellie's hair.

"I wouldn't—I didn't! It wasn't like that at all! We cared, and when you feel like that, you've got to meet somehow, and it was too difficult in the day—people talk so in a village, and Edna is so jealous."

Mary felt an immense relief. It was bad enough, but it might have been worse. She said,

"Oh, Ellie! What would you feel like if it was your husband who was meeting silly girls in the middle of the night?"

Ellie pulled herself up in the bed.

"It wasn't—it wasn't like that at all! You simply don't understand! It was all tied up with Adriana! Geoffrey hasn't any money, and she would have cut off his allowance if he had left Edna. He was only waiting—we were waiting—until—until—he got the money she has always promised him."

"You mean in her will?"

Ellie nodded.

"And then he would be able to get Edna to give him his freedom, and we could be married."

There was a silence. Ellie fidgeted with the sheet. Even as she spoke, the words were bitter in her mouth. The thought of marriage with Geoffrey Ford brought no glow with it. There had been a time when it would have warmed and quickened her. It did not warm her now. When she said, "We loved each other," the words had no strength in them. They did not drive away the cold, sick feeling at her heart. The defiant stare which she had fixed upon Mary began to waver. She looked away.

Mary Lenton said,

"Adriana might live for twenty years. Were you going to

221

wait all that time and wish for her to die? It's not very nice—is it? And do you suppose that Geoffrey would stick to you for twenty years? Don't you know that he isn't sticking to you now? Don't you know perfectly well what anyone else can see? He is just a philanderer who will flirt with any woman who lets him. Why, it's the talk of the village that he is having an affair with Esmé Trent!"

The tears were pouring down Ellie's face.

"She is wicked—"

"She is doing what you were willing to do—she is taking another woman's husband. Here, you had better have my handkerchief. . . . Ellie, I'm not saying this to be unkind, but I've got to make you see. Where did you go last night?"

Ellie said in a choking voice,

"He was—with her—I went to see—"

"Oh, Ellie dear!"

"They were there—together. I was—outside—in the cold—"

Mary leaned forward and caught her wrist.

"Then how—how did you get your skirt and jumper wet?"

She got a terrified stare and a gasped "I didn't!"

"They were soaked through."

Ellie said, "No—no—"

She slid down against the pillows and fainted.

222

CHAPTER 35

Ninian followed Janet into the nursery and shut the door.

"Janet, I want you to go away."

"Adriana wants me to stay until after the inquest."

"Why?"

"I don't know. I said I would."

"I don't want you to be here. You had to come back to see the police, but there's no earthly need for you to stay. I'll drive you into Ledbury, and you can get up to town by daylight."

She shook her head.

"I said I'd stay."

"And I say I don't want you to. For all we know, we've got a homicidal maniac on the premises, and I want you off them before anything else happens."

She said, "That's nonsense!"

"Is it? That's just you keeping up your character for being sensible, and you ought to know that it won't go down with me. Are you going to tell me you didn't get the wind up when the Superintendent was talking about niblicks? If you didn't, why did you go hiding your face on my shoulder and quivering like an aspen?"

"I didn't!"

"My child, you did. Quite the best imitation of an aspen in my long and varied experience. If I hadn't put my arm round you, you would probably have swooned."

"I don't swoon!"

"You don't know what you can do until you've done it." He put his arms round her and said in a melting voice, "Darling, please go away. I do love you so."

She gave a little shaky laugh.

"You don't really."

"Really—absolutely—finally. My jo Janet!"

"Ninian, I can't."

"Why can't you?"

"I said I'd stay."

It was in her mind that if she gave way to him now she would be giving way all along the line, and before she knew what was happening they would be married and she would be living in the flat with the flowery curtains. The mere fact that this made her feel as if she had just had two glasses of champagne was proof positive that it must be resisted. Marriage was the sort of thing to go into soberly and advisedly, with a due regard for the possible recurrence of another Anne Forester. It was by no means to be embarked upon with a swimming head, a beating heart, and a strong disposition to cry upon Ninian's shoulder. She said,

"You think you love me now because we've been away from each other and we're all worked up."

He shook his head.

"I don't *think* I love you—I know it. I always have, and I always shall. And I want you to go up to London tonight."

They went on talking. She wouldn't move from her point. Adriana had asked her to stay until after the inquest, and she thought it was the right thing to do. Also Star was almost certain to ring up and want more things brought up to town for her or for Stella.

These considerations and the frame of mind they induced

served to insulate them from the atmosphere of dullness and gloom which prevailed in the family circle. Adriana had withdrawn into an almost complete silence in which she contemplated the break-up of her present way of life. Geoffrey Ford talked fitfully about the weather, about the political situation, about anything that came into his head except the subject which filled their thoughts. Nobody mentioned golfclubs, or the police, or the fact that they would all have to attend another inquest within the next day or two, and that this time the verdict would not be accidental death but wilful murder.

There was some general conversation during the evening meal, but when the party had moved to the drawing-room Adriana took up a book, Geoffrey retired behind a newspaper, and with the chairs so disposed as to leave a sofa between the windows for Ninian and Janet, the talk in the circle about the fire was confined to Miss Silver and Edna Ford.

Conversations in which Edna participated could usually be taken as heard. There was a kind of plaintive pattern about them, since whatever the other person had to say, Edna did not so much respond as just go on talking about the rise in prices, the difficulty of getting household help and the deterioration in its quality, together with such kindred subjects as her own health, the lack of consideration it received, and the general decline of everything in every direction. The extreme inconvenience of old houses was her present theme.

"Of course one can't really expect comfort in any house which is more than a hundred years old. This house is a great deal older than that—and so low-lying. Of course they had to build down by the river in those days because of the water supply. Most insanitary."

Adriana lifted her eyes from her book. She was at a sufficient distance to make it possible that the criticism had not

225

reached her, but on the other hand it was not impossible that it had. Her look did not, however, convey any impression of offence. It rested thoughtfully upon Edna for a moment and then went back to a page which had not been turned for quite a long time. She turned it now.

Edna sat there quite undisturbed in the old black dress which she considered appropriate to the fact that there had been a death in the family. Like the coat and skirt which she had worn for the funeral the day before, it sagged over the shoulders and made it plain that she had been losing weight. Above the high neck, unrelieved by so much as a row of pearls, her skin was lifeless and sallow. There was no colour about her anywhere—not in the pale eyes, the straw-coloured lashes, or the faded hair. Even the tints of her embroidery silks were faint. She took a stitch and said,

"The plumbing is dreadfully old-fashioned. It takes far too much fuel to heat the water, and I do not—I do *not* consider that Mrs. Simmons understands the range. It simply eats coal, and she has no idea of economy. Now, in one of those nice modern little houses one would get about twice as much hot water for a much lower expenditure."

Miss Silver smiled encouragingly. She held quite pronounced views upon the general inconvenience of old houses, but she would not have considered it courteous to say so in the—possible—hearing of her hostess. She had, however, no desire to prevent Edna Ford from saying anything she chose. Having smiled, she observed that many of the houses now being built were of a quite convenient type, though they had not, of course, the romantic associations of the older buildings.

Edna responded in a complaining voice.

"All these old houses were built when people had armies

of servants. Now a small modern villa would be so easily run, and it is so much more comfortable to live in a road with proper pavements and street-lighting. I have never really got accustomed to going out by myself in the dark. It always makes me nervous. Why, last winter after I had been having tea at the Vicarage I was coming up the drive. Of course I had my torch—I wouldn't go anywhere without one—and Geoffrey said perhaps that was what attracted it. But it was really most startling—a great owl swooped right down over my head. It gave me quite a bad shock, coming down suddenly like that without any sound and looking all white."

Miss Silver pulled on her ball of wool.

"A most unpleasant experience."

"I haven't been out by myself since—it made me so nervous. Now before I married, when we lived in Ledchester, I used not to mind going out at all. There were four of us, so there was always someone to come and go with, and the streets were very well lighted. And of course there are more men in a town. In the country there are so few." She leaned towards Miss Silver and dropped her voice. "That is the worst of it—those that there are get so run after. It doesn't matter whether they are married or not, they are *pursued!* And the young women don't seem to have any shame about it. That woman they were talking about upstairs, Esmé Trent—always ringing Geoffrey up and wanting to play golf with him!"

"Indeed?"

Edna nodded.

"It isn't easy to find excuses when you are asked point-blank. Of course she never asked *me*. Not that I should have played if she had—I am not really strong enough. I gave it up years ago."

"Mrs. Trent is fond of the game?"

"She is fond of anything that will help her to get hold of a man. She has quite *persecuted* Geoffrey. And you know what men are—they grumble about that sort of thing, but it flatters them."

Miss Silver wondered if any of this was reaching the ears of Geoffrey Ford. He and Adriana were on one side of the wide hearth, and she and Mrs. Geoffrey on the other. The *Times* screened him from view, and he appeared to be reading it page by page. Every now and then he turned it inside out with a loud rustling noise. He might be listening, or he might not. She thought it was unlikely that his wife's conversation would arouse any interest, unless Mrs. Trent's name had caught his attention. In any case it would be quite difficult for him to hear what had been said. It was obvious that Edna Ford desired to minimize the effect which she might have produced upon Miss Silver with her outburst about Esmé Trent. Geoffrey was to be presented not as the hunter but the hunted, Mrs. Trent as the brazen woman in pursuit of a reluctant prey. And if there were to be any enquiries about golfclubs, it was to be made quite clear that Esmé Trent was a devotee of the game.

Glancing momentarily in Adriana's direction, she thought the fine eyes held a sardonic gleam. They met hers for the briefest possible space, but she no longer felt sure that Mrs. Geoffrey's conversation had not been overheard.

When they went up to bed this suspicion was confirmed. Adriana followed her into her room, enquired perfunctorily whether she had everything she wanted, and closing the door behind her, moved to a comfortable chintz-covered chair by the fire and sat down upon one of the padded arms. She nodded in the direction of the electric blaze.

"I told Meeson to light it. It's chilly tonight, and it's horrid coming up to a cold room, and even though Edna says so, old houses in the country are cold." Her eyebrows lifted in a quizzical manner and she continued. "Well, you know now practically everything there is to know about her—don't you? They live here because they haven't enough money to live anywhere else, and she hates every minute of it. Geoffrey, on the other hand, finds it extremely agreeable. As she was observing, personable men are at a premium in this sort of neighbourhood. Geoffrey is a personable man, and he likes being at a premium. I don't think his affairs are very serious. But of course there is this drawback to the country, that everyone is bound to know about them, and they certainly don't lose anything in the mouths of the gossips. Meeson tells me there's been talk about the parson's cousin. Nice for the Vicarage!" She laughed without amusement. "She's the one who teaches the children, and it's rather too bad of Geoffrey, but I daresay she met him half way. Those delicate clinging creatures often do. They want a man to prop them, and there just aren't enough to go round—at least not in a place like Ford."

Miss Silver had sat down on the other side of the hearth. She said,

"I think I saw her when I walked into the village. She did not look at all strong."

Adriana frowned.

"No. Of course there's nothing in it, and Edna is absurdly jealous. She got Geoffrey herself against not very serious competition and under the very capable management of her mother. When he tried to wriggle out of it the father stepped in. I believe Geoffrey thought I should cut him out of my will if he figured in a breach of promise case, so he threw in his hand. Edna's idea of heaven is to go back to Ledchester or

229

one of the London suburbs and live in a six-roomed house with every modern convenience. One of the suburbs would really be best from her point of view, because there are always plenty of men in a suburb. They work in London, but they come home to play, so Geoffrey wouldn't be the only pebble on the beach. All the same she is every kind of a fool, because wherever they go there will be other women, and wherever there are other women Geoffrey will run after them. She'll never change him."

Miss Silver said, "Why don't you let her go?"

Adriana shrugged.

"She wouldn't go without Geoffrey, and I shouldn't care to live here without a man in the house. Edna can do as she likes when I'm gone. Did I tell you I had left their share to her for her life?"

Miss Silver said, "Yes."

Adriana gave a short laugh.

"I don't want Geoffrey to leave her. He would if the money were his, or even half of it. She would crack up if he did, and as long as she holds the purse-strings he won't. Besides, he's a fool about women, and I don't care for the idea of, say, Esmé Trent spending my money."

Miss Silver had put down her knitting-bag. She sat with her hands folded in her lap and looked earnestly at Adriana.

"Miss Ford, you are making a mistake."

"Am I?" The dark eyes met hers with a touch of scorn.

"I think so. And as you have engaged my professional services, I feel that I owe you an honest opinion. It is a mistake to employ financial arguments to induce or constrain the actions of others. Deplorable repercussions may be set up. Since I entered this household I have been struck by the absence of any kindly feeling between its members. I exclude Mr.

230

Rutherford and Miss Johnstone who do not properly belong to it, and who are very obviously in love with one another."

Adriana looked at her with something like anger. She sustained the look, and continued with quiet authority.

"You yourself were able to believe that someone in the house was attempting your life. It seemed to me that you were not really able to exclude anyone from this suspicion."

Adriana said, "Not Star—not Ninian."

"I did not think that you were sure even about them. That was the first thing that struck me, that there was no reaction such as would be felt where there was genuine confidence and affection."

Adriana's lips were dry. She moved them to say, "Are there many people of whom you can feel quite sure?"

Miss Silver was conscious of a humble thankfulness as she said, "Yes."

The dry lips spoke again.

"You are fortunate. Go on."

"I found a painful sense of strain between Mr. and Mrs. Geoffrey, and between Miss Meriel and everyone else in the house. She neither liked anyone, nor was she liked. Last night she met with a tragic death, and it is difficult to avoid the conclusion that she was killed because she knew too much about the death of Mabel Preston. We know that four people overheard Meeson say that a scrap of her dress had been found by the pool. We know that this scrap indicates that she was in the neighbourhood of the pool at about the time that Mabel Preston was drowned. Any of those four people may have passed on what they had overheard. If this information reached the murderer, there must have been an instant and dangerous reaction. The person who might have been seen at the pool on that Saturday night stood in immediate danger. Only immediate action could prevent disclosure. I believe that action was taken."

Adriana said, "Yes." Just the one word coming from the depths of her voice.

There was a silence in the room. When it had lasted for some time Miss Silver said in a thoughtful tone,

"In addition to the four people who heard what Meeson said about Miss Meriel's presence at the pool, there are three more names which should perhaps be mentioned."

"What names?"

"My own, for one. I would like to take the opportunity of assuring you that I did not speak of the matter to anyone. Can you say the same about yourself?"

Adriana's hand lifted from her knee and fell again.

"I did not speak of it." Then, after a pause, "You said three names."

Miss Silver watched her closely.

"I was thinking of Meeson."

She saw Adriana start and flush. She spoke with anger and emphasis.

"Oh, no! Not Meeson!"

"She had the knowledge."

"I said, 'Not Meeson'."

"You have said that Mrs. Geoffrey would like to leave Ford. Is she the only one? Does Meeson like living in the country?"

"What do you think!" Adriana gave a short laugh. "She loathes it. She's a Londoner. It's not a suburb she hankers after, but the real thing. She's always at me to pack up this place and go and take a flat just round the corner from where we used to be."

"She knows that you have provided for her in your will?"

"She knows most things about me. And you won't get

232

me to believe that it's Gertie Meeson who has been playing tricks on me for the sake of what I've left her! You will never get me to believe that!"

"So there is one person about whom you do feel sure."

Adriana got up.

"Oh, yes, I'm sure about Gertie," she said.

CHAPTER 36

When Superintendent Martin left Ford House he had a good deal to think about. In the upshot he betook himself to see Randal March, the Chief Constable of Ledshire. After some preliminaries on the subject of the death of Meriel Ford and the fact that there was now indisputable proof that she had been murdered, Martin said in rather a tentative manner,

"There is a Miss Silver staying in the house there."

There had been a time when the handsome and robust Chief Constable was a spoiled and delicate little boy. He had not been considered strong enough to go to school, and had therefore shared his sisters' lessons for some years beyond the usual time. Over that schoolroom Miss Maud Silver had presided with a firmness and tact which won his entire respect and affection. She had always kept up with the family, and when in later years their paths crossed again he found both the affection and the respect enhanced. He was then Inspector March, and she no longer a governess. They came together over the affair of the Poisoned Caterpillars, and he most gratefully admitted that her skill and courage had saved his life. He had encountered her in her professional capacity a good many times since then.

He looked in a considering fashion at the Superintendent and said,

"I know Miss Silver very well indeed."

"I thought I remembered her name, sir. Hadn't she something to do with that business at the Catherine-Wheel?"

Randal March nodded.

"She has had something to do with quite a number of cases in Ledshire. How does she come into this one?"

Martin told him.

"And what does she say about it all?"

Martin told him that too, finishing up with, "And what I was wondering was just what notice—"

The Chief Constable laughed.

"I should advise you to take quite a lot of notice of anything she puts forward! I won't say she is never wrong, but I will say that she is usually right. She has a very just, acute and penetrating mind, and she has what the police can never have, the opportunity of seeing people off their guard. We come in after a crime, and we get everyone in a state of jitters. This may make a guilty person give himself away, but it also makes innocent people act as if they were guilty, especially in a murder case. It is astonishing how often there is something they want to hide. We turn a searchlight on them, and they all start trying to cover up. But Miss Silver sees them when we have shut the door behind us and gone away. They draw a long breath of relief and relax. The innocent ones confide in her—she is astonishingly easy to confide in—and the guilty get the feeling that they have been too clever for the police. I have seen it produce remarkable results."

Martin said, "Well, sir, she's easy to talk to, and that's a fact. I was hoping I hadn't said too much."

"She is perfectly discreet."

"And she was right about the footprints under that window and the fingerprints on the sill. Someone stood and listened there all right. Only it wasn't Meriel Ford—the fingerprints are not hers." He went on talking to the Chief Constable.

It was not until next morning that he returned to Ford House. He asked for Miss Silver, and waited for her in the small room where they had talked before. When she came in he took the hand she offered him, waited for her to be seated, and then came out with,

"Well, we've investigated the fingerprints on the outside of the sitting-room at the Lodge, and they're good enough and clear enough, but they weren't made by Miss Meriel Ford."

Miss Silver allowed herself to say, "Dear me!"

He nodded.

"You thought they would be hers, didn't you? Well, they're not, and that's that. Both the footprints and the fingerprints are out. And they're not Mrs. Trent's, or the boy's either. She made no trouble about letting us take them for comparison. Well, we compared them with the prints from up here. It did cross my mind that they might be Mrs. Geoffrey's, but that's out too, and so are all the others. Of course there's nothing to say just when they were made, but they were fresh. Then whilst we were about it we went over the front door, and the passage, and the door into the sitting-room. Miss Meriel's prints were there all right. Nothing you could swear to on the handles—too much of a mix up with Mrs. Trent's and the little boy's—but a good clear print of her left hand on the wall of the passage, as if she had come in in the

235

dark and been feeling her way, and one of the right hand on the jamb of the sitting-room door as if she had stood there to listen.''

"Then she was there.''

"Oh, yes, she was there all right! And the question is, did Geoffrey Ford walk home with her? Or follow her? And how did he get her to go to the pool?''

"You suspect him of the murder?''

"What do you think yourself?''

"If Miss Preston was deliberately pushed into the pool— and it begins to look as if she was—then we have to consider why anyone should have pushed her. The only shadow of a motive suggested by anyone is the one put forward by yourself. You say she was wearing a coat of a very marked and unusual pattern which belonged to Adriana Ford, and you suggest that the person who attacked her did so under the impression that she *was* Adriana Ford. Now there is no evidence on this point at all, but whereas, so far as we know, no one benefited by the death of Mabel Preston, quite a number of people stood to benefit under the will of Adriana Ford. Miss Ford was quite frank on the subject. She has provided handsomely for the Simmons and for the maid, Meeson, who used to be her dresser. There is a legacy to Mr. Rutherford, but the main beneficiaries are Mrs. Somers, Meriel Ford, and Mr. and Mrs. Geoffrey Ford. Any one of these people had a motive for her death. Any one of them could have slipped out of that cocktail party and pushed Mabel Preston into the pool under the impression they were pushing Miss Ford. Well, there we are—and no evidence to show that any of them did it.''

Miss Silver sat in an attitude of gentle composure. Her eyes rested on Superintendent Martin's face with an expression

236

of most gratifying attention. Detective Inspector Frank Abbott of Scotland Yard was wont to say that she had the same effect upon him as the match-box has upon the match—she enabled him to produce the illuminating spark. He was, as Miss Silver very frequently pointed out, addicted to talking in a very extravagant manner when not on duty. But it is certain that Superintendent Martin was experiencing a somewhat similar feeling. He was conscious of an unusually clear train of thought and of the power of putting it into words. He would not, perhaps, have admitted that Miss Silver had anything to do with this, but it is a fact that he found her a very stimulating listener. He continued in the same vein.

"Then we come to the death of Meriel Ford—a strong young woman and, unlike Mabel Preston, sober. She couldn't just be pushed down into the pool and drowned. She was hit over the head with a golfclub and put in the pool to make sure. And when you come to the motive in her case, we get that shred of stuff which you found caught in the hedge. It proves that she was down by the pool between half past six and the time Meeson saw her with coffee all down the front of her dress. That would be about an hour. The medical evidence puts Mabel Preston's death within that time. The moment these facts became known the person who murdered Mabel Preston would realize that he was in danger—if there was such a person. Just for the moment I am assuming that there was. Well then, out of the possible suspects, Mrs. Somers is the only one who is in the clear. She wasn't at the cocktail party, she didn't know about that shred of stuff, and she wasn't here when Meriel Ford was killed. But all the others knew. Simmons and Ninian Rutherford were in the hall when Meriel was accusing Meeson of telling tales about the piece of stuff, and the Geoffrey Fords were on the landing.

237

Geoffrey Ford went down to see Mrs. Trent that evening. Meriel Ford followed him out of the drawing-room. You suggested that she might have followed him to the Lodge. I think there is evidence that she did so, and that she stood listening at the sitting-room door. Would it have been in her character to let it stop at that?"

"I think not, Superintendent. She had an impulsive temperament and a fondness for scenes."

He nodded.

"So I am told. From what I've heard of her, I should say she would have burst in on them, especially if they happened to be talking about her. Well, this is where I put some more questions to Mr. Geoffrey Ford." He got up, but before he reached the door he turned again. "I suppose you would say that you are representing Miss Ford?"

"She has engaged my services professionally."

He nodded.

"That being the case, and as far as I am concerned, I should make no objection if you care to be present. Of course he may object, in which case—"

Miss Silver smiled graciously.

"You are too good, Superintendent. I should be very much interested."

Martin rang the bell, and when Simmons appeared asked him to tell Mr. Ford that he would like to see him.

Geoffrey came into the room in his usual easy manner. He had had a good night—he could not in point of fact remember that he had ever had a bad one—and with even the short lapse of time since his interview with the police he had been able to persuade himself that he had made a favourable impression, and that all would now be well. These things were a nine days' wonder, but they soon died down and were forgotten. Once the inquest and the funeral were over, they would all be able to go back to their usual way of life. Meanwhile he supposed that there were formalities which the police had to attend to, and that they would naturally have recourse to him as the man of the house. His manner was pleasant and assured as he said,

"Oh, good-morning, Superintendent. What can I do for you?"

"There are just a few questions I should like to put to you, Mr. Ford. As Miss Silver tells me she has been professionally retained by Miss Adriana Ford, you will not, perhaps, object to her presence."

Geoffrey stared. He wasn't going to refuse, but his voice stiffened as he said,

"Oh, no, of course not."

"Then shall we sit down?"

Geoffrey's colour deepened a shade. He didn't care about being asked to sit down in what he regarded as his own house. He took a chair and sat as for a business interview. The Superintendent followed his example. His tone was grave as he said,

"Mr. Ford, I have to ask you if you have nothing to add to your account of the events on the night of Miss Meriel Ford's death."

"I don't think so."

"When I asked you whether she accompanied you on your visit to Mrs. Trent at the Lodge, you said of course not—she would not have gone there without being asked. You are quite sure she did not go there with you?"

"Of course I'm sure! Why should she?"

"Mr. Ford, please think very carefully before you answer this. You say that Miss Meriel Ford did not accompany you to the Lodge. What I am asking you now is, did she follow you there?"

"Why should she?"

"She left the drawing-room in search of you. You had not been gone very long, but you say that you had already left the house by way of the study window."

"I must have done."

"Why must?"

"Because I didn't see her."

"Going out by the French window like that, you must have left it unlocked behind you?"

"Yes."

"Then she had only to try the handle to know that you had gone out."

"Why should she try the handle?"

Martin said in an authoritative voice,

"Mr. Ford, I have a pretty extensive account of the conversation in the drawing-room both before and after you left it. Miss Meriel Ford was sarcastic on the subject of your having letters to write, and made it quite clear that she believed you were going to see Mrs. Trent. You said you were going to the study to write letters. When she found that you were not there, it seems to me that it would be quite natural for her to try the glass door, and if she found it open to follow you."

Geoffrey Ford looked at him haughtily. He considered himself to be an easy-going man, but his temper was becoming rasped. He said,

"That is just supposition!"

Martin returned his look very directly.

"Not entirely. We have found a good fresh print of her left hand on the wall between the front door and the living-room

240

at the Lodge, and another of her right hand high up on the jamb of the living-room door. Any prints on the handle would, of course, have been overlaid, but the two I have mentioned are clear and recent. The one on the jamb points to the probability that she stood by that door and listened. Both you and Mrs. Trent must know whether she entered that room or not. It seems very improbable that she would come to the door of the very room you were in and go no farther, and it is not in keeping with what I have heard of her character. She was not a timid person, and by all accounts she had no objection to a scene."

Geoffrey Ford had begun to feel cold. If he went on saying that Meriel hadn't followed him and they found any more of those damned fingerprints inside the living-room, he would be sunk. He tried to remember just what Meriel had done. She had burst into the room and made a scene. This blasted policeman was right about that—there was nothing she liked better! But had she touched anything? He didn't think she had. She had stood there and waved her hands about, all very theatrical. And just before she went she had stooped down and picked something up. He hadn't noticed what it was at the time—he hadn't really thought about it. But now, when he was trying to remember, it came back to him. The thing she had picked up was a handkerchief. Her hand had gone down empty, and had come up with a little screwed-up handkerchief clutched in the palm. An amber-coloured handkerchief. Esmé hadn't seen it. It was when she had turned towards him and away from Meriel. Esmé didn't see it, but it was her handkerchief. Her handkerchief, with her name on it. And it had been found in the summerhouse by the pool. He had forgotten about Meriel's fingerprints. Meriel must have taken Esmé's handkerchief to the pool. She must

241

have dropped it in the summerhouse. Deliberately. He stared at Superintendent Martin, and heard him say,

"I shall have to ask you to accompany me to the Station for further questioning."

CHAPTER 37

Miss Silver made good progress with the white woolly shawl that morning. She found the process of knitting very conducive to thought, the gentle rhythmical movement of the needles forming a barrier against small inevitable distractions. Behind this barrier she found herself able to pursue the careful examination of motive, character, and action. When she had reached certain conclusions she put her work away in the flowered knitting-bag and went up to her bedroom.

Emerging a little later in the black cloth coat, the hat which she considered suitable for a morning walk—older and with less trimming than the one in which she had travelled down—the neat laced shoes, the woollen gloves, and the elderly fur tippet, she encountered Meeson, charged with a message. Adriana would like to see her—"And if you ask me, Miss Silver, it's time somebody did. There's just one thing she ought to be doing and doing it quick, and that's packing up and getting out of here before the whole lot of us get murdered. And if I've said it to her once I've said it to her twenty times since poor old Mabel got pushed in the pool. 'If anyone would do it to her, they'd do it to you or to me!' I said. 'As soon as look at us! And sooner! For once murdering takes hold of anyone they don't know how to stop, and that's a fact. First poor old Mabel that you wouldn't have thought had an enemy in the world, and then Meriel, and no one knows who next!' And all I get out of her is, 'Gertie, for God's sake stop talking!' "

Adriana was standing by the window staring out. She turned as Miss Silver entered, and came over to her, limping more noticeably than she had done since her visit to Montague Mansions. When she spoke her voice was harsh.

"Geoffrey isn't back."

"It is only twelve o'clock. He would hardly have had time."

"What does 'further questioning' mean? I should have thought they had asked us everything in the world already!"

Miss Silver said gravely, "They are not satisfied with his answers."

"Why?" She threw the word at Miss Silver.

"They do not think that he is telling the truth."

"What do you think?"

"That he has not been frank with them."

Adriana made an impatient gesture.

"Oh, Geoffrey will shuffle if he is in a tight place. But that is not to say that he would murder anyone. He wouldn't. He likes everything to be easy and pleasant, and if he gets in a mess he tries to blarney his way out of it. If you think he would do anything violent, you're not such a good detective as you're cracked up to be."

Miss Silver infused a slight distance into her manner.

"I am not prepared to offer any opinion at the moment."

Adriana dropped wearily into a chair.

"I don't know why we're standing, except that I can't rest. Do you know what Edna said? That's one of the things that has got me worked up like this. I met her on the landing after

243

Geoffrey had gone away with the Superintendent, and she said—she had the nerve to say—that at any rate if they kept Geoffrey in Ledbury, he wouldn't be able to go running after Esmé Trent! I didn't lose my temper—not then—but I wasn't going to let that pass. I asked her pointblank whether she knew what she was saying—'Do you mean to tell me you would rather he was detained on a suspicion of murder?' And all she had to say was that Esmé Trent was a wicked woman and anything that kept Geoffrey away from her would be all to the good. I did lose my temper then, and I let her have it. Nothing annoys me so much as stupidity—stupidity and obstinacy! And that's Edna all over! To hear her talk, you wouldn't think she had a mind at all, but whatever she has got, once she gets what she would call an idea into it, nobody and nothing will ever get it out again! Don't let's go on talking about her—it upsets me, and I've got enough without that! This business of Geoffrey—I can't think why he doesn't come back."

Miss Silver said gravely,

"The Superintendent was not satisfied."

Adriana made an impatient movement.

"Then he's a fool! Anyone who thinks Geoffrey is capable of violence is a damned fool! Now if it was Esmé Trent—well, I wouldn't put it past her!"

"You think she would be capable of a violent crime?"

"I think she is a completely ruthless and hard-boiled young woman. Her instincts are predatory and her moral standards low. That comes amusingly from me, doesn't it, but she neglects and illtreats her child, and I don't like women who do that. I think she is capable of anything which would be to Esmé Trent's advantage, and if she thought Geoffrey was

244

going to come in for my money, I think she would do her best to get him away from Edna and marry him."

Miss Silver gave a slight disapproving cough.

"Does she know the terms of your will—that you have left Mrs. Geoffrey a life interest in her husband's legacy?"

Adriana raised her eyebrows.

"Who is there to tell her? Geoffrey knows, because I thought it would be good for him to know, but I didn't tell Edna, and I'm perfectly sure that he wouldn't tell her—or Esmé Trent. It would take him down too many pegs! I don't see him giving Edna the whip hand or crying down his stock to Esmé! Oh, no, he'd keep a still tongue!" She made an abrupt change in her manner. "Are you going out?"

It was as if she had only just noticed that Miss Silver was in her outdoor clothes.

"I thought I should like to walk into the village. I have a letter to post."

Adriana laughed.

"Geoffrey had letters to write, and you have a letter to post! The time-honoured alibi! No one believes in it, but it serves! I don't wonder you want to get away from this house, if only for half an hour!"

On reaching the road Miss Silver turned to the left. Passing the Lodge she did not so much as glance in its direction. She had no desire to give Mrs. Trent any grounds for supposing herself to be an object of interest to Adriana's visiting friend. The point upon which her attention was fixed was the distance between the Lodge and the Vicarage, which she was now approaching. It was a very short distance, really a very short distance indeed, and both the front and the side windows of the Vicarage would command a view of the road. She had had it in her mind to call upon Mrs. Lenton with an enquiry after the health of her cousin Miss Page, but when she had still a little way to go she saw Ellie emerge from the farther gate, take a few hesitating steps along the road, and turn in to the churchyard. She wore a scarf pulled forward on her head in such a way as to hide most of her face. Miss Silver caught but one partial glimpse of it, but she received a strong impression of pallor and fragility.

Slackening her pace a little, she passed the Vicarage and followed Ellie at a discreet distance. The girl walked with painful slowness and never looked round. She took a path which skirted the church and went in through a small door at the side. It always gratified Miss Silver to find a church kept open. The weary, the wayfarer, and the sorrowful should never be denied the shelter of its walls. As she opened the door and closed it again quietly behind her she found herself in a mellow twilight. Ford Church was rich in stained glass, most of it old and carefully preserved. There was a stone tomb on her right with the figure of a Crusader. There were old brasses on the walls. The step which she had crossed had been worn by the feet of many generations.

Moving quietly forward and passing a pillar which blocked the view, she was aware of a small recessed chapel on the right. It contained a large and very ugly tomb of the late Georgian period with a portly marble gentleman in a wig supported by a number of stout cherubs. Almost concealed by these funerary ornaments, there were two or three chairs, and upon one of these chairs sat Ellie Page, her face covered with her hands and her forehead pressed against the marble of the tomb. Miss Silver passed into the nearest pew and sat down. It was plain that they were alone in the church. They might have been alone in the world, the atmosphere was so dead and still. There was a smell of old hassocks and old wood and the fine imponderable dust of centuries. There was no sound at all until Ellie began to draw those long painful breaths. They went on for a while and then ceased. The choking sobs which Miss Silver half expected did not follow. Instead there was complete silence. By moving slightly nearer the end of the pew she could see the girl's lifted profile as white and frozen as if she were part of the tomb against which her forehead had been bent. It was raised now, and her eyes stared.

CHAPTER 38

Miss Silver rose quietly to her feet and passed into the chapel. Ellie did not move. It would have been hard to say that she breathed. She seemed frozen. It wasn't until Miss Silver spoke her name and touched her gently on the shoulder that she turned her head. For the moment her eyes were blank and unaware. They looked at Miss Silver as though they did not see her. Then she drew another of those painful breaths and leaned back against the chair.

Miss Silver sat down beside her.

"You are ill, my dear."

There was a faint movement of the head, a faint sighing "No—"

"Then you are in trouble."

Consciousness came back to Ellie's eyes. The voice which spoke to her was kind—not anxious like Mary's or stern like

John Lenton's. It had a comforting warmth, a supporting authority. She had come to the end of anything she could do or think. She turned a little towards Miss Silver and said in a piteous voice,

"I don't know what to do—"

In Miss Silver's experience this usually meant that the person in distress had a perfectly clear idea of what ought to be done, but shrank from doing it. She said very gently,

"Are you quite sure that you do not know?"

She saw the girl quiver.

"They are going to send me away."

"Do you want to tell me why?"

Ellie Page said, "Everyone will know, and I shall never see him again."

"Perhaps that is what is best."

Ellie made a quick movement.

"Why do things hurt like this? If I don't see him again, I can't bear it. And if I see him—" Her voice stopped as if she had no more breath.

"You are speaking of Mr. Ford." It was not put as a question.

Ellie gasped.

"Everyone knows—Mary said so—"

"There has been a little talk. I do not think that it amounts to very much. Mr. Ford has that kind of way with him. People do not take him very seriously."

"I did."

"That was a pity, my dear. He has other obligations. To neglect them was bound to cause unhappiness."

Ellie repeated what she said before.

"They are going to send me away."

"That might be wise, at any rate for a time."

Ellie's hands held one another tightly.

"You don't understand."

Miss Silver said, "In order that I may do so, I should like to ask you one or two questions."

There was a shaking movement. Ellie said,

"Oh—"

"It may be important for you to answer them. I hope that you will do so. Some of the Vicarage windows have a good view of the road leading away from the church. Is your bedroom window one of them?"

There was a faint movement of the head which said, "Yes—"

"Will you tell me which window it is?"

"It is the one at the side where the pear-tree is."

"If you were to look from that window on a clear night you would be able to see if anyone came down the road from Ford House. The moon was almost full last night. Even though there was a good deal of cloud, the night was not dark. Mr. Ford came down that road on the night before last at about half past eight. If you had been looking out of your window you could have seen him. I do not mean that you could have recognized him, but if he came down that road and turned in at Mrs. Trent's you would be in very little doubt as to who it was. And you might have been sufficiently distressed to feel that you must make quite sure."

Ellie stared.

"How—do—you—know?" The words could hardly be heard.

Miss Silver said in a compassionate tone,

"You were very unhappy. Did you climb down the pear-tree? You had done it before, had you not? And you went to the Lodge, but you did not knock at the door or go in. You went round to the sitting-room window, and you stood there and leaned on the sill and listened. The window was open, was it not? Miss Page—what did you hear?"

It was like the Day of Judgment. These were things that no one knew. But this stranger knew them. She was Adriana Ford's friend who had come on a visit on the day of Mabel Preston's funeral. How did she know the secret things that were hidden in your heart? If she knew them, it wasn't any good to try to hide them. And because she was a stranger it didn't matter so much. It didn't matter what you said to a stranger like this. She wouldn't be grieved like Mary, or condemn like John. And if she told the terrible things that crowded in her mind, perhaps they would go away and leave her to find some kind of help and peace again. She said faintly and with stumbling words,

"I heard—them talking—Geoffrey and—her—"

"Mrs. Trent?"

"Yes—"

"What did they say?"

"Geoffrey said, 'She saw us there,' and Esmé said, 'She couldn't speak the truth if she tried.' They were talking about Meriel."

"You are sure about that?"

"I thought it was Edna at first when Esmé said, 'She's as jealous as hell.' But it wasn't, because Geoffrey said Meriel would like anyone to make a pass at her, and that she was out to make trouble."

"Did he say how she could do that?"

"Esmé said she could have seen them slip behind the curtain at the cocktail party, but she couldn't know they were anywhere near the pool, and who cared if they took a stroll in the garden? And then—and then—"

250

"Yes?"

"It was Meriel. She flung back the door and came into the room. She must have been listening. They quarrelled dreadfully. It was all about how that poor Miss Preston got drowned. Meriel talked of telling the police, and Esmé said didn't Meriel know rather a lot about it herself? She said she and Geoffrey went for a stroll on the lawn, and they were never anywhere near the pool. And Meriel said she saw them in the summerhouse."

Ellie was shaking all over. Miss Silver laid a hand on her arm.

"Wait a minute, my dear, and think of what you are saying. Do you mean that Meriel Ford stated that she had seen Mr. Geoffrey Ford and Mrs. Trent in the summerhouse by the pool on the Saturday evening that Miss Preston was drowned?"

"Oh, yes, she *did!*"

"Did she say at what time this was?"

"She said—she saw—Miss Preston—coming across the lawn when she went away. And it was true—I know it was true! Esmé said they were only taking a stroll in the garden, but they were there in the summerhouse together—I know they were! Geoffrey didn't deny it—not until she made him. They were there—*together!*"

Miss Silver said in a kind, firm voice,

"My dear, you must control yourself. I do not think you can be aware of the implications of what you have just said. It is not a question of whether Mr. Geoffrey Ford and Mrs. Trent were carrying on a most reprehensible flirtation in the summerhouse, but whether either or both of them was present at the time of Mabel Preston's death."

Ellie had been looking in front of her. She jerked round now and stared into Miss Silver's face.

"It is a question," said Miss Silver, "of whether either or both of them was responsible for that death."

Ellie said, "No—no—oh, no!" The words came out in gasps. "That is what Meriel said—she said the police would think Geoffrey had done it. But he didn't—he couldn't! She was just saying it to hurt him! She said the most terrible things! She said, 'Supposing I say I saw you push her.' And she said it was because she was wearing Adriana's coat and he thought it was Adriana. Because of the money she was going to leave him."

Miss Silver said,

"To desire what belongs to another person is a frequent cause of crime."

"Geoffrey *wouldn't*! He wouldn't do a thing like that! He didn't! Do you suppose I would have told you all this if I thought it was Geoffrey?"

Miss Silver said, "No—you do not think so."

Ellie put up a hand and pushed back her hair.

"After Meriel had gone they talked. Each of them thought the other had done it. They had heard someone coming, and they had gone different ways. Esmé asked Geoffrey if he came back and pushed Miss Preston in, and he said, 'My God, no! Did *you*?' She might have been pretending, but he wasn't. He was quite dreadfully shocked. And Esmé said he must go after Meriel and not let her ring up the police. She said he would be able to talk her round—and if everything else she said was lies, that was true. Oh, yes, that was true—he knows how to do that."

"And he went?"

"Oh, yes."

Miss Silver's thoughts were grave. Did this poor girl have no idea of just how damning all this was for Geoffrey Ford? She had heard Meriel accuse him of having pushed Mabel Preston into the pool. She had heard Esmé Trent tell him to go after Meriel and talk her round. She was a witness to the fact that he went. Could she be blind to what these things implied? There might be so extreme a case of infatuation, but she was not prepared to allow it to convince her. She said,

"And what did you do then?"

There was no colour in Ellie's lips. They parted to say,

"I went after them."

Miss Silver experienced that sense of satisfaction which comes to the thinker and to the craftsman, the poet and the artist, when the tool follows the thought, the concept takes its shape, the right word comes into its own place. There had been at first the faintest stirring of an instinct which she had learned to trust. There was as yet no evidence, but the instinct had grown stronger all the way. It might be that now when it was most needed the evidence would be forthcoming. She said in her quiet voice,

"Tell me what you did."

Ellie repeated like a gramophone record.

"I went after them. I don't know why I did. I was afraid. I wish I hadn't done it. I wish—" Her voice died away.

"Pray go on."

"They went up the drive. Geoffrey didn't catch her up. It would have been quite easy if he had wanted to, but he didn't. When they got up to the house he went in by the study window—it is round at the side. But Meriel went on."

"He did not speak to her?"

"Oh, no. She just went straight on round the house and across the lawn."

253

"You followed her?"

"I didn't know where she was going. I don't know why I wanted to know, but I did. She had a torch. When she put it on I could see her going away across the lawn to the garden where the summerhouse is, and the pool. I wondered why she was going there—I wanted to know. Then—then I got the idea that someone was—following me. When I stood still I could hear a footstep behind me. I was just by the corner of the house and Meriel was away across the lawn. I stood quite still behind a bush, and someone went by."

"Someone?"

Ellie shuddered.

Miss Silver said, "Was it Geoffrey Ford?"

Ellie's dumb reluctance was gone. The words which had been so painfully come by were pouring out. She caught at Miss Silver's arm with both her hands.

"No—no—*no!* Geoffrey went into the house. He didn't come out again—it was someone else. It wasn't Geoffrey—it *wasn't!* That's why I can be quite, quite sure he didn't—he *didn't* do anything to Meriel! It wasn't Geoffrey! It—it was a woman!"

"Are you sure about that?"

The grip on her arm was painful.

"Yes—yes—I'm sure! She came up behind me, and she went on over the lawn after Meriel. She had a torch, but she didn't put it on until Meriel had gone through the gate to the garden. She had the torch in one hand and a stick in the other. She went into the garden."

"You say she had a stick?"

Ellie caught her breath.

"It was a golfclub—one of those ones with an iron head. The light caught on it when she switched it on. She went

254

into the garden, and I stood under the bush and waited. I thought perhaps if they came back together, Meriel might be saying what she was going to do—about the police. Or if she came back alone, perhaps I could speak to her—could ask her. Oh, I know it sounds silly now, and she wouldn't have listened to me, but I felt—I felt as if I had got to do something—for Geoffrey! And then I saw the light for a moment down by the gate into the garden, and one of them came back across the lawn. I didn't know which one it was. She switched off the torch. She came past me in the dark and went into the house by the study window."

"Are you sure about that?"

"Oh, yes, I'm sure. I'm sure about all of it. I wish I wasn't. I keep going over and over it in my mind. I can't forget any of it—not the least little thing. Why do you keep on asking me whether I'm sure?"

"Because, my dear, it is very important. Everything you saw or heard that night is important. Will you pray go on?"

Ellie's hands dropped from her arm.

"I waited—I kept on waiting—"

"Why did you do that?"

"I didn't feel as if I could go away. I thought Meriel would come back."

"But you said just now that you did not know which of the two women came back from the garden."

"It wasn't Meriel—it wasn't tall enough. I knew when she went by me."

"How long did you wait?"

Ellie pushed back her hair again. She had a bewildered look.

"I don't know. It was a long time. I don't know how long it was."

255

"But in the end you came home."

Ellie repeated the words.

"In the end I came—" There was a very long pause before she said, "home."

Miss Silver said, "Did you know that Meriel Ford was dead?"

There was a look of startled horror.

"I—I—"

"I think you did. Will you tell me how?"

Ellie said in an extinguished voice,

"It was a long time. I thought she would come—but she didn't. I was giddy and I sat down. I don't know whether—I fainted—I think I did. The moon had moved a lot—I could see it behind the clouds. I thought I would go to the pool and see why Meriel didn't come. I thought I would have heard her if she had come already. I went across the lawn and through the gate to the pool, and she was there—" An uncontrollable shudder went over her.

"Pray go on."

Ellie's eyes were wide and staring.

"She was fallen down—in the pool. I tried to get her out. I couldn't lift her."

"You should have summoned help."

There was a faint negative movement of the head.

"It wouldn't—have been—any use. She was dead."

"You could not have been sure about that."

"She was dead. It was a long time. She was right down in the water. She was dead."

"You didn't tell anyone?"

"I went—home. Mary was there—in my room. I didn't tell her—I didn't tell anyone."

Miss Silver spoke slowly and gravely.

256

"You will have to tell the police."

There was a terrified movement.

"No! No!"

Miss Silver said, "Do you know that Mr. Geoffrey Ford is being detained for questioning?"

"No—" It was more of a gasp than a word.

"He is under grave suspicion, and the police have detained him for questioning. You cannot withhold this evidence."

Ellie burst into tears.

CHAPTER 39

Superintendent Martin looked at Miss Silver with that mixture of exasperation and respect which it was not unknown for her to arouse in the official breast. There had been quite a neat case against Mr. Geoffrey Ford. In addition to his own admissions, the butler Simmons had heard raised voices proceeding from the study when he passed through the hall at half past eight. It had been his intention to make up the study fire, but on hearing those angry voices he thought better of it and went back to the housekeeper's room. He had no difficulty in identifying the voices as those of Mr. Geoffrey and Miss Meriel, and he had attributed no importance to the fact that they were quarrelling, since Miss Meriel was always in a way about something. Taxed with this evidence, Geoffrey Ford admitted that Meriel had found him in the study, and that they had quarrelled there, but he continued to deny that she had accompanied him to the Lodge, or so far as he knew, that she had followed him there. On the top of this Miss Silver produced Ellie Page with her story of having overheard Meriel Ford accuse Geoffrey and Mrs. Trent of having pushed Mabel Preston into the pool. According to this statement she had accused them and threatened them with the police, after which she left the Lodge and Geoffrey followed her. Evidence that would hang Geoffrey Ford if she stuck to it in the box. She had stuck to it with him all right, and at this second time of telling there had been very little of the agitation reported by Miss Silver. She had been anxious to tell her story and careful in telling it, and again, according to Miss Silver, the narrative though more coherent and rather more ample in no way differed from its original form. All very satisfactory up to a point. But if that point was to be accepted, the whole case against Geoffrey Ford broke down, because Miss Ellie Page deposed, and stuck to it, that Geoffrey Ford had entered the house by the study window, and that it was a woman coming up from behind her who had followed Meriel across the lawn and through the gate into the enclosed garden beyond. Miss Ellie Page could be lying to protect a man with whom she had been carrying on, but her evidence did not strike him that way. She was so set on this point and so sure of it, it really didn't seem to occur to her that the earlier part of her evidence would bring him under suspicion. It was just something to be got out of the way before coming to the real point. And the real point was that she had seen a woman following Meriel Ford with a golfclub in her hand. She had seen this woman come back alone from the pool, and some considerable time later she had found Meriel lying there dead with her head and shoulders under the water. If that was to be accepted, bang went the case against Geoffrey Ford. A difficult business, taking part of a girl's evidence to build your case on and rejecting the climax to which it led. A jury either believes a witness or it doesn't. He thought the odds were that it would believe Ellie Page. Well, that left you with the good old three-card-trick and 'Spot the lady!' If a woman followed Meriel Ford, what woman was it? Again an easy answer, if it were not that Ellie Page's evidence didn't lend itself to easy answers. A woman coming up from behind and following Meriel carried the overwhelming suggestion that it would be Esmé Trent. Quite in character that she should distrust Geoffrey Ford's capacity to silence Meriel with fair words, and make sure of it by some more drastic action. She could have taken up a golfclub and followed them, seen Geoffrey go into the house, and pursued her purpose. A nice easy theory ruined by the evidence of Miss Ellie Page to the effect that she had afterwards seen the woman enter Ford House by the study door.

He had gone so far in a frowning silence. He broke in now upon his own train of thought.

"Miss Page says she saw this woman go into the house. You say you believe her evidence. Do you believe that?"

Miss Silver said composedly,

"I think she was speaking the truth."

"Your reasons?"

"She was in such a state of shock and agitation as to preclude any design in what she said. And when she repeated it to you she did not vary it. I feel sure that if it had not been securely based on fact there would have been discrepancies."

"She wants to help Geoffrey Ford."

"She believes him to be innocent. If she did not, she would recoil from him in horror."

He said,

"Well, well—about this woman. She ought to be Mrs.

259

Trent, but if you believe that she went into Ford House, why in heaven's name should Mrs. Trent do that? If she had just killed Meriel she would have every incentive to get back to the Lodge and make out that she had never left it. She could have had no possible motive for going into Ford House."

"I think as you do, Superintendent. The woman who entered Ford House was returning to it."

"Then it wasn't Mrs. Trent. And that leaves us with the six women who are known to have been in the house that night—Adriana Ford, Meeson, Mrs. Geoffrey Ford, Miss Johnstone, Mrs. Simmons, and yourself. I think perhaps we may exclude the last three."

He smiled slightly, but Miss Silver remained grave.

"Yes, I think so."

They were in the study at the Vicarage where he had interviewed Ellie Page, now handed over to Mary Lenton's care. He sat a little drawn back from the table at which John Lenton was in the habit of writing his sermons. On the right of the blotter lay a Bible and the Book of Common Prayer. Since to Miss Silver all law and justice drew its authority from these two books, the association did not seem incongruous. That the police force was upheld by what she called Providence in exactly the same way as the ministry of the Church she regarded as axiomatic.

Martin was frowning.

"Well, to start at the beginning, there's Adriana Ford herself. There doesn't seem to be any motive for her to kill her old friend—but there are old grudges as well as old friendships. Granting the first crime, she would have the same motive as anyone else for the second. She knew Meriel Ford had been down at the pool, and she was afraid of what she might have seen."

Miss Silver shook her head.

"She is a very tall woman, and she has a limp. It becomes especially noticeable by the end of the day. The woman seen by Ellie Page was not tall, and there was no mention of a limp."

The Superintendent said, "Meeson—" in a meditative voice. "Now what would Meeson's motive have been? As regards the first crime, some provision under Miss Ford's will, I suppose. Do you happen to know if it was considerable?"

"I believe that she is handsomely provided for."

"And she doesn't like living in the country. Somebody told me that—I believe it was Meriel Ford. Anyhow she's a regular Londoner—it sticks out all over her."

"She has been forty years with Miss Ford. She is devoted to her."

He nodded.

"Sometimes people have been too long together, they get on one another's nerves—you'd be surprised. Well, the other possibility is Mrs. Geoffrey Ford. Either she or Meeson would do as far as height is concerned, and so would Mrs. Trent if one could think of any reason for her going in through that study window. You don't think it was a put-up thing between her and Geoffrey Ford? Say it was like the Macbeth business—'Infirm of purpose, give me the daggers!' He hadn't the nerve to pull it off, and she had."

Miss Silver observed him with interest.

"You are a student of Shakespeare?"

"Well, I am. He knows a lot about the way people go on, doesn't he? You don't think Mrs. Trent might have come into the house to tell him she'd done the job? I don't mind saying she is the one I would pick out for it. Not many scruples, I should think."

Miss Silver gave her slight cough.

"No, Superintendent," she said. "But not one to rely upon another, or to risk anything for Geoffrey Ford. If she had committed the crime she would, I feel sure, have returned at once to the Lodge as you yourself opined."

Sitting at an angle to the writing-table, she looked down the study to where Mary Lenton's dahlias bloomed brightly in the sun. She saw Edna Ford walk up to the front door.

CHAPTER 40

Mary Lenton came through the hall to let her in. Nothing could possibly have been more inconvenient, but then Edna was one of those people who always did time her visits at the most inconvenient moment. She had a shopping-bag on her arm and was extracting from it three small account-books which she held out in a complaining manner.

"I really ought not to have undertaken anything to do with accounts. I remember I told you so at the time. I have no head for figures."

"But you offered—"

"I am too kind-hearted," said Edna in a fretful voice. "When I heard that Miss Smithson was ill, I know I said that I would carry on, but I really can't make head or tail of her writing. So I thought I would come down and tell you it's no use. Unless, of course, we can just go through them together—"

Mary Lenton struggled with an acute feeling of irritation. She never had been able to like Edna Ford, though she had sometimes felt sorry for her. And to come at this moment, with Superintendent Martin in the house, Ellie upstairs looking as if she was going to faint again, and lunch to see to! Now she came to look at her, Edna didn't seem any too well herself. Such a bad colour—and that dreadful old black coat and skirt! It ought to have been on the scrap-heap years ago. She really oughtn't to go about looking like that. And that steel buckle would be off her shoe any minute now. She said,

"I'm afraid—Edna, I'm very busy just now. Ellie isn't well."

"She gives way," said Edna Ford. "I've always said so. She should rouse herself. I'm sure no one can tell me anything about bad health, but it shouldn't be made an excuse for neglecting one's duties. Now if we can just come into the dining-room and go through the entries for July. I see Miss Smithson has put down six yards of pink flannelette, and I really can't think what it was for."

Mary Lenton was just going to say "night-gowns," when the study door opened and Miss Silver came to her rescue.

"Mrs. Ford, I wonder if you would mind coming in here for a moment."

Edna looked surprised. She could not imagine why Miss Silver should be inviting her into the Vicar's study—she could not imagine why Miss Silver should be there at all. She walked into the room with the shopping-bag on her arm and the three account-books in her hand, and was still further surprised to see that it was Superintendent Martin who was

263

sitting in the Vicar's chair. The door closed behind her. He said,

"Ah, Mrs. Ford—won't you sit down?"

She took the chair on the other side of the table and put the bag down on the floor. Miss Silver seated herself. Edna said,

"What is it?"

"We think you may be able to help us."

"I can't see—I really don't think—"

He leaned towards her with a hand on the edge of the table.

"It has been found necessary to detain your husband for questioning."

She went on looking surprised.

"I don't see how you can think of any more questions to ask. I don't suppose he can tell you anything he hasn't told you already."

"That is as may be. At the moment, I've asked you to come in here because Miss Silver would like to speak to you."

"Miss Silver?" The surprise deepened.

He got up and walked away to the window. Miss Silver said,

"Superintendent Martin does not wish to be involved in this, but I think you ought to know that your husband is under a good deal of suspicion in regard to the deaths of Miss Preston and Miss Meriel Ford."

Edna said, *"Geoffrey?"*

"There is quite a strong case against him. In fact up to a point it is a very strong case indeed. I think you know that he went to the Lodge to see Mrs. Trent on the night of the murder, and a witness has now come forward to prove that Miss Meriel followed him there. This witness overheard the violent quarrel which ensued. She heard Miss Meriel say to your husband that she would tell the police she had seen him push Miss Preston into the pool under the impression that the person wearing Adriana Ford's coat was in fact Adriana Ford herself. Miss Meriel then left, and after being adjured by Mrs. Trent to follow her Mr. Geoffrey Ford did so."

Superintendent Martin looked over his shoulder and saw Edna Ford sitting stiffly upright. She was clutching the three account-books, and there was a perfectly blank expression on her face. As he looked round, she said,

"I don't know why you are telling me all this. I don't approve of Geoffrey going to see Mrs. Trent—you have heard me say so before. She is an immoral woman—I don't approve of her at all."

Miss Silver said firmly,

"There is a witness to the fact that Miss Meriel Ford threatened your husband, and that he followed her when she left the Lodge. Within a very short time of that she was struck down by a murderous blow and her body left in the pool."

Edna had a gleam of animation.

"I can't think what she was doing there. So damp—and such unpleasant associations."

"Mrs. Ford, your husband was seen to follow her. Do you not realize that that could be very serious for him? She threatened him. He followed her. She was found dead."

The trace of animation became stronger.

"Well, he had to get home. I hope you do not suppose he would have stayed at the Lodge all night."

Miss Silver sighed. She looked round at the Superintendent, and he came back to his place at the writing-table.

"Well, Mrs. Ford, it is no part of my job to make you

anxious about your husband, but the evidence of this witness whom Miss Silver has mentioned extends beyond his case."

"Really, you know, I came here to do these accounts with Mrs. Lenton."

"Just a moment, if you please. This witness states that she followed Miss Meriel and Mr. Geoffrey all the way to Ford House. She says Mr. Geoffrey went in, but that someone else came up from behind her after she had reached the farther corner of the house and followed Miss Meriel across the lawn and into the enclosed garden which contains the pool. She states that it was a woman, and that after a little time this woman returned and went into Ford House by way of the study window. But Meriel Ford did not return."

Edna fidgeted with the account-books.

"How very strange."

"You realize that this witness was seeing the murderer?" She nodded.

"Then it would have been Esmé Trent."

"You think so?"

"Oh, yes. She is a bad woman—I have always said so."

"But she would not have gone into Ford House."

"Oh, yes—she was always running after Geoffrey." She put a hand on the edge of the table and got up. "I really mustn't keep Mrs. Lenton waiting."

And just at that moment the handle moved, the door opened, and Ellie Page came a half step into the room. She wore a dark blue jumper and skirt, and she looked like a ghost. When she saw Edna she said "Oh!" and stopped where she was.

"There was something I had forgotten. I thought perhaps—I ought to say—"

266

Edna began to move towards the door. As she did so, the loose steel buckle on her left-hand shoe fell sideways and almost tripped her. Ellie stared at it, and at her. Then she came right into the room, shut the door, and went back against it.

"That was the thing I remembered," she said.

The Superintendent got to his feet and came round the table. He saw Ellie's eyes fixed and staring, and he wanted to see what they were staring at.

Edna Ford stooped down and pulled at the buckle. The loose threads broke and pulled away. She stood up with it in her hand.

"Dear me—it nearly tripped me!"

Ellie's eyes followed the buckle. She said,

"That's what I remembered. I saw it when she was crossing the lawn after she put the light on. The torch hung down in her left hand and shone on the buckle. It moved because it was loose, and the light shone down on it. I remembered, and I thought I ought to tell you." She looked from the buckle to Edna's face and shrank back against the door. "Oh, you killed them! You killed them both!"

Edna Ford had a small complacent smile. She tilted the buckle on the palm of her hand and said,

"It was very clever of me, wasn't it?"

CHAPTER 41

The way she smiled and the sound of her voice, the foolish inconsequent sound of it, were there in the room. They were there in a silence that no one seemed able to break. Thoughts beat against it, but it resisted them. In the end it was Edna Ford who broke it. She held the three account-books in her right hand. She glanced down at them now, still with that foolish smile, and said,

"Well, I mustn't keep Mrs. Lenton waiting."

Ellie gave a kind of gasp. Superintendent Martin said,

"Mrs. Ford, you have just made a very serious admission. Do you wish to make a statement on the subject? I have to tell you that anything you say may be taken down and used in evidence."

She turned round, the buckle in one hand and the account-books in the other.

"It was clever of me, wasn't it? And if that buckle hadn't been loose, no one would ever have known. I suppose I ought not to have put on the torch until I was out of sight of the house, but you don't expect people to be looking out of their windows at that time of night. And what was Ellie Page doing in our garden in the dark? I should like to know that. Running after Geoffrey, I suppose—just like all the other silly women. But they won't get him, because I happen to know that Adriana has left the money to me. So they won't get him away from me—none of them will!"

268

The Superintendent addressed Ellie Page.

"Miss Page, would you be so kind as to ask Watson to come in here. He took down your statement, and I asked him to wait. And please come back yourself—we may want you."

Edna Ford went on talking about how attractive Geoffrey was, and the folly of the women who imagined that they could get him away from her. She did not seem to be addressing Superintendent Martin or anyone else in particular. The words just ran on as if they were her thoughts, and as if by saying them aloud she could make them come true. She was still talking when Ellie came back with a dark young man who sat down by the side of the table and opened a notebook. Miss Silver's eyes rested on her gravely and compassionately.

When Watson was seated the Superintendent checked the flow.

"Now, Mrs. Ford, if you are prepared to answer questions or make a statement, Detective Watson will take down what you say in shorthand. When it has been typed it will be read over to you and you can sign it."

She said in a fretful voice,

"I don't see why he wants to take it down. We were getting along very nicely without him."

"It is better to have it on record. Then it can be read over to you, and you can say whether it is all right."

She had an approving nod for that.

"Well, of course there is that. I wouldn't want you to put things in afterwards."

Ellie Page had found a chair beside Miss Silver. Her face was hidden in the hands which rested against the hard upright back. Martin said,

"Now, Mrs. Ford, when Miss Page said, 'You killed them

both!' you made this reply, 'It was very clever of me, wasn't it?' Did you mean that as an admission that you had pushed Mabel Preston into the pool and drowned her there, and that you subsequently struck Meriel Ford with an iron club and pushed her into the same pool?"

Edna Ford shook her head.

"Oh, no, I didn't push Meriel—I didn't have to. She fell into the pool. It was very convenient."

Young Watson felt a pringling at the back of his neck. He wrote down what she had said.

"Why did you drown Mabel Preston?"

"That was rather a tiresome mistake. You see, she was wearing Adriana's coat—the one with the big black and white squares and the emerald stripe. Such a noticeable pattern and not at all suitable at Adriana's age—in fact at either of their ages. I do think elderly people should dress quietly—I am sure you agree about that. Anyhow, there was the coat, and of course I thought it was Adriana inside it. Very misleading of Mabel to put it on like that, and quite her own fault if it turned out as it did. I didn't like her very much, but I'm sure I hadn't the slightest desire to drown her. I just switched on my torch for a moment, saw that very noticeable pattern, and gave her one good push. After that, of course, I had to hold her down until she stopped struggling. But it really was quite easy. I am stronger than I look. You see, I used to play golf quite a lot, and it develops the muscles."

"You say that it was your intention to drown Miss Adriana Ford?"

Edna gave a casual self-satisfied nod.

"It seemed such a good opportunity," she said.

"How did you come to be following Miss Preston?"

270

"Oh, but I wasn't. It was quite a surprise to me when she came through the gap in the hedge."

"Then why were you there?"

She primmed up her mouth.

"Well, it is all rather delicate. You see, Mrs. Trent was behaving so very badly about my husband—she really never left him alone. And when I saw them slip behind the curtains—the room was so hot and I had just opened a window—I thought I had better see where they had gone to, but that tiresome Mrs. Felkins caught hold of me. Such a talker, and I couldn't get away from her. And then there were two or three other people, so it was quite a time before I could go after Geoffrey and that woman. I guessed they would be in the summerhouse down by the pool, and so they were. But I think they heard me coming, because Geoffrey went off one way and she another. I didn't know that Meriel had been there too, and that she had seen them. At least I don't know whether she saw them, or whether she saw me, because I don't know when she was there, but she tore her dress on the hedge, and she must have stained it too, because when I saw her again up at the house she had spilt coffee all down the front of it, and I thought, 'Well, she wouldn't do that for nothing'. I had a good close look at the dress, and under the coffee stain it was all wet with water and slime. So then I knew she had tried to move the body, because that was the only way she could have got herself stained like that. And do you know what I think? She didn't give the alarm, so she must have thought it was Adriana who had fallen into the pool. And she must have thought it would be a pity if she was found too soon. Because of course she wanted to get her share of the money so as to be able to go on the stage."

Ellie Page dropped her hands from her face and turned an

incredulous gaze on Edna. It sounded as if she thought it was all quite a matter of course to push people out of your way, to push them out of life, because they had something you wanted. She thought, "She's mad!" And then, "But I was pushing for something I wanted too. How far would I have pushed her because I wanted Geoffrey?" A bleak horror fell on her. Her hand went out gropingly. Miss Silver took it and held it in a firm, kind clasp.

The Superintendent was saying, "Why did you kill Meriel Ford?"

"Well, I didn't know how much she knew. As soon as I heard about her having left a shred of her dress on the hedge I knew she would be questioned about it, and I didn't know what she might say. And the more I thought about those stains, the more I thought they might mean that she had seen me coming away from the pool. And then, night before last when I knew she had gone out after Geoffrey, I thought perhaps it would be better to get her out of the way anyhow. You see, I'm tired of people running after Geoffrey. And if Meriel had seen me by the pool she would have loved to make a scene about it. She was a very tiresome woman."

"So you killed her."

She gave another of those casual nods.

"I thought she would be just as well out of the way."

The young detective wrote. Martin said,

"Will you tell us how you set about it?"

She was still smiling.

"It was quite easy. We went up to bed at half past nine, Adriana, Miss Silver, and I. I waited till they had gone into their rooms, and then I slipped down the back stairs. First of all I went to the study, just to make sure about Geoffrey. The glass door was unlatched, so I knew he hadn't come in.

272

I went to the cloakroom and fetched a niblick, and then I went out. I had just got to the corner of the house, when someone came by. I knew it was Meriel, because she was laughing to herself. She sounded as if she was angry and pleased at the same time. I couldn't do anything about it then because there was someone else coming up behind her, so I had to let her go past. It seemed a pity, but it turned out all right in the end, because she didn't go into the house. She just went straight on past the study door and round to the back. And then Geoffrey came by. He went as far as the study door and stood there. Then he gave a sort of groan and said, 'Oh, my God! What's the use!' and he went in, but he didn't fasten the door, so I knew he was leaving it for Meriel. He must have seen her go on round the house and thought what was the good of going after her." She paused.

The Superintendent said,

"Where were you when Mr. Ford went into the house?"

"I was just off the path behind a lilac bush. Do you know, I very nearly went after Geoffrey and missed what turned out to be such a good opportunity. I actually did go up the steps and into the room, but it was all dark and Geoffrey wasn't there. He must have gone straight through and up to his room. So if Ellie was following him, that is when she must have gone past, because I didn't see her and she didn't see me—at least not then."

"Miss Page says she went past the study door after Mr. Ford had gone in. She says she was watching Miss Meriel Ford on her way across the lawn when you came up from behind her."

"Yes, that's right. Only I didn't know she was there. She hadn't any business to be there! I wanted to know what Meriel was doing, so I followed her. When she had gone in through the gate in the hedge I put on my torch, but I let it hang down in case there should be anyone looking out of a window. I was quite careful about that, and it is just a bit of bad luck that the buckle was coming off my shoe."

"Go on, Mrs. Ford."

"It was all quite easy. I put the torch out before I came to the gate. I wanted to see what she was doing. She had gone through the inner hedge to the pool, and she had a light. I came up to the arch in the hedge and saw her go into the summerhouse. She had that handkerchief you picked up here afterwards. She held it in the light and laughed, and I could see that it was one of Esmé Trent's. I don't know anyone else who has bright yellow handkerchiefs—not what I should call in good taste—not at all. Meriel dropped the handkerchief and switched off her torch and came and stood by the pool. It was all very convenient. I only had to hit her once."

CHAPTER 42

Miss Silver was ready to go. The modest suit-case was packed. The woollen gloves, black cloth coat, the elderly fur tippet, were ready to put on. The black felt hat with its loops of ribbon had been assumed. A handsome cheque had passed. It remained only to bid Adriana Ford farewell.

She found her in an upright chair, her head high, her dark red hair meticulously arranged, her make-up carefully applied.

"Well," she said, "so far as you are concerned it is over.

As far as we are concerned it is just going to begin. Pity one can't drop the curtain and call the whole thing off, isn't it? I keep wondering what would have happened if I had never written to you or come to see you."

Miss Silver coughed.

"I do not feel that I had much part in clearing the matter up."

Adriana lifted a hand.

"You got the truth out of Ellie. Mary Lenton says she did nothing but cry and turn faint. They didn't know what to do with her, and they were going to send her away, and if they had done that, or if she had just slipped into an illness, I don't suppose she would ever have spoken. In which case poor Edna would probably have murdered somebody else before anyone found her out, and the most likely person to be murdered next would have been me. So you must expect me to have some bias in the matter!" She gave a short laugh. "Odd, that one should still feel an affection for living! My household has been broken up, two people have been murdered on the premises, Geoffrey has had a narrow escape of being hanged, his wife turns out to be a homicidal lunatic, and my family affairs are front-page news. I ought to feel finished, but I don't! I'm looking for a flat in town, and Meeson is as pleased as Punch. She has always hated Ford. The one bright spot seems to be that there are no two opinions about Edna being mad, poor thing. She hadn't a great deal of mind to go out of, but I suppose she might have kept what balance she had if she hadn't let herself get so eaten up with jealousy about Geoffrey."

Miss Silver said,

"Jealousy is a terrible and corroding poison."

Adriana made an impatient gesture.

"People don't always go off their heads with it. Why, we didn't even take it seriously."

"That was a mistake."

"It's all very well to say so now, but if you could have seen her all these years, doing that tiresome fancy work, interfering in the household, bickering with Meriel, fussing about Geoffrey—why, we used to make a joke of it. The Superintendent says you suspected her, but I don't see how you could."

"She was one of the people whom I was bound to suspect, because she was one of the people who was aware that Miss Meriel Ford had been down by the pool at or about the time when Miss Preston was murdered. This fact at first placed Miss Meriel herself in the position of being my principal suspect, but when she had met the same fate as Miss Preston it became clear that she had been removed because she was a danger to the real murderer."

"Edna—why did you pitch on Edna?"

"She was in an abnormal mental state. I have some experience of these matters, and she seemed to me to be given up to what the French call an *idée fixe*. Her outbursts on the subject of her husband's infatuation for Mrs. Trent were indications which I could not neglect. Both before and after these outbursts there were characteristic periods of apparent inertia. She also exhibited a strong and settled desire to return to the life of a town or suburb, but as she herself informed me, that was not financially possible. I believe that she allowed herself to dwell upon this idea incessantly, and that it provided the motive for the first crime. She knew that you had left her a life interest in the bequest made to her husband, and she dwelt on the idea of removing him from the neighbourhood of Mrs. Trent."

"Then why didn't she just murder Esmé Trent and have done with it?"

"She might have done so if the opportunity had occurred. That first murder was not planned. The time, the place, the opportunity, presented themselves at a moment when her jealousy was most strongly excited, and the second crime was committed to cover up the first. Her mania had by then progressed to a point where it seemed to her that it was a perfectly natural and inevitable thing to do. By the time she made her statement to Superintendent Martin she no longer felt any sense of guilt."

Adriana said in her deep voice,

"Well, they won't hang her, and it lets Geoffrey out. He is a good deal broken up."

Miss Silver's natural kindness of disposition did not incline her towards sympathy with Mr. Geoffrey Ford. He was certainly very much shocked and upset, but she did not think it had failed to occur to him that he might himself have been a victim, and she felt assured that it would not be very long before he was again reaching out for feminine admiration and sympathy. The fact that Adriana now turned the conversation to Ellie Page did not dispose her to regard him with any more favour.

"I can't imagine why you should have thought that Ellie came into it at all."

"You yourself told me that there had been some talk about her and Mr. Geoffrey Ford, and the footprint under the Lodge window had to be accounted for. It was quite a recent one, and it was not made by Miss Meriel, neither were the fingerprints on the windowsill hers. The footprint was that of a much smaller foot. It was a deep one. Whoever made it had stood at the living-room window to listen. A chance remark informed me that Mrs. Trent had a passion for open windows. It was therefore more than possible that the person who stood by that window to listen might have heard what would throw valuable light upon the crime. In considering who this person might be, it was reasonable to deduce that she must have had a deep personal interest in what was going on inside the Lodge. Ellie Page came into my mind at once. I had seen her, and had been struck by her look of deep unhappiness. She is slightly made, her hands and feet are small. Immediately after the crime she is said to be ill. I decided to see her if it were possible to do so. Walking along the road, it was apparent that any of the Vicarage windows on that side would command a view of the road between Ford House and the Lodge. As we now know, Ellie Page was in the habit of watching this stretch of road from her bedroom window. Mr. Geoffrey had become alarmed by the strength of her feelings. He had been cooling off, and she was tormented by his attentions to Mrs. Trent. As I walked in the direction of the Vicarage I became convinced that it was Ellie Page who had listened at the Lodge window. The rest you know. When I saw her leave the house and go into the church I followed, and found that she had reached the point where unhappiness compelled her to find an outlet. Fear and shame withheld her from confiding in her cousins. She had grieved Mrs. Lenton and angered the Vicar, and they were sending her away. She had to speak to someone, and she unburdened herself to me. The hardest part of my task was to get her to see that it was her duty to give this information to the police. It was only when she realized the serious nature of Mr. Geoffrey Ford's position that she was induced to do so."

Adriana made one of her impatient gestures.

"Oh, well, she'll get over it," she said.

CHAPTER 43

Miss Silver made her farewells, and was seen off at Ledbury station by Ninian and Janet. Janet herself would be leaving next day. She had received her belated cheque from Hugo Mortimer and was feeling pleasantly independent. She told herself what a relief it would be to get away from Ford House. There had been two murders, two inquests and two funerals in the brief time she had spent there. And anyhow her job was at an end, since Stella was with her mother and Nanny would join them at Sunningdale, though how long she would get on with Sibylla Maxwell's own nursery autocrat was another matter. She watched the smoke of Miss Silver's train die away in the distance and felt Ninian's hand upon her arm.

"Come along with you!"

They went out to the car, but instead of taking the road to Ford he turned in the opposite direction. To her "Where are you going?" she got no answer but "Wait and see." After which she sat in what he felt to be a deceptive silence whilst they ran out of the old narrow streets into broader and more modern ones and were finally clear of the straggle of bungalows and small houses which Ledbury had gathered to itself since the war.

On this side the ground rose. They came to a wooded slope that looked to the south-east, and there he stopped the car. Janet opened her lips for the first time in half an hour.

"What do we do next?"

"We get out."

"Why?"

"I'm tired of sitting in the car."

There was no hedge on the right. A path meandered downwards between the trees. After a little way there was a clearing with a view. They could see the smoke of Ledbury, the flat green fields they had left, and the bend the river made at Ford. There was a sky flecked with blue and grey, a clear pale sunlight, and a temperate breeze. A fallen tree made a convenient seat. They sat down on it. Janet folded her hands in her lap, lifted her eyes to his face, and said,

"Well?"

She caught a momentary gleam of mischief, and then it was gone. If it hadn't been Ninian, she might have thought he was embarrassed. There was the sound of it in his voice as he said,

"Well, what?"

"Oh, just well. Did we come here to look at the view?"

"It's quite a good view."

"Oh, yes. Did we come here to look at it?"

"Woman, you've no sense of romance!"

She lifted her brows.

"And just what am I supposed to be romantic about?"

"Wouldn't you call fixing our wedding day romantic? In the old books the girl was expected to swoon. Rather embarrassing, so I don't insist on it, but a little sensibility would be appropriate."

"It might if we were doing what you say."

"Oh, but we are. Janet—we are, aren't we? And I wasn't going to do it in that unchancy house, cluttered up with murders and inquests and funerals and what not. I'm romantic if you're not, and I thought this would be a nice sort of place for you to say yes, and—and—Janet, you're going to, aren't you?"

He had slipped down on his knees beside her. She said,

"I—don't—know—"

"You do! You must!"

"And what happens when you meet another Anne?"

"Nothing—absolutely nothing!"

"It did before."

"It won't again. Annes are definitely out."

"Until next time. You see, I know you, Ringan."

He put his head down suddenly on her hands.

"It's only you—*really!* It's always you—*Janet!*"

His head came up with a jerk. His eyes were wet, and her hands. The wind blew on them, and she felt his tears. He said in an angry voice,

"I don't go away! You've got me for keeps! I can't get away if I want to, and you've got me so that I don't want to! And if you want to know what you are, you're just a chip of Scots granite and a gey cantankersome wumman! And now, for the last time, will you marry me? You're going to anyway, and you might as well do it as if you liked it, my jo Janet! And it had better be next week, because of Hemming's flat. We don't want it to get cold, or be burgled or anything, do we? And for God's sake let's get away from Ford! Janet— you will, won't you?"

He saw her eyes soften and her lips tremble into a smile. She said,

"I suppose so."

THE END